The Tigers in the Tower

A Little Princess – with tigers! Orphan and outcast Sahira Clive is a brave and plucky heroine with a brightly burning heart. I was rooting for her all the way to the end of this thrilling – and thought-provoking – adventure.
Ally Sherrick, award-winning author of *Black Powder*

A delightfully engaging global escape! Golding pulls readers into a tale of London's Tower Menagerie with the classic feel of Kipling's *The Jungle Book*. *The Tigers in the Tower* is not only a well-researched adventure for animal lovers, it is a story of hope, love, and family that will capture the heart and imagination of readers young and old.
Lauren H. Brandenburg, author of *The Books of the Gardener* series and *The Death of Mungo Blackwell*

An almost magical adventure into an exotic corner of London's history. Colourful characters and vivid imagery bring to life the remarkable story of a feisty girl. *The Tigers in the Tower* is a must read for animal lovers of all ages. Like Sahira, I'll be dreaming of tigers for days to come!
Luke Aylen, author of the *An Adventure in Presadia* series

Sahira's adventure of towers, tigers, and treachery is underpinned by deep values carried along by a story where you can never guess what will happen next.
Andrew Briggs, Professor of Nanomaterials, University of Oxford

The Tigers in the Tower is a beautifully written story that will take you on a journey from India to Victorian Britain. It tells of how one girl's courage, kindness, and love of tigers is key to getting through the highs and lows of life. This book is an adventure you won't want to miss!
Sharon Dirckx, author of *Am I Just My Brain* and Senior Tutor at the Oxford Centre for Christian Apologetics (OCCA)

THE TIGERS IN THE TOWER

JULIA GOLDING

LION FICTION

Text copyright © 2020 Julia Golding
This edition copyright © 2020 Lion Hudson IP Limited

Published by
Lion Hudson Limited
Wilkinson House, Jordan Hill Business Park
Banbury Road, Oxford OX2 8DR, England

www.lionhudson.com

ISBN 978 1 78264 317 3
eISBN 978 1 78264 318 0

First edition 2020

Acknowledgments
Cover illustration by Keith Robinson
Henna Paisley Patterns © Blue67/Dreamstime.com

A catalogue record for this book is available from the British Library

Printed and bound in the UK, June 2020, LH26

For Dr Nigel Pearson.
For over a decade, you have always helped me with my books whenever I have a tricky medical question so I thought it past time I wrote one just for you! Thank you for your years of dedicated work as a doctor to the poorest people in the world. I hope you enjoy Sahira's story.

PART 1
LONDON

The King's Royal Menagerie
TOWER OF LONDON

This ancient edifice, built in 1465, in the reign of Edward IV,
for the reception of
FOREIGN **BEASTS, BIRDS**, &c.
presented to the Kings of England, could never, since its foundation,
boast a more significant and splendid VARIETY than it does at present.

First Department – A Beautiful,
Majestic, Fully grown

BENGAL LION

AND HIS CONSORT, IN ONE DEN

*

YOUNG LIONS

◆

ROYAL TIGERS

*

THE STRIPED or
UNTAMEABLE HYENA

◆

Leopard & her cubs

*

PAIR OF ORIENTAL PORCUPINES

◆

OCELOT, OR TIGER CAT

A Beautiful ZEBRA

KANGAROOS

◆

SOUTHERN OSTRICHES
Pelicans of the Wilderness

*

EAGLE of the SUN

And Golden Eagle

◆

**Majestic Elk, from the
East Indies**

Tapir, or Hippopotamus
of South America
Boa Constrictors, or
Great Serpents of Java

PROLOGUE

Last night one of the tigers escaped. Slipping free of her tether, she climbed the ladder and slunk past the sailor on watch. Sniffing his canvas trousers, whiskers twitching, she contemplated taking a bite before the scents of the shore lured her onward. The man nodded sleepily at the wheel, unaware death had passed him by.

Padding on velvet paws, she leaped to the rail and dived into the star-filled expanse of the Thames. No one noticed just one more splash in the busy Pool, the mooring place in the river where trading vessels from the Indies unloaded their cargo in the world's biggest city. There she trod water for a moment.

Should she head north or south?

The reek of Billingsgate fish market drew her to the northern bank and with powerful strokes she made short work of swimming to shore. She dragged her sodden pelt up the beach, startling the young mudlarks scavenging at low tide, and so began a new legend of the beast that crawled from the slime at night to snatch the unwary. With a rolling shrug of her shoulders, she shook free of the river water, then surveyed her new home. Odours of horse and human, cats, rats and dogs, refuse and dung assaulted her nostrils. Searching, she could find no smell of jungle or village, no bullock at the plough or cotton field, no spices in the air, no fragrant wood smoke – only coal dust.

But then she caught it: a hint of green. Using her well-honed tracking skills, she padded up the ramp from the beach, past the frightened beggar children shivering sleepless in upturned boats. They whimpered and clung to each other but tonight they were not her prey. Paws met cobblestones. The narrow ravines between houses made the tiger's fur bristle. Any of these darkened windows could hide a hunter armed with more than claws and teeth. She had lost too many of her family to cowardly bullets. Keeping to the shadows, she wound through the mazy streets of Wapping, heading west.

Finally, just as the tiger was beginning to think that the houses would never cease, the cramped walls of brick released her onto an open plain. There, in the centre of the grassland close to the river, was a white tower. The ancient edifice stood proud, surrounded by double walls and a moat. What was it? It was much bigger than the wooden walls of the ship she had sailed in but it smelled confusingly of the jungle. She could hear the roar of lions, the chatter of monkeys, and the shriek of eagles as they scented the threat that was at their door. Intrigued, the tiger approached, coming like dawn from the east, a creature of a hot orange sun, striped by bars of black cloud.

The keeper in his bed in Lion House felt the tiger's arrival in his dreams. Mumbling to his wife, he turned on his side and pulled the covers over his head.

CHAPTER 1

Sahira Clive sat cross-legged in front of the iron-barred cage. Rama and Sita prowled at her back, girl and tigers watchful for the next attack. They were a little team of three against the world, braced for whatever misery it would serve up to them.

Rain flattened Sahira's dark hair against her face, soaked her clothes, and speckled her companions with diamond droplets. Their fur was so much better than cotton and wool at repelling water. Not for the first time, Sahira wished she could be one of them.

Sita sneezed.

"I know, Sita, I know," Sahira murmured. "But what can I do?" She could feel the tigress's desire for freedom pushing at her back, ordering her to lift the latch and let her and her mate roam free. But their ship was floating in the heart of London and they were waiting to disembark; getting loose would end in musket fire and an afterlife as a tiger-skin rug. Sita could only prowl unfettered in Sahira's dreams.

"What are we going to do with the girl?" The East India Company official who had met the boat huddled with the wives of the officers Sahira had travelled with from Calcutta. He held a black umbrella over his head, struggling to keep control in the stiff breeze.

Nothing about this place was as colourful as home. The bobbing motion of the umbrella reminded Sahira of the last procession she had witnessed in India as she waited for her ship to sail. A great prince had been embarking on a neighbouring vessel, bound for his education in England. His umbrellas had come in silk of many colours, with tassels and beads, and were used to keep off the sun. Did the sun ever shine here in England, or was Sahira's nurse right? Bala had said the foreigners were so pale when they arrived in Calcutta because they were like naan dough, uncooked and pasty. Then, under the hot sun, they freckled and burned, just like the bread baked in the tandoor.

"Her parents' death was unfortunate in so many ways. I feel sorry for the girl." Mrs Tailor glanced in Sahira's direction and smiled apologetically.

Sahira looked down at her lap. There was an empty place in her chest where her heart had once beaten. Sometimes she wondered if she were still alive, because she felt like a ghost of herself, going through the motions of eating, drinking, speaking. She'd never been apart from her family; she'd always been able to reach out at any moment and touch her mother's soft fingers or her father's prickly beard. Now when she reached out there was no one there, only the tigers. Sahira felt the bitter tears gather inside but she could not shed them; it was as though the rope on the well bucket had been cut and she couldn't bring her emotions to the surface. She did not hate Mrs Tailor, not like she did the other women. Only Mrs Tailor had entered quarantine in the cabin with Sahira and helped nurse her parents when everyone else had fled the fever. As for the other British wives, Sahira had no time for them because they had none for her. In their dull brown and blue seagoing coats, they looked more like vultures gathered to peck a carcass. They could scent that Sahira was stricken – desperate. Sahira hated to appear like that to her enemies. The wild was not kind to one that became separated from the herd. Only the very tough, or those protected by others, survived.

"Can you take her, Mrs Tailor?" asked the official hopefully.

Sahira's heart lifted. Of all her options, that wouldn't be so bad. But the thought immediately followed: *what about the tigers?*

Mrs Tailor's mouth thinned, brow furrowed. "I'm afraid not, sir. It would be misunderstood by my family if I returned a widow with a native child in tow. That kind of thing will not do in Hampstead."

Sahira's brief hope flickered out. No, she and the tigers would not do in Hampstead.

"Of course not. I apologize." The man blushed. "That was insensitive of me. Did Captain Clive have family, do you know?"

"They cast him off," boomed Mrs Bingham, the largest of the vultures with a black bonnet framing her pinched face. "Marriage to the native woman was a step too far for them. She won't receive a welcome from Lord Chalmers at Fenton Park from what I hear."

Fenton Park was Sahira's father's ancestral home. Captain Clive had spoken of it with great affection, describing the fish and frogs in the clear streams, the squirrels and deer in its woods, the ancient yew tree in the churchyard. *"No better place for bird watching,"* he had told her as they sat around the campfire in the jungle. Sahira could recall the evenings of storytelling with crystal accuracy, still hear the crickets rasping in eardrums with their shrill rhythms. Nights in the jungle were punctuated by strange cries from the depths of the trees and every step had been a negotiation with death. When their journey became too hard or too frightening, Captain Clive had conjured up Fenton Park in his stories, a fairy-tale palace set in a fertile landscape, home to the modest brown animals of this realm. He had taught Sahira to value the small and overlooked as well as the great creatures of India. He had praised the virtues of a gentle landscape, a balance to the terrors of the magnificent one they had travelled through collecting their animals. God's creation was infinitely varied and he marvelled at all its facets.

The Company man was shaking his head in sorrow that an easy answer was denied him. "We will send word to Lord Chalmers, nonetheless. Until we get a reply, I suppose we'll have to place her in an orphanage. They might overlook her origin. You would hardly know she was a native with that auburn hair of her father's."

"But one look at that unfortunate complexion and they'll know," sniffed Mrs Bingham. "There's no whitewashing her scandalous birth."

From feeling nothing but numb grief, outrage now sparked and burned hot in Sahira's heart. Her fingers formed claws on her palms. Feeling her distress, Rama rattled the cage, provoking shrieks of alarm from the ladies.

"Surely the girl is too close to the bars. Those beasts will hurt her!" exclaimed Mrs Tailor.

"Not that one," replied a gruff old seaman who was standing by to hoist the cargo. "She's more like their cub."

The captain gave his crewman a reproving look for speaking out of turn. "Don't worry, ma'am, we've rifles and whips ready. No need to fear the wild beasts."

This wouldn't do: she was putting the tigers at risk. Sahira tried to calm herself. She couldn't let the tigers be punished for sympathizing with her. As her parents had taught her, she reached for stories of the past. They had both been tale tellers to rival Shahrazad of *One Thousand and One Nights*, so she sought help from her storybook of memories.

Her father's smiling facing came into her mind's eye, hazel eyes twinkling above his rusty moustache. *"You are as beautiful as your mother, little one. Let no one persuade you otherwise."* He held her above his head, swinging her between him and the sun. *"You are the exact same colour of my favourite spice, nutmeg."* She could still feel his whiskers on her arm as he pretended to nibble her elbow. *"And you smell like nutmeg too."*

That always made her giggle.

Baba. A wave of grief overwhelmed her and she buried her head in her knees.

The grown-ups had carried on talking about her, dissecting her with their disapproval. "And look at what she's wearing. No decent English girl would be seen wearing trousers!" declared Mrs Bingham.

"It's a *salwar kameez*," said Mrs Tailor, who had lived on a small station upcountry rather than in one of the big cities. She knew more about the natives than the women who had not emerged from their barracks. "Quite decent for India, I assure you, Mrs Bingham."

"But this is London!"

"Quite. Eleanor, dear, do you have some other clothes you can put on?" asked Mrs Tailor.

Sahira lifted her head. There it was again: the foreign middle name they insisted on using for her, finding her first name too exotic.

"I do have your kind of dresses." She'd brought a trunk of European dresses her father had had made for her in the bazaar of Hyderabad. The seamstress had copied pictures in one of the lady's magazines belonging to the Resident's wife. They had been a few years out of date but Sahira's mother had said they would do. At twelve, Sahira wasn't expected to be in the first rank of fashion.

"Then run along and find one of your gowns," coaxed Mrs Tailor. "We need to put our best foot forward if we are going to persuade the kind people who run the orphanage to take you."

If they were kind, what did it matter how she was dressed? Biting her tongue, Sahira returned to her cabin. She had been sleeping on a mat on the floor, too scared to stretch out where her parents had lain. The beds had been stripped after their death, the linen buried at sea with their bodies. Also gone overboard were most of their clothes and possessions, all for fear of contagion. There was little left to say they had ever been here. Except the animals, of course. And Sahira.

Delving in her trunk, brought up from storage by a considerate sailor, she found one of her favourites. It was a pale green cotton dress with a border of elephants marching around the hem. Sahira folded up her salt-stained loose trousers, unbuttoned the flame-orange tunic, and slipped into the new dress. It had a scooped neck, small puffed sleeves, and fitted tightly at the waist before flaring out in silly amounts of material that were bound to get in the way. Only the elephants reconciled her to the gown. She had insisted that each London dress had some animal decoration to make it bearable. Sahira looked down at her bare feet in their sandals and remembered the women on deck in their boots and thick stockings. She had been chilled since the ship left the Azores and had wrapped herself in blankets most of the grey days and hopeless nights. It was true that her toes were cold and wet; she would have to adapt to this new climate. She dug further down in the trunk and pulled out a pair of stockings, an undergarment her mother had laughed at but what her father had blushed and called "pantalettes", and finally a pair of blue leather boots, dyed by the old shoemaker in Narrow Alley to suit Sahira's taste for colour.

"So my little girl is going to walk the London pavements in sky boots, is she?" Father had asked with a smile.

"I don't want to walk them at all," Sahira murmured to the empty cabin, tugging the laces. She just wanted to go home, so badly she could taste it, like ginger hot on the tongue.

But there was no home any longer. Nowhere on Earth was "home" to her. Sahira no more fitted in India than she did in England. Only being with her parents had made sense of her existence, so maybe her true home lay at the bottom of the sea with them?

Finally ready, Sahira buckled the trunk closed on her Indian clothes. She was Sahira Eleanor Clive, daughter of Captain Richard Clive of the East India Company service and Begum Noor un-Issa, noblewoman of one of the oldest families of Hyderabad. She had nothing about which she should be ashamed. She had given her father her sacred promise that she would look after the tigers.

And she was *not* going to an orphanage.

CHAPTER 2

All was not well on deck. The rain had eased but the tigers had become distraught.

"What have you done to them?" Sahira scrambled up the ladder and grabbed the nearest crewman. The tigers were roaring and clawing at the planks of their crate. None of the sailors dared approach. Wood splintered around the bars, amber eyes wild with fright. Much more of this and Rama and Sita would be able to escape in truth and not just in dreams.

"Miss Clive?" The Company representative looked very relieved to see her emerge from below decks, quite unlike his earlier disapproval of her existence. "I know your father trusted you to care for his animals. The fact that they have all arrived alive and well is proof of your skill, even after…" he cleared his throat, "well, enough said. Did Captain Clive mention how best to transfer these brutes from the ship to their new home? I was expecting him to be here. I foresee no difficulties with the parrots and the snake, but the tigers are," he searched for a word, "fretful."

Rama growled so loudly he rattled the chains binding the crate to the deck.

Adults could be so foolish sometimes. "There is no secret, sir. They just need a familiar face," said Sahira. "They don't like it when I'm out of sight."

Hands clasped behind his back, the official rocked on his heels. "If you would be so kind as to accompany them on their journey to the Tower menagerie this morning, afterward I'll take you myself to the most superior orphanage Mrs Bingham has recommended. It is run by a cousin of her husband so you can be reassured that it is a very good place."

And I am a one-eyed fakir, Sahira thought sourly. She had no intention of crossing the threshold of an establishment recommended by the vulture. However, the Company man's request fell neatly in with her own plans to stay with the animals. They were her only family now.

"Of course I'll help. It's what my father would've wished." Sahira bowed, forgetting she was supposed to be acting like a European girl.

"Quite, quite." His hands flapped like the pert tail of a sandpiper foraging for insects in the mud of the Musi River. "Carry on then."

There were more scandalized flutterings from the women.

"That dress," hissed one to Mrs Bingham, "is not appropriate. Elephants are not suitable for decent company."

Did Sahira care? Not a whit. In fact, she was pleased they didn't like it. And they were wrong: there was nothing indecent about elephants. She approached the crate and kneeled before the bars, murmuring in her mother's tongue of Persian. "I'm afraid, my brother, my sister, that this is where our journey ends. I'm heartily sorry you no longer have the jungle and the swamps to roam, but you would otherwise have been shot by the hunters on their elephants." Sahira mourned their freedom. Her father had disliked removing them from the wild but he had had his orders: capture or kill the tigers that had strayed too near human settlements. He'd said that God would understand that he was doing his best to look after these most beautiful but deadly of creatures. "Surely this life is better than no life?" continued Sahira. "We've all got a new place here in London and we have to make the best of it."

Her tone rather than her words calmed her friends. With a groan, Rama settled on his straw bed. Sita wrinkled her nose, a rough tongue emerging from her mouth. It was an expression that could be mistaken for a snarl but Sahira knew Sita was just testing the scents of the world around her. Sahira often wondered if the tigress could smell a lie. Her reassurance must have passed the test, for Sita crouched down, preparing herself for the next journey. Sahira hoped for their sake that it would be short and uneventful. "They are ready to be moved, sir."

"Is the lighter in position?" called the captain.

"Aye, sir," replied the boatswain.

"Then heave away!"

The sailors hurried forward and hooked the crate to a wooden crane. It took eight men to lift the tigers off the deck and another to use a guide rope to swing the bar of the crane over the barge, what the captain called a lighter, which had moored alongside the Indiaman.

"Careful!" squawked the Company official, nervous now his valuable cargo of exotic beasts was dangling over the brown waters of the Thames. "Don't drop them!"

Hearing his note of alarm, Rama sprang up and came to the bars, changing the balance in the crate. The lurching motion distressed him further and he began to pace and roar. Sita joined in, tail flicking in agitation as the crate rocked violently from side to side; ropes squeaked in the block and tackle. Now was not the moment for the tigers to start testing the limits of their cage. The Company man screeched like a parrot with its tail feathers plucked. *Didn't he realize that his nervous tone was upsetting them?* wondered Sahira. What was worse, the tigers couldn't see her below them on the deck as the crate spun in the air. They needed to have her in sight to reassure them.

"Hold tight! I'm going to them," Sahira warned the sailors as she ran to the rail and scrambled up. Pushing off with the stronger of her legs, she cleared the short distance between deck and crate. Her new skirts puffed out like a cobra's hood, almost making her misjudge the leap. She had a sickening glimpse of water below.

The ladies screamed and seamen swore.

"What is the girl doing? She will surely kill herself!" cried Mrs Bingham. "Stop her, someone!"

They were nothing more than the chattering of monkeys in the canopy. Grabbing one of the lines, Sahira scrambled more securely onto the roof of the crate and then hung her head over the barred door. "Lie down, Rama. You're safe."

Rama looked up at her distrustfully and snarled, but retreated to his bed.

21

"Hold on, Miss!" Slowly the crate was winched down to the deck of the lighter. Its crew of two nodded respectfully to Sahira as she made her unconventional entrance.

"All right up there, lass?" the master of the boat asked.

"Yes, sir. The tigers can go ashore now."

"And you too, I suppose?"

"Yes, I'm staying with them." For the first time, she felt contented. Surely they wouldn't separate them now? She'd proved that the tigers needed her.

Using the long sweeps, the men battled the tidal flow of the Thames and took the tigers and Sahira toward St Katharine Docks. The masts of the other ships rose around them like trunks in a spindly forest, the lighter scuttling like the prey beneath their rope branches. Sahira wasn't sure she was going to like London.

"Know these tigers well, do you, lass?" asked the second man.

Sahira pulled her attention back to the crew. "Very well, sir. I was there when we caught them and spent the months of the voyage in their company. That's since October."

"Then I reckon you'll not mind doing a little more of your animal magic to keep 'em safe as we load 'em on the cart."

"It's not magic."

"Whatever it is, Miss, just keep on doing it." He puffed as he hauled on the oar, knitted black cap beaded with raindrops. "Strong spring tide this morning."

"This is spring?" Sahira looked up at the drizzly skies. Father had made spring in England sound joyous, a season of blossom and blue heavens with white puffy clouds like fat sheep, temperature perfect for a long walk with none of the humidity that made it difficult at times to ramble in India. Today the clouds had closed on London like the lid of her trunk. The smoke from the higgledy-piggledy houses around the docks seemed to rise and then get trapped, hanging in the air like a shroud. Everything looked grey. Everything looked dirty.

"Aye. It's nice mild weather for March, Tiger Maid."

Clutching her thin arms to her sides, Sahira shivered in her cotton dress. "If you say so."

He chuckled. "All you new arrivals from India say the same. You'll find it warmer off the water."

The operation to lift the tigers was repeated at the dockside, this time ending on the flatbed of a cart pulled by the biggest pair of horses Sahira had ever seen. They did not like her, though, shying away as she went to make their acquaintance. Sahira was taken aback: usually all animals took to her. She decided she must have smelled too strongly of tiger and the carter warned her to keep her distance.

"Shire horses," her friends from the lighter told her when Sahira asked what breed they were. "London's pride, capable of pulling the heaviest loads."

Sahira was impressed. They were far bigger than any horse she had ever ridden, much closer in size to the most common Indian load carrier, an elephant, and of a fine cinnamon colour.

The Company representative, Mrs Tailor, and Mrs Bingham caught up with the tigers as the last rope was tied to secure the crate on the cart.

"All shipshape?" asked the Company man, tipping the dockers and lightermen who had brought the cage to rest with no mishaps.

"Yes, sir, thanks to the Tiger Maid." The master of the lighter gave Sahira a wink and flipped her one of the coins. She quickly pocketed it. Her first shilling.

"*Mam'noon*, thank you." Palms together, Sahira bowed.

"Miss." The lighterman touched his cap and cast off to fetch another cargo of exotic creatures.

"Oh, before I forget, don't tip the python's basket over!" Sahira called after them. "It really doesn't like that!"

"Good advice, Tiger Maid. *Mam'noon* to you too."

"None of that heathenish chatter, if you please." Mrs Bingham ushered Sahira along to where a two-wheeled hackney cab waited to take them to the menagerie. It was pulled by a sway-backed horse wearing blinkers. Both horse and carriage looked on their last legs. "You're in England now, not India."

Sahira wasn't likely to forget. "*Mam'noon* is Persian, my mother tongue."

"As I said, heathenish babble."

"I've found you a shawl," said Mrs Tailor quickly, before Sahira could protest that it was one of the oldest and most elegant of world languages. She tucked a grey woollen garment around Sahira's shoulders as they squeezed together on the bench seat. "I thought you must be cold in that thin dress of yours."

"You're very kind." Sahira hugged it to her chest. It was scratchy but did keep out the chill.

"And we really should do something about a hat for the child," said Mrs Bingham. "It's not decent for her to hare about, jumping onto boxes, hanging upside down within a hair's breadth of those wicked creatures – she is a complete hoyden!"

Mrs Tailor held Sahira's hand under the cover of the shawl. "It's only because she's not been taught better manners. I spent weeks with her in the sickroom. Eleanor's a sweet, biddable child underneath, I assure you."

Whatever gave Mrs Tailor that idea? Sahira wondered. Her mother had often called her "Little Ox" as she said her only child had proved the most stubborn daughter under God's heaven.

"I don't need a hat," Sahira said, thinking of the money she did not have to spend on such useless items.

Mrs Tailor turned to her, holding her gaze with her warm brown eyes; while not as beautiful, they were still a little like Sahira's mother's so commanded respect. "Maybe you don't think you need a hat, Eleanor, but society needs you to wear one for decency's sake. You understand about rules, don't you? I believe ladies like your mother remain in seclusion, not mixing with men outside their family?"

"Yes, in the *zenana*, the women's quarters." Until they went on animal hunts with their British husbands and dressed in male clothing like her mother did, much to the horror of her stuffy old relatives. Sahira's mother had been a scandal in Indian society for her choice of foreign spouse.

"You'll find girls here have much more freedom, but they are expected to go about modestly dressed. And that includes a hat, cap, or bonnet."

"So they carry their *zenana* on their heads?" asked Sahira.

"If you like," replied Mrs Tailor.

Explained like that, it seemed a reasonable demand. "I will wear a hat then."

"There you are, Mrs Bingham; if one takes the trouble to explain matters to the child she is quite rational."

"We'll see." The woman folded her arms across her thin chest, regarding Sahira with deep distrust.

That was fine: Sahira didn't trust Mrs Bingham either. She felt they were probably natural enemies, like mongoose and snake.

It did not take the carriage long to rattle over the cobbles to the tigers' new home in the Royal Menagerie in the Tower of London. Sahira's father had told her in the early days of the voyage, as they'd watched the stars of the southern skies sparkle over the Indian Ocean, that it was the oldest animal collection in the kingdom, founded to house the gifts European sovereigns were in the habit of giving to each other. What was more impressive to a northern medieval king than the gift of a lion from the lands of the Crusades? It was why so many big cats appear on royal coats of arms, a boast that the monarch had something no other noble in the kingdom did: the king of beasts.

This gift giving must have got quite out of hand, explained her father, because centuries later, the Tower had several courtyards in the western corner nearest the river devoted to its collection and had even opened to the public. Commoners as well as kings could now gaze upon lions, if they could pay the entry fee of a shilling.

"*Is that a lot of money?*" Sahira had asked.

"*It is, but you can also bring a dead dog or cat to feed to the lions and that gets you in.*"

"*Ugh!*"

"*Maybe, but it is practical and cuts the costs of keeping the animals in meat.*" Captain Clive had not been squeamish.

He had gone on to tell her that the menagerie was struggling. Even the extraordinary becomes stale when always available. With competition from other sources of amusement in the capital – freak shows and pleasure gardens, theatres and exhibitions, balloon rides and comic operas – the keeper had sent word to the East India Company for more specimens. Nothing brought in the visitors like the arrival of a new, previously unseen species. Captain Clive's tigers were the result.

"I'm not sure they will be enough," Captain Clive had said. *"Times are changing, and menageries are too. The men of science want them to be places of learning, not entertainment. The Tower menagerie is a dying breed. I fear in your life you will see it go extinct. Still, maybe the novelty of a tiger pair will keep it alive a little longer, eh, Sahira?"*

As the Company man knocked on the gate of Lion Tower, Sahira wondered whether this London appetite for new things had killed her parents. If they had not been on this voyage, they might not have caught a fever from a sick sailor soon after the ship left the Cape. They might even now be exploring the jungles of India, content in their little paradise of three living outside society's rules, collecting animals for zoological gardens. Her mother and father would be alive. Sahira would not have to wear a bonnet. Or be alone.

The gate creaked open and a man stood in the entrance, squashy hat clamped on his bearded head, rumpled clothes of rough material speckled with wisps of straw. He reminded Sahira of a jungle tree festooned with moss.

"At last!" He clapped his hands together – they were as big as coal shovels. "My tigers?"

My tigers, Sahira thought mutinously.

"Sit still, Eleanor," warned Mrs Tailor.

The Company man shook hands with the keeper. "Yes, Mr Cops. You'll find they're in fine fettle. Take a look."

Mr Cops walked round to the bars on one side of the crate. "Magnificent! Well worth the wait. A male and female too – just as I ordered."

"Eleanor!" Mrs Tailor's protest came too late. Sahira had slipped free of her two guards and jumped down from the hackney cab.

"Sir? Mr Cops?"

The keeper looked down at the girl with a bemused expression. "Yes, young miss?"

"I'm the daughter of Captain Clive."

"Ah yes. The great animal collector. Where is he?" He looked over her head, expecting her father to emerge from a carriage.

"He... he died – as did my mother – on the voyage." Sahira swallowed against tears. It was the first time she had been forced to say the words.

"Ah." Mr Cops hunkered down beside her and placed a hand on her shoulder. "I'm sorry to hear that, Miss Clive. The captain was the most talented man in his profession – never failed to find what I asked for, always delivered them in tip-top condition. Don't worry; I'll make sure the payment for your father's services reaches his heirs. How many are there of you?"

At first his question didn't make sense, but then Sahira realized he was asking if she had brothers and sisters.

"Just me, sir." Another reminder that she was quite alone in the world. How had that happened? Not long ago she was part of a household with her parents and many loyal servants, so much noise and chatter that she'd wished at times for more solitude.

"Mr Godstow, you heard my promise to the young lady? The payment should reach her without the Company skimming off any of it for expenses or whatnot. I'm wise to your tricks."

The Company representative, Mr Godstow as Sahira now belatedly found out he was called, bristled with indignation. "As if I would do such a thing. I do not cheat orphans."

Mr Cops stood up. "But you wouldn't call it cheating. It would show up on your accounts as your commission, a percentage, an administrative fee: how else do all you nabobs make your fortunes out of India?" He turned back to the tigers. "But you are worth the money, my beauties. I must send a notice to the papers to tell of your arrival. These marvels will bring the people flooding back."

"Sir." Sahira tugged the back of his jacket. "Sorry if I seem impertinent, but I have a request – not to do with money. You see, my father gave me a sacred charge. He said the Bible taught we must be good stewards of creation and look after our creatures, just like Adam and Eve in the Garden of Eden. My father gave the tigers into my special care."

He scratched his head, dislodging his hat so it sat far back on his scalp. "What's that?"

"So can I please stay with the tigers?" It came out in a tumble. "You see, I know them best. They won't settle without me. I'm really good with animals – all animals, not just tigers – and I'll work hard, I promise."

He stared at her for a moment. "You want to be a keeper of the Royal Menagerie?"

She nodded, hope rising. She felt the tigers' eyes on her. She had to persuade him – had to!

But then he laughed. "Dear girl, it ain't no Garden of Eden here. I don't employ children, let alone little ladies, to deal with dangerous beasts! Don't you know how strong they are? Look here: I almost got eaten by a boa constrictor myself three years ago." He bared his arm, showing the fang marks. "I'm hardly going to feed you to it, am I?"

"I wouldn't let a snake eat me. I know better than that, sir."

Rama growled. Sahira took that for agreement.

Unfortunately the keeper heard this comment as a criticism of his handling skills rather than proof of hers.

"It's out of the question. I'm the one to care for them now. I'm sorry for your loss but you have to make your way in the world somewhere else. The East India Company will look after you, I'm sure. They're rich enough to house you in a silk-lined palace."

From his expression, Mr Godstow did not agree. "We don't as a rule sponsor the native offspring of our employees. It sets a bad example."

"So does abandoning the cub to starve. I remind you she is half English and not penniless. She will receive her father's fee, I trust?"

"Yes, yes," nodded Mr Godstow.

"See that she does. I will check it has been done. Now, I really must get on. I have two tigers to unload in their new pen."

"But sir!" Sahira's one frail prospect of any happiness was disappearing fast. She made a last ditch appeal and grabbed his sleeve. "They're all I've got left!"

He brushed off her fingers. "None of that, child. You can't make a life with tigers! Go with Mr Godstow. There's no place for you here."

With a nod to the carter, he signalled for the tigers to be driven inside. The shire horses heaved in their harness and the crate rattled over the drawbridge and into the Tower. As the gates closed on Rama and Sita, she caught a last glimpse of their glittering eyes.

CHAPTER 3

The orphanage was in a poor district of East London, an area Sahira learned was called Whitechapel. Gazing out of the window, she could see nothing white, or even a chapel, among the cramped streets and rundown houses. Alleys were draped with grimy washing like grey creepers flung from cliff to cliff. Dirty-faced children sat listless on doorsteps, like rock lizards waiting for the invisible sun to warm them. The air smelled of coal dust and something much worse. It reminded Sahira of the badlands at the meeting of the rivers Nerbudda and Sher Nadi, a place where only the jackals flourished in the rocky ravines.

Mrs Tailor became more uneasy as the carriage made slow progress through the busy streets, alarmed by the signposts they passed. "Mrs Bingham, the orphanage: it's not a workhouse, is it?"

Mrs Bingham shook her head, bonnet moving like a pelican's beak from side to side. "No, but it lies close by that institution. It is a charitable home run on the most modern enlightened lines. Take notice, child: if you don't behave, the workhouse is where you'll end up!"

"But I like to work," Sahira said. Travelling with her parents, she had always had tasks to do for each camp, collecting firewood or tending their donkeys. "I'm not afraid to earn my way."

"Not in that place, you don't," corrected Mrs Tailor. "I'm afraid 'workhouse' is not a good name for it because it's the last stop before the grave for most of the poor who go through its gates."

Sahira shuddered. The carriage slowed, going past great iron gates in front of blackened brick buildings. People in grey uniforms milled about the yard or hung on to the bars. *Workhouse?* thought Sahira. It looked like the prison in Calcutta. The smell was terrible: sweat, toil, and hopelessness.

Mrs Tailor saw the direction of Sahira's gaze. "Yes, that's the workhouse. Believe me, an orphanage is a far better option." She pressed the girl's wrist. "Do try to fit in, Eleanor, for your parents' sake. They would not want to see you in that hellish place."

Despondent at being separated from the tigers, forced to break her word to her father that she would look after them, Sahira was finding it hard to care at all what happened to her. She knew, though, she should listen to the advice of her last remaining friend.

"I will try."

The carriage turned into a road with the interesting name of Duck Street and drew up in front of a five-storey house squeezed in among others like it, much as the three passengers were squashed up on the bench of the cab. The lowest floor was below street level and the topmost set behind a parapet on the roof. Black railings barricaded the front area from the riff-raff on the street, and she spied a tradesmen's entrance down at basement level. Brown curtains hung limply at the windows. Above the door was written:

Pence's Orphanage for Pauper Children

Sahira knew that word. "But I'm not a pauper. I have money – not a rajah's fortune, I know, but some." Surely it would be enough for her to rent a room somewhere with a family and find employment as a maid or seamstress? Maybe the Company would employ her when she was a little older to teach her languages to those ladies going out to India? As well as English and Persian, Sahira could speak Hindustani and a little Telugu, thanks to her ayahs, or nurses, who had lived in her father's household in India.

"You have a shilling in your pocket and only a promise of more from Mr Cops," said Mrs Bingham severely. "And what is he? A menagerie keeper!" She said it as if were the most despised profession on Earth when to Sahira it sounded perfect. "To all accounts and purposes, today you are a beggar depending on other people's charity and so you should be grateful that some of us have been prepared to go out of our way to accommodate you. You have no idea, do you, of what it costs to live in London?"

Sahira shook her head. "But I'm willing to work for my keep. I can make camp; build a fire; capture animals without harming them."

"Make camp! Capture animals! Ridiculous! No one will employ someone of your background. You've just had that proved to you at the menagerie. Did you not think of either of us when you embarrassed us with your outrageous request to Mr Cops?"

Mrs Bingham was the kind who liked to press on a bruise. Of course, Sahira hadn't been thinking of them. She had been thinking of what was best for her tigers and her future.

"I don't understand this place at all," Sahira appealed to Mrs Tailor but she could see from her expression that the nicer lady was in agreement with her companion.

"That is quite apparent," continued Mrs Bingham. "Now, Eleanor Clive, listen and learn. Children, especially girls, should act modestly; they should not cause trouble; and they should keep a still tongue in their head. Remember these three things and you will do well enough."

Impossible. Sahira knew she was not that girl, either in India or in England.

Mrs Bingham got out of the carriage and was joined by Mr Godstow on the pavement from a second cab.

"Let us go ahead and broach this delicate matter with my cousin, Mr Pence," she said. "Mrs Tailor, will you watch the child?"

They clearly thought Sahira was in danger of fleeing, which was true. She would have run if she had the least idea of where to go. The streets around her looked perilous – black chasms housing the desperate lairs of bandits and beggars.

"I don't want to live here," Sahira whispered, looking up at the ugly building. "It's not a happy place."

"How can you tell that?" Mrs Tailor asked with forced cheer. "You will make lots of lovely new friends and learn a suitable trade."

"Do you really think that?" Sahira asked.

Mrs Tailor fell silent. A Christian missionary to Bengal, she had promised Sahira that she would always try to tell her the truth.

After fifteen minutes of what must have been difficult negotiations, Mr Godstow emerged with a broad smile on his shiny face.

"Good news, Mrs Tailor! Mr Pence has agreed to overlook Eleanor's origins and admit her to the house. We've assured him that she barely looks like a native and will behave with English propriety. I trust you will not prove us liars, Miss Clive?" he said sternly.

With a nudge from Mrs Tailor, Sahira murmured a "no, of course not". It was ridiculous though: there were no more well-mannered people than her mother's. Compared to them, English people were ill-bred louts.

"Then, please come in. Mrs Tailor?" Mr Godstow helped the lady from the carriage, leaving the girl to make her own way. Sahira jumped down and went to the head of the cab to stroke the grey in thanks.

"Best keep away from Dobs," called the cab driver from his position high behind the passenger compartment. "He bites."

The horse snorted.

"Only those that deserve it, I bet," Sahira murmured. With a last pat, she moved away and followed Mr Godstow inside.

And so, with no other choice, Sahira broke her promise to herself and crossed the threshold of the orphanage.

"So this is the child?" asked Mr Pence, a tall stick of a man with stooped shoulders. He stood in his study like a heron on a riverbank. Sahira could just imagine him spearing her with his cane held ready in his left hand, her the glittering fish thrashing about for escape.

"That's right, sir," said Mr Godstow. "Her father was one of the Company's most loyal servants."

"But her mother was a native."

"A Hindoo princess," said Mr Godstow quickly.

Sahira's mother was neither Hindoo nor a princess but she wasn't going to correct him. If the story helped, then she would let it stand.

"Royal blood, eh? Well, that counts for something, even if it is *Indian* royal blood." Mr Pence sniffed. "Well, Miss, what have you got to say for yourself?"

Many inappropriate comments came to mind but Sahira chose one that would allow her a roof for the night. She wasn't planning to stay long.

"I'm very grateful for your charity, sir," she said, hoping this choice of words would appeal to her audience. Mother had always said Sahira should be gracious under all circumstances.

"Quite so. You are to be admitted to the girls' dormitory on a month's trial. If by then you prove unworthy of your place, you will be passed over to the workhouse to deal with. I hope that provides you with enough incentive to curb your behaviour?"

Mrs Bingham evidently had spread tales about her already.

"Sir." Sahira bobbed a curtsey. *Be gracious: remember you are a daughter of a noble family on both sides.*

"Matron will find you a change of clothes. Colourful gowns such as the one you are wearing might do for Sunday best, but they are not permitted for daily use. The heathen elephants must be removed, of course."

How could elephants be heathen? Sahira wondered.

"I will enter you in our admission book," continued Mr Pence. "I take it you were christened?"

Sahira's father had raised her in his faith, her mother in her Islamic traditions, so she was able to nod. "Yes, sir, by the Company chaplain in Madras."

"Full name?"

"Sahira Eleanor Clive."

"Sahira? No, that won't do. I'll put you down as 'Eleanor Sarah'."

"But that's not my name, sir."

He thumped the ledger closed. "It is now. Say goodbye to your friends, then follow me."

Sahira already hated the orphanage. She stared at the three adults who were abandoning her here, leaving her as trapped as a caged tigress. It was hard to find any word of thanks. Rage seethed powerlessly behind bars.

Mrs Tailor patted her cheek awkwardly, soothing some of the anger with her attempt at kindness. "Be brave, Eleanor. I wish things had happened otherwise for you but you'll soon get used to the change. It's a lesson we all have to learn at some time in our lives."

Despite herself, Sahira leaned into the lady's hand, drinking up this last tender touch. She missed her mother so much. "Thank you for your kindness, Mrs Tailor."

"I'll remember you in my prayers. God watch over you, child. I'll call in when I'm next in town."

Mr Godstow gave her a curt nod. "I've arranged with Mr Pence for the money owing for the tigers to be set against your account with him. He'll take your expenses out of it."

"What? Please, no, I need that money!" Sahira wanted to add that Mr Pence had the shifty look of a swindler at the bazaar. If he got his hands on her small inheritance then she'd never see a penny of it.

"What can you, a child, do with such a sum? Someone would take it from you in a trice. No, it is much better that it goes to a responsible adult to manage on your behalf."

Now Sahira knew why Mr Pence had agreed to take her.

"Have you ever known such ingratitude?" asked Mrs Bingham. "Anyone would think from her expression that we were leaving her in the hands of pirates."

Their ship had fought off buccaneers in the seas near Madagascar but Sahira knew well from her travels in India that piratical people sailed on dry land as well as the high seas. Father had taught her not to be taken for a fool. But what could she do? As Mr Godstow made plain, all these arrangements were being agreed over her head. She hated being a child – hated being at the mercy of these merciless grown-ups.

"Good, that's settled then." Mr Pence exchanged a snide smile with Mrs Bingham. "Come, Eleanor Sarah Clive. I'll introduce you to Matron."

With a final pleading look at Mrs Tailor, Sahira let herself be led away.

Matron appeared an easier person to manage compared with the conniving Mr Pence. Her frizzled brown hair curled from her mob cap; her little eyes sat like currants in dough before it is cooked.

There was an air about her of someone who had seen everything, done too much, and so given up caring. She rummaged through her linen store and pulled out a set of clothes for Sahira, making wild guesses as to size. Sahira ended up with a shift that finished at her calves and a drab woollen dress that trailed on the floor. A close-fitting white cap and apron completed the uniform.

"There you are, lovey. I'll look after your pretty dress for you. Ooo, I like these what-you-ma-call-its." She held it up to the light, swaying slightly.

"Elephants," Sahira supplied. She reminded herself that she had to be as strong and excellent as an elephant to survive in this jungle.

Matron took a swig from a silver flask before dropping it back in her deep apron pocket. "That's the word. Saw one once, can you imagine it, at the Exeter Exchange?"

"What's an exchange?" Sahira asked.

"An exhibition hall on the Strand. We used to have lots of wild animal shows once upon a time – a real treat they were. Anyway, they had to shoot the elephant when it got too frisky – poor Chunee."

Sahira could guess exactly what had happened. "Did they not know that the bull elephant goes into must? Males cannot be caged when driven to mate."

Matron clicked her tongue. "Little girls shouldn't talk about mating. Terrible massacre it was. The place stank for days. Then the scientific men took over and they carved it up to study. You can still see the bones. Hard to believe the good Lord made such creatures – so big, and to think they eat through their noses!"

How could she get this basic fact wrong? "They don't actually eat through their trunks. They have mouths."

Matron wasn't interested in Sahira's correction. "Here's a sheet and blanket. You take the bed by the window. Jenny left us last week so it's free."

Sahira blinked three times to erase the image of the elephant shot to death and dissected – a trick her father had taught her to get rid of bad thoughts. It only half worked. "Where did Jenny go?"

"Churchyard, of course." Matron took another swig. "It was a harsh winter. Don't worry: I've turned the mattress."

Sahira knew better than to sleep in the same bed as someone who had recently died. As her ayah had told her, their spirit might return and occupy your body and Sahira had no amulet to ward them off. Her father told her this was merely superstition and had given a more scientific explanation that diseases might linger. Both views led to the same conclusion: she would sleep on the floor until she could find a way out of here.

"The other children will be out of their lessons soon for dinner. We then have prayers, chores, an hour of playtime, and then bed, understood?"

"Yes, Matron," Sahira said solemnly.

"Mr Pence said not to mention that you're Hindoo."

"I'm not…" Sahira stopped herself from betraying the lie about her identity.

"So I won't tell them anything about that when I introduce you. Best you forget all those foreign ways of yours, eh? And the name Eleanor, well that sounds too much like you're taking on airs. You need something plain and serviceable for your new station in life. Better to be Ellie." She hiccupped. Everyone here seemed intent on giving Sahira names she didn't want: first "Eleanor Sarah", and now "Ellie". A bell rang downstairs. "That's the signal for dinner." Matron took Sahira's hand, noticing for the first time that the new girl limped. "Hurt yourself, lovey?"

"A long time ago. It's nothing. I'm not in pain." Not from that old injury, she wasn't.

"That's the spirit. Soldier on. I never complain about my nerves, though they plague me something dreadful." Taking another quick swig before returning the hip flask to her apron pocket, Matron led Sahira down two flights of stairs and into a large bare room with two long tables. Children were already standing behind the benches, one side for boys, the other for girls. Matron took Sahira to the top of the girls' table to sit among the older orphans. "Here, squeeze in between Emily and Ann. Girls, this is Ellie."

With curious looks, the two girls made a space for her. Matron carried on to the table at the far end, the only one covered by a cloth. Mr Pence and people Sahira assumed were the other members of staff, teachers and nursery maids, assembled around it.

Mr Pence rapped on the table. "Hands together and eyes closed."

Like well-drilled troops, the children all assumed the attitude of prayer, Sahira following only a beat behind. Mr Pence then began a long prayer about how they should be grateful for his charity towards them and how wicked they all were and in need of forgiveness. He made special mention of all benighted heathens in foreign lands, especially India. Sahira could feel his eyes on her, even though she wasn't looking. Eventually, after wandering through the highways and byways of all the possible sins the children might have committed since breakfast, he blessed the food.

"Be seated."

With a rumble like thunder, forty children climbed over the benches and sat down. The forty-first copied them, again lagging a little behind.

"You have blue boots!" whispered the fair-haired girl next to Sahira – Emily or Ann, she wasn't sure.

"Yes."

"Don't let Mr Pence see or he'll confiscate them," the girl on the other side hissed. She had tightly curled black hair and a gap-toothed smile. Her skin was a shade darker than Sahira's. *Where had her parents come from?* Sahira wondered.

"Are we not allowed to talk?" Sahira asked.

The girl shook her head. "It's not seemly," she whispered.

So far in this orphanage Sahira had been told so many things she couldn't do, she wondered what was allowed.

"I'm Sahira." She kept her voice low.

"Not Ellie?"

"That's the name Matron calls me." Sahira flicked her eyes to the adults at the top table. "I won't let it stick. I'm really Sahira."

The black-haired girl nodded, putting a hand to her cheek to shield her mouth. "I'm Ann."

"I'm Emily," murmured the other.

A spoon rapped on the tabletop. "Eleanor Clive, stand up," a stern voice said. It was Mr Pence.

Sahira's companions gave her alarmed looks as she got to her feet.

"Eleanor Clive, you are not to talk at mealtimes. You are forgiven as it is your first day but I trust you will respect our rules from now on?"

"Sir." Sahira almost bowed but remembered in time to bob a curtsey.

"Sit down."

The orphans who worked in the kitchens served the meal. These included a little lad who narrowly avoided being tripped by a mean-looking boy on the other table. The food appeared to be some kind of stew. Unidentified meat swam among the vegetables.

"What is this?" Sahira asked, masking her question with her hand as Ann had done.

She coughed. "Pork."

Sahira spat out a mouthful in her hand and put her spoon down. Pork was *haram*, forbidden.

"You have to eat everything or you'll be punished," Ann warned.

"It's against my religion."

Ann looked furtively around her before whispering, "But you're a Christian, aren't you?"

Sahira looked at her miserably. Was she? Father had called her his little amphibian, like a frog living on land and in water: she had hopped along as a Christian with him in his world, and then swum as a Muslim with Mother in hers. Sahira had observed both religions' festivals, followed their dietary practices and fasts, worshipped in their holy buildings. It had felt natural to cross between the two.

Ann's gaze went over Sahira's shoulder to where one of the monitors was patrolling the children's tables. "Quick, give it here."

They swapped bowls, her empty one for Sahira's full. Better to go hungry than let her mother down, thought Sahira. She knew, though, that she would have to come to terms with her new life in this Christian country. Being amphibian was no longer a choice she was allowed in this narrow world.

After prayers and chores, during free time, Ann and Emily went to visit their younger brothers and sisters in the nursery. In the snatches of conversation the three girls managed, they told Sahira that they both had been orphaned in a recent outbreak of cholera in Spitalfields just a stone's throw from the orphanage. They counted themselves lucky still to be with their surviving siblings in the same institution rather than in the workhouse. When Sahira, a determined collector of stories, had asked Ann where she had got her tawny complexion, she had laughed. Apparently, London had a history of people coming here from many nations, right back to the Romans, even though it was rarely discussed. One of Ann's own ancestors two generations ago had been a freed slave.

"Ann, that is a huge comfort to me," Sahira said seriously. "The women on the ship had acted as if I were an oddity, like a white elephant."

Emily nudged her friend. "Hear that? Sahira speaks like a swell, don't she?"

Sahira frowned, wondering what she had said. "I speak like my father."

"I don't know about your voice, but to look at?" said Ann. "I'd say that in Whitechapel and Spitalfields, you'd slide right in without a splash. We have people of all nations so close to the docks – Hindoos, Chinamen, Africans: you name it, we've got it. Good thing too, because you're stuck here now with us."

Do I really have to stay here though? Sahira wondered. She had not seen the sky since her arrival, penned by drab walls and grimy windows. She stayed downstairs when the girls left to visit their baby siblings and followed the noise of children's voices to the courtyard at the back of the house. There was a small patch of grey overhead with a light rain falling. Some girls played hopscotch while older boys hit a ball against a wall using their palms as bats. Her weak leg made her a poor player at skipping games so she took a seat in a corner to watch. It was fairly easy to read the relationships among the children – the ones in charge of their little packs, the lone wolves, the rivals. Sahira hoped they would just leave her alone. Like the tigers, she preferred her own company most of the time.

How were Sita and Rama coping? Did the keeper understand that they needed space for exercise? They'd been cooped up in a crate for months and months. If only they had somewhere to run, stretch, and roll! They'd enjoy swimming in the moat if he'd let them. If Mr Cops only had experience with domestic cats, he might not realize that they were used to water and liked it.

A finger poked Sahira in the shoulder. "New girl, what's your name?"

Startled to be disturbed while minding her own business, Sahira looked up. Two boys stood over her, at first glance identical down to their freckles and prominent ears. She had spotted them earlier at the centre of the boys playing ball. They must be brothers.

"I am Sahira Clive," she said proudly.

"What kind of name is that?" asked one.

"My kind."

He wrinkled his nose like someone testing a food they did not like. "Where are you from?"

"Hyderabad." He had to have heard of that, of course.

"Where?"

Did English people not look at maps? "It's in India. Shall I tell you about it?" Folding her hands in her lap, back straight in proper storyteller mode, she got ready to embark on a tale to entertain.

"Nah. What you doing 'ere then?" asked the other.

It was bewildering. Did they not want her stories? Tales had been what people swapped between them around the campfire, a way of making friends as the stories passed like well-worn coins from person to person. She wasn't sure what to reply.

"Don't you know why? Are you an idiot?" The first boy elbowed his brother. "She's daft."

"No, I'm not!" Why was she here though? The first answer she thought of – "I'm in exile like Rama the Steadfast" – probably would not be understood by these London boys. They clearly did not know the same stories.

"You've got blue boots," declared the first one to talk to her.

"They're Indian too."

He glanced over his shoulder. "What size?"

"My size." Why was he asking?

"I'll give you good money for 'em."

"I don't want your money. They're my boots." What did her boots have to do with him?

He seemed taken aback by her refusal, but then came forward almost to step on her toes. "Don't you know who you're talking to?"

"No, I'm afraid I don't." She was obviously missing something here.

"I'm Tommy Newton, and this is my brother, Alf."

"Hello, Tommy Newton. Hello, Alf Newton." *"Be polite,"* her mother had told her, *"even when others are not."*

"Yeah, we run this place," cut in Alf who she noticed had a scar over his left brow and a wild look, distinguishing him from his brother. She'd seen a jackal look like that once, with its red jaws deep in a lamb's entrails. Moments later her father had shot it. She would definitely not turn her back on Alf. "We keep it ticking over. Forget Mr Pence. Stay on the right side of us and you'll be fine. Get on our wick and then…" He drew his finger across his throat.

Sahira didn't know whether to take his threat seriously or not. Some maharajahs had trained up boys as assassins so she knew that there were many of his age prepared to take a life over the slightest insult. Should she be afraid? She decided caution was her best option.

"I'll attempt not to 'get on your wick', Alf."

He scratched his head, still not sure what to make of the newcomer. His looked down at her feet. "And the boots? Tommy wants 'em."

Sahira tucked them away under her skirts. "What boots?"

"Humph! You're a cheeky one. We're not sure we like you," Alf said, his brother nodding.

"The feeling is mutual, I assure you," she said absent-mindedly as she looked for an escape.

He regained her attention with a poke in the arm. "You speak like a swell – all airs and graces. Don't like that neither."

Did he really think she was going to apologize for being educated by her father?

"And another thing: why were you limping earlier?" asked Tommy.

Was there no end to their questions? "Because I was injured a few years ago and my leg has never recovered."

"What happened?"

"I was stepped on." Normally she would freely offer the story but she sensed they wouldn't appreciate it.

"By what? A horse?"

"No, an elephant."

Alf laughed. "Blimey, you're not making it up, are you?" His tone changed from threatening to curious.

"No. Where I come from, accidents involving elephants are commonplace."

He stared at Sahira, trying to judge if she was taking advantage of his ignorance. "Watch it, Clive."

"I was just answering your questions."

Ann arrived breathless at Sahira's side. She pressed a hand to her chest. "Tommy, Alf, I see you've met Sahira."

"We don't like her," said Alf.

Ann wrung her hands. "Give her a chance. She's only been here a few hours."

"I want her boots," said Tommy.

"He's not getting my boots," Sahira said quickly before yet more of her possessions were bargained away without her say-so.

"I'll talk to her," said Ann.

"You do that." He cast another dubious look at Sahira, then grabbed his brother's arm and tugged him away to find more orphans to torment.

Now they had moved on, Ann slumped down beside Sahira. "Oh Lord, I should have realized they'd be on to you."

"Who are the Newton brothers and why should I give them my boots?"

She sagged against the brick wall behind them. "More than brothers – twins. Unlike the rest of us, they're not orphans. Their ma is dead but their dad is the king of the East End underworld. He takes a percentage from all the ships that dock, runs the thieves and bullies, rules the markets."

"What are his sons doing here then?"

"Harry Newton can't be bothered raising them – he has a dangerous household – so he has an arrangement with Mr Pence to keep them here until they're old enough to be useful. They've copied their father's ways, putting themselves at the top of our pecking order."

"I see." Sahira rubbed her chilly hands together. She had been in more danger than she realized. "So they've marked out their territory. Lots of animals do that."

Ann gave her a strange look. "I suppose they do."

"They usually pass water on the trees, scratch the bark, and so on."

Ann giggled. "I haven't seen Tommy or Alf doing that – though I wouldn't put it past Alf. If you didn't cotton on, he's the mad one of the pair. Tommy is the only one who can rein him in."

"I didn't mean they'd really do it. They needed to scratch on me a bit, threaten me so I would recognize their dominance." But they didn't realize she was a tiger, not some stray dog they could intimidate.

"Yes, so you might want to think about how much you want your boots. Tommy'll give you money for them now, but later he'll just take them."

"I don't give in to bullies."

Ann's frown deepened. "Please, Sahira, don't take on two enemies so much bigger than you. You have to be cautious around them."

The sun finally broke through the clouds, turning the rain to silver.

"Don't worry. Like Sinbad, I've travelled to places they've never been, faced down threats they can't imagine. They haven't met anyone like me before."

PART 2

FOREST OF THE NIGHT

CHAPTER 4

Sahira had disturbed dreams that first night as she lay on the draughty floor of the girls' dormitory. The white tower featured prominently, a castle she couldn't reach, a wall she couldn't climb, a paradise she couldn't enter as Mr Cops stood at the gate with a flaming sword. In her dream, the Holy Roman Emperor processed through the doors easily enough, three leopards on a leash. He gave them to the English king Henry III as a gift. Sometimes the beasts prowled in the forbidden garden as spotted cats, sometimes as lions, because her father had told her the chroniclers of the time used the words "leopard" and "lion" for the same creatures. In the dream the big cats changed skin like chameleons, sniffing the block where traitors were executed, raking at the stone steps where prisoners entered from the river. Climbing Tower Hill, the three lions then leaped from the grass to take their places on Henry's Plantagenet crest, flapping above the tower turrets.

Sahira awoke to find a cat curled up on her stomach. So that was why she had dreamed of lions.

It was a scruffy tabby with a white chest and three white paws. She stroked his coat, marvelling at the black and brown stripes, a miniature English tiger. His jade green eyes blinked once at her.

"Who do you belong to?" she murmured. Seeing the light was dawning through the cracks in the shutters, she got up and pulled on the scratchy grey gown. She picked up her boots and stockings and crossed the bare floor, trying not to step on any squeaky boards. The cat wound around her ankles, almost tripping her. Tiptoeing past the sleeping girls, Sahira had a quick wash in the cold water on the stand by the door, stuffed a cap in her apron pocket, and went down four flights of stairs to the basement. The only person in the kitchen was a little boy, the same who had almost fallen over while serving supper; he was lying curled up by the hearth. He looked over at Sahira as she crept through.

"What are you doing?" he whispered. "You're not supposed to be 'ere."

She had to see the sky. "I won't be here in a second. I'm going outside. Have you got any crusts?"

Brushing off the ash from his clothes, he climbed on a chair and brought down a basket of iron-hard bread. "The cook softens it in water and adds it to broth," he explained.

"She won't mind if I take a bit, will she?" Sahira asked.

He grinned, face lighting up like a lamp flaring under a glass mantle. *Perhaps*, she thought, *there was much more spirit in him than first meets the eye.* "She won't know, will she?" the boy asked.

Sahira shook her head and returned his smile. "Not from me." She selected a blackened piece that would doubtless spoil the broth and then helped her new partner in crime put the basket back in its place out of reach of the rats.

"I'm Sahira," she said, bowing to him Indian fashion.

"I'm Ned," he said, bowing to her like a little English lord. "You're the Hindoo princess, Cook says."

So much for her origins remaining a secret. "Not Hindoo, not a princess, but I am from India. It's a long tale."

"You must tell it to me when you 'ave time but Cook will be 'ere any moment. What do you want with the bread?" He yawned and scrubbed at his hair that was sticking up like hedgehog pins. His ears poked out from the side of his head.

"Come and see if you like." Sahira nudged the cat toward the hearth. "Sorry, puss, you need to stay inside."

Shutting the door on the tabby, Sahira and Ned slipped together out into the courtyard. It was chilly as the dawn broke to yet more leaden skies and Sahira was glad of her warmer clothes even if they were ugly. The stones were cold under her feet.

"Hold the bread a moment." Sahira thrust the crust in Ned's hands and pulled on stockings and blue boots. At least the Newtons hadn't launched a raid in the night to gain them; she'd slept with them under her pillow to prevent them being stolen and they were probably responsible for half of the dreams.

"You should get dressed in the dormitory, you know," said Ned matter-of-factly, nibbling on the crust.

"I thought I probably should but I didn't want anyone to hear me. It's always a good idea to stalk your quarry in bare feet so you can feel the terrain under your toes and avoid loose stones, snapping twigs, or squeaky boards."

"Until you get caught – then you'll be whipped."

"You have a point." Sahira took the bread and crumpled it into pieces.

"Are you going to tell me what you're doing?"

"Ssh! Just wait." Yesterday, Sahira had noticed on the top of the wall some of her favourite birds, ragged London examples, not the soft grey and white of the ones in the Nizam's pigeon house. These specimens had black and slate feathers, but they were pigeons nonetheless, with the distinctive iridescent sheen around their neck that made them noble even in rags. Sahira made soft cooing noises, telling them about the feast she had in store. She had always been good at mimicking animal noises, particularly birds. Soon the pigeons flocked to the wall, then flew down to peck at their feet, little courtiers with their ladies.

"You like smelly old pigeons?" asked Ned. "Cook calls 'em rats of the air."

"Cook is wrong." Sahira kneeled down. "And rats are very intelligent so not to be despised." The birds flapped away, then returned with their self-important strut to eat from her palm. "As for pigeons, they are noble birds. Ladies in my country keep them and fly them for sport. To have a rare breeding pair is to have much renown in the durbar of Hyderabad."

"What's a durbar?"

"A court where the Nizam sits and rules his people."

"Is a Nizam like a judge and you get scragged?"

"Scragged?" Sahira couldn't get her head around this London English.

"Hanged."

Sahira shuddered. "No, not like that. More like King George's court. A Nizam is a ruler."

Ned picked up a couple of crumbs and held them out as she had done. A bold male sidled up to him and took one from his small palm. "Look at that! Pigeons ain't so bad, are they?"

"Not so bad at all." Sahira smiled.

Breakfast over for the pigeons, Sahira brushed off her hands. "Tell me, Ned, are you an orphan like the rest of us?"

He grimaced, his young face suddenly looking decades older with worry. "Yes, but I'm not on the register. My mother wasn't married when she 'ad me so I'm not allowed in official like. My ma was Cook's second cousin so she persuaded Mr Pence to let me in as 'er boot boy."

"Boot boy?" Boots were clearly an important part of orphanage life if they even had a boy assigned to them.

"I clean shoes, sweep up, do the dirty jobs. It's fine though as long as Cook's not been drinking. At least I don't 'ave to go to school like the others." He paused, then added anxiously, "Mr Pence wants to get rid of me so you'd better go back upstairs – I don't want to give 'im a reason to carry out 'is threats." Somewhere in the city a clock struck six, perhaps in the white chapel Sahira was yet to see. "Cook'll be in to make breakfast and it wouldn't do for you to be found down 'ere with me." He rubbed his knuckles as if he could still feel the sting of the last blow.

"Thank you, Ned. It's been good meeting you." Sahira bowed.

He blinked up at her. "You're not how I thought you'd be."

"And how was that?"

"Lawks, for one thing, you're odd but not that odd. Being a Hindoo princess, I thought you'd 'ave blue skin and lots of arms or something." He'd clearly seen pictures of Hindoo gods and got the wrong idea.

"No one in India has blue skin and lots of arms." Sahira didn't think it worth repeating the fact that she was from another faith and not a princess – the differences didn't seem to matter here. Distance blurred the distinctions that were so important in India.

"Shame. It sounds like it could be useful, you know, for carrying things?" He demonstrated his idea of having many arms with a little pantomime of juggling eggs.

Sahira laughed and shook her head. "Careful you don't drop one. See you later, Ned." She paused at the door. "Oh, by the way, who does the cat belong to?"

"The cat?" Ned shrugged. "No one really. 'E just lives 'ere. We all call him 'Cat'."

"Then his name is Jeoffry," Sahira announced.

"'Ow do you know?"

"He told me." She winked and ran upstairs as quickly as her bad leg would allow, Jeoffry at her heels.

After the breakfast of a decent serving of porridge that helped silence Sahira's rumbling stomach, the official orphans were expected in the schoolrooms, boys on the first floor, girls on the second. As they left, Sahira noticed Tommy Newton going from boy to boy, flicking necks, patting pockets, and removing whatever he had a fancy for, marble or coin, while Alf kicked a damp-eyed lad down several steps and laughed at him for being a crybaby – all this while Mr Pence was in the room reading his newspaper.

"Why does Alf do that – and why doesn't Mr Pence stop him?" Sahira asked Ann and Emily, ready to go to the bullied child's aid.

"Don't!" warned Emily, taking her arm. "Are you mad? You'll only make it worse. Hubert knows he gets a kick in the morning and a kick at night. He expects it."

This was outrageous but Ann and Emily had firmly taken charge of her, steering her into the classroom to see the schoolmistress, Mrs Pence. She looked as welcoming as her husband, staring down her long nose at Sahira as if she were something dubious Jeoffry had dragged in from the street. A glittering jet necklace coiled around her throat like a Black Mamba snake.

"Mrs Pence, this is the new girl," Ann said, pushing her gently forward. Out of the corner of her eye Sahira noticed Jeoffry leap to a windowsill and settle down in a patch of weak sunlight.

The woman surveyed Sahira. "I see a lock of hair escaping."

Emily came up behind and tucked the offending curl under the cap for her.

"Have you been to school, girl?" The woman's tone could cut ice from a Himalayan glacier.

"No, ma'am."

"Can you read?"

"Yes, ma'am. My mother taught me." *Be patient,* Sahira reminded herself.

"The Indian woman." Mrs Pence pursed her lips. "So I suppose you cannot read the King's English?"

"Indeed I can – and Persian script."

"There's no call for that here. Can you write?"

"Yes."

"When you reply you will say 'ma'am' or 'yes, Mrs Pence'."

"Yes, Mrs Pence." Sahira looked down at her boots for encouragement.

"Know your numbers and tables?"

"Yes, ma'am."

"Sew?"

"My mother thought my embroidery very fine, ma'am."

"Not embroidery – good plain sewing – shirts, pillowcases, and so on."

"I dare say I can learn, Mrs Pence." She hoped that would satisfy the woman.

But no. Mrs Pence scowled at Sahira. "I dare say you can. You'll join the top form and we'll see if you are as skilled as you claim." She pointed to the ring of girls who surrounded her chair. Sahira rather wished she had pretended to be ignorant and been invited to sit among the younger ones. Their teacher had a kindly face and soft voice.

Sahira took her place next to Ann. The top form began by copying out the Ten Commandments on their slates, a tedious process for Sahira as she was used to pen and ink, not chalk. Her handwriting was not at its best. They then moved on to an hour of sewing hems while Mrs Pence read aloud. This was a little better as the book she chose was *The Pilgrim's Progress,* which had enough action and adventure between the moral stuff to keep Sahira interested. In the final session before dinner, each girl was invited to recite the piece she had learned. Emily had chosen one of Isaac Watts's poems, which starts, "How doth the little busy bee." Sahira felt tears prick her eyes – it was one of the verses her father had taught her, containing splendid stuff about gathering honey and building cells. She was transported far from grey London into the steamy heat of the jungle. Once, in an old temple in the forest, he had shown her a honeycomb dripping from a crack in a frieze of the Lord Shiva with his cobra necklace and trident. A colony of bees had moved in when the holy men had abandoned it, new followers for the Hindoo god of destruction and re-creation. She was shocked, therefore, to come back from her daydream to hear new verses as Emily continued. The poem went on to say how if children weren't kept busy, the devil, Satan, would find mischief for their idle hands to do. Somehow Sahira's father had not thought she needed to hear that part. His God had been the God of love, not punishment.

Mrs Pence turned her beady eye on the newcomer. "Eleanor Clive, I see you are impressed. I imagine that this is the first good poetry you've ever heard?"

"No, ma'am." After the bee part, Sahira didn't think it very good. Father had said good poetry should tell you a story, or open new vistas of feeling and thought, not beat you over the head with a moral. "I've heard quite a lot."

"Indeed?" the teacher said severely.

"My father adored poetry and taught me lots by heart. He even made me my own *diwan* but I think it was lost on the voyage."

"What is a *diwan*?" Mrs Pence spoke the foreign word like it was an apricot stone she had to spit out.

"A collection of his favourite poetry, written out by hand. There were many English poems in it."

"And many heathen riddles too, no doubt," she said smugly.

"Not riddles, ma'am, though he put in some English ones. The Persian poems were mainly love songs, like the *ghazals* of the great poet Hafez, and Father also translated the best speeches from the epic of Rama the Steadfast."

"We'll have none of that foreign stuff here, young lady. You may, however, recite one of the English verses your father included. Make sure it is suitable."

Thinking of this morning's adventure, Sahira decided that no one could object to her favourite poem about a cat.

> For I will consider my Cat Jeoffry.
> For he is the servant of the Living God, duly and daily
>   serving him.
> For at the first glance of the glory of God in the East he
>   worships in his way.
> For this is done by wreathing his body seven times round
>   with elegant quickness.

And so it went on, for many lines, extolling the virtues of this most excellent of creatures, teacher of benevolence to children and member of the tribe of Tiger. The girls listened to her with delighted expressions, unclear if the tongue-firmly-in-cheek poem was mockery or sincere – the poet probably meant it as both. But because it mentioned God, Moses, and the Lord Jesus, Mrs Pence could hardly object.

When Sahira finished, the teacher was silent. "A fine piece," she eventually declared, though she didn't sound sure, "but next time you will learn something more conventional. The opening of John Milton's *Paradise Lost* will suffice. First twenty lines."

Sahira curtseyed. That was already lodged in her memory. Father had enjoyed declaring it with a swing of his long knife as he cut a path through thick undergrowth, saying there was nothing better than a bit of Milton to clear a way through obstacles.

During dinner, Sahira didn't try to talk behind her hand because she was too busy pondering all the things she had learned about the orphanage in the day she had spent there. It was like a dangerous forest, full of snares. The owner was crooked like a forked-tongue viper, she was sure of that. Not only was his arrangement with Mr Godstow about her inheritance unfair, he was clearly in cahoots with the local bandit lord. If Tommy and Alf were to be believed, he didn't really care for running the place but left the children to sort out their own caste system under his nose. Bright little Ned was down at the bottom – the *chamar*, or untouchable, of the house; the Newtons considered themselves the brahmin, or top caste. As to where Sahira fitted, that was still undecided.

What she didn't realize was that in a very short time she was about to find out the hard way.

CHAPTER 5

Several days passed at the orphanage, all much the same as the first. It was hard to know which day of the week it was, the only sign of change being that the orphans had fish broth on Friday. It was as unpalatable as it sounded, Sahira discovered. The cook could do with a lesson from her family's *khansaman*; he knew how to add spices to make the most boring vegetables tasty. This English food was like cotton in the mouth and about as exciting to the taste buds.

It didn't take Sahira long to unearth more dishonest dealings in the orphanage. According to Ned, Cook sold on the best cuts of meat bought for the orphans. She replaced them with poor-quality but cheaper stuff from the market. The plain sewing the girls were expected to do was sent to Mrs Pence by a local seamstress. In other words, they were cheap labour as the dressmaker didn't have to pay them, though Sahira had no doubt Mrs Pence saw the benefit in her purse. Most worrying of all was what happened to the orphans when they left the establishment at thirteen or fourteen. Mr Pence told his patrons that they all found good jobs with reputable employers. Ann whispered to Sahira that two boys from last year could now be found acting as runners for thief lord Harry Newton and that one of the girls now worked in an inn he owned. The rumour was that if you dined there, you didn't leave with your watch or wallet.

Mrs Bingham came a few days later to check on "the girl from the boat", as she called her. It was dinnertime. She sat with her cousin at the high table, a small smile of satisfaction on her lips that made Sahira want to do something drastic just to wipe it off her face, but she knew, like the tiger, she had to wait for her chance to pounce. For the moment, she had to pretend she was a pussy cat. She hated that Mrs Bingham thought she had successfully clipped Sahira's wings. What Mrs Bingham didn't know was that Sahira was just waiting for her opportunity to fly. She only lingered because she couldn't decide where she was heading. Sahira often imagined herself running free into the green fields of this country with her tigers for company, but what would happen next, she couldn't fathom. Nothing good, she feared.

Saturday brought an early dinner and longer free time than on other days so that Cook could take a half day. The sun had finally shown herself so Sahira sat in a shaft in the corner of the yard, turning up the hem of her Sunday best gown. Preparing for the day when she would be free of here, she had decided she wasn't going to cut off the elephants so had opted to hide them in a fold and risk reproof for having too short a skirt. A shadow fell across the material. When she looked up, she found Tommy, Alf, and a couple of their friends had gathered around her.

Sahira knew that this was not good. Groups of animals ganging up on a solitary one never went well for the victim. Even mallard ducks, one of the most friendly seeming of creatures paddling across ponds in London parks, could turn into murderous brutes when in a flock. They mobbed and drowned one of their number if they took against him, according to her father. Nature was not kind, he'd said. Sahira knew that you had to be a creature of teeth and claws, not a white belly shown in submission.

"Give Tommy your boots," said Alf, getting straight to the point.

"I told you 'no'." Sahira snapped the thread, keeping the needle in her hand. She looked around, hoping to find someone to help, but the yard had rapidly emptied once the others smelled trouble.

Tommy clucked his tongue and sighed. "You've been here long enough, Clive. You should know how things work by now. You're here on our say-so. If we demand payment, then you cough up. That's how it works."

"No, it doesn't." Sahira stood up. "Not with me."

"Who are you to challenge us, eh?" Alf thrust his face right in hers, forcing her back a step. His breath smelled of onions.

"I know exactly who I am, but do you?" *I am a tiger,* Sahira told herself, *not a mouse.*

"Yeah, you're a grubby foreigner who's due a lesson in doing what she's told by her betters."

"I have no betters here. I am from the house of un-Issa and the house of Lord Chalmers. The blood of two noble families runs in my veins."

"Let's see what colour you bleed then!" Faster than a cobra strike, Alf took a swipe at her, blade in hand, meaning to scare rather than make contact.

Sahira flinched back, shocked. She hadn't expected that. Until now all scuffles in the orphanage had been purely shoves and fists, but Alf had changed the rules on her.

So she threw the dress at him. It fell over his face, blinding him with the folds of green cotton. He stabbed blindly. Sahira ducked his swipes and stuck the needle in his forearm. He yowled like a bee-stung dog and ripped the dress from his head, tearing it from neck to hem. She wouldn't be wearing elephants again.

"What the 'ell was that?" he protested. "Tommy!"

Tommy pulled the needle from his twin's arm, staring at the little droplet of blood in disbelief. "You hurt Alf!"

"Tommy, teach her a lesson!" moaned Alf.

What could she do? Sahira flung her hands out at the ring of the twins and their snarling pack of dog-boys. "Keep back, or I'll curse you!" She began chanting under her breath. *"Tyger, Tyger, burning bright, In the forests of the night."* She curled her fingers into claws, praying that the spirit of the tigers would protect her.

Tommy waved his hand at his minions. "For Gawd's sake, she's bamming you. She's no witch. That's no curse. Bill, what are you waiting for?"

A big lad took a swing at her, but he was slow and Sahira dodged his blow. Behind her, another boy took hold of a handful of hair and shoved her into the wall. Pain and outrage boiled inside Sahira.

"Get those boots!" shouted Tommy.

One of the boys – she couldn't see which – tackled her to the ground and tugged at her ankles. The bootlaces were tied in a double knot so it was no easy matter to wrestle them off the feet of a kicking, struggling captive.

"Boys, Eleanor Clive – what are you doing? Get up this instant!" Mr Pence entered the yard with a guest in tow.

The weight on Sahira lifted and she struggled to her feet, her bad leg singing its protest. When she pushed the hair out of her eyes, she saw the orphanage owner was accompanied by an unexpectedly familiar figure: Mr Cops from the menagerie.

All thoughts of the fight vanished. "Is something wrong with the tigers?" Sahira asked, wiping a trickle of blood from her nose.

Mr Cops scrunched his hat up in his hands, fury in his eyes. "Aren't you going to say something to the lads? They were picking on the little lass," he muttered to Mr Pence. "That isn't right."

"Of course." Mr Pence turned magisterially to the Newtons and their pack. "Boys, that was very wrong of you."

"Yes, Mr Pence," they intoned. The twins smirked at each other.

"Even if the girl started it –" said Mr Pence.

"What!" Sahira gasped.

"– you must not give in to the provocations of the unfortunate. She cannot help her savagery; you, as Englishmen, can. You are dismissed."

The boys walked cockily past Mr Pence and Mr Cops and burst out laughing as soon as they were out of sight.

"I'll leave you to tell her your business." Mr Pence strutted off to find another orphan to annoy.

Mr Cops scowled after them. "I'd've given 'em all a hiding. Bullies, the lot of 'em. You all right, Miss?"

Sahira nodded and felt the egg-sized swelling on her head where she had collided with the wall. That was the worst of her bumps and bruises.

"Humph! Well, I don't expect you'd admit if you weren't," Mr Cops added.

"I am, sir," Sahira said quickly.

"Then, if you're up to an outing, you're needed at the Tower." There was a note of desperation in Mr Cops's voice.

"Why, sir?" But Sahira knew – oh, she had feared this would happen!

"I'm at my wits' end, Miss. And I remembered what you said."

"What's wrong, sir?" Sahira pleaded.

Mr Cops looked at her, his expression grave. "One of the tigers is dying," he said. "If you can't save her, then nobody can."

CHAPTER 6

Sahira had so desperately wanted to enter the gates of the menagerie, but not under these circumstances. She hurried along with Mr Cops, debating what could be the matter. Bad or unsuitable food and water? But if Rama were not ill then that was unlikely to be the cause.

"What are the signs that Sita's unwell, Mr Cops?" she asked.

He counted them off on his blunt fingers. "I've had her a week and she hasn't eaten. She lies in the corner with her head on her paws. Nothing I offer her tempts her. She's dropping weight, fur dirty, eyes dull." He steered Sahira around a pile of manure dropped by a carthorse. "It can't be an Indian sickness as you've been at sea for months and anything of that nature will've worked its way out of her system. It has to be something she's caught here. It started from the moment we took her out of the shipping crate."

Already Sahira was beginning to see a possible explanation. "And Rama, how is he acting?"

"He's not as happy in his pen as I'd hoped. Spends his day pacing to and fro."

"How big is the pen?"

Mr Cops scratched his throat wearily. "Not as big as I would like but they have as much space as the lions. They've a shelter and a fenced yard that I let them into from time to time. There's a viewing gallery overhead so the visitors can watch them. I keep them strictly separate from the other creatures."

"Indeed, they would fight another animal if they were put together. You mustn't let that happen," Sahira said.

By keeping up a swift pace they reached the Tower in half an hour. Sahira's leg was hurting – brisk walks were always a challenge – but she refused to show any weakness to Mr Cops and if he noticed her limping he did not mention it. At any rate, he'd probably attribute it to the fight with the Newtons. Sahira knew that this was her big chance: she wasn't going to waste it. They went in through Lion Gate, the main entrance to the Tower from the western side. At some point in the fortress's history, someone had decided to keep the animals separate from the royal inhabitants, troops, and prisoners who occupied the main buildings. The round Lion Tower and pens for the animals were the result. All people entering from land had to pass through it, then enter the rest of the fortress across a second bridge. The moat gave added security against animal escapes.

Not that it would stop a tiger.

A file of soldiers marched past Sahira, muskets on their shoulders, boots and buckles shining in the sunlight. With the Saturday crowd coming in to view the animals, jostling for space with the military, the Tower struck her as a very busy place, not at all like the menageries she had seen that belonged to the rich rulers in India. These were set apart in palace gardens, havens of peace where peacocks strutted and doves cooed under leafy canopies. Here the sergeant in his barracks and the fishwife on the wharf could hear the lions' roar and smell the stench of over a hundred animals kept in close confinement.

"She's down there." Mr Cops stopped Sahira on a bridge built over the yard. The semicircular walls of the enclosure were lined with cages set in archways. Her heart sank. She had hoped her tigers would have much more space, but they were in a prison little bigger than their crate. No wonder Sita was sickening.

"If you can make her at least eat, I'd be grateful," said Mr Cops. "I'll take you down to the gate we keepers use."

He led her through a door marked "No Entry" and down a steep flight of stairs. A passageway ran along the back of the cages. They passed lion and lioness, ocelot, black bear, and grinning hyena, until they reached Rama and Sita.

"*Salam*," Sahira said, running to the bars. Immediately, Sita's ears pricked and Rama bounded to the bars. He stared at Sahira, the unnerving amber gaze of the tiger. Sahira felt her heart quicken.

If only I could have stayed with them, this never would have happened, she thought.

"What will you do?" asked Mr Cops, keeping back. "Go in with them and check on her?"

Sahira turned to him, astonished he'd suggested such a reckless thing. "These are tigers, Mr Cops, not kitchen cats! We are friends, that is true, but we respect our differences. I would never treat them so lightly and none of your keepers should. Just because they are beautiful and have fur that begs to be stroked doesn't mean that you should try to pet them."

Mr Cops looked rather embarrassed by his words. "I thought you had a special gift, Indian magic or whatnot?"

Sahira shook her head. "My father was a man of science – a zoologist – not a wizard. The only special knowledge I have is that I understand them."

"So you know what is wrong with the tigress?"

"Oh yes." Sahira couldn't believe that it hadn't been obvious to Mr Cops too, or to anyone who bothered to stop and look.

Mr Cops's eyes brightened. "And you know how I should dose her to make her better?"

"Indeed I do." Sahira kept her gaze fixed on Sita.

He sighed. "I hope it's not going to be expensive. What does she need?"

"She needs a dose of me – at least once a day." Sahira smiled as Sita heaved herself off her straw and padded to the bars, mouth open in her familiar yawn which Sahira took as her equivalent of a smile. Sahira spread her hands in a gesture of helplessness to change things. "You have to eat, Sita," she told the tigress, gently but sternly. "This is how it is going to be now, this life here in this land, and there's no point sulking."

"She was *sulking*?" asked Mr Cops dubiously.

Sahira shrugged. "Maybe, though I think she was really pining for me. I'm the human she trusts."

Mr Cops paused, his brow furrowed in thought. "Can you teach me how to gain her confidence?"

And do herself out of a job? Not likely! "I think it would be better and much cheaper in the long run if you just let me come here daily until she's settled." *Please, please let me come!* Sahira sent a little prayer up to God, hoping he was watching and would nudge the keeper in the right direction. The Almighty had answered so few of her prayers recently, surely she was due?

Mr Cops looked from Sahira to the tigers. "How long will that take?"

As long as Sahira could spin it out. "I don't know. Sita will decide."

As if to strengthen the girl's plea, Sita ambled over to the feeding trough and picked out a meaty bone. She carried it back to her corner and began to chew, all the while her eyes on Sahira to be sure that she didn't slip away again.

Mr Cops dug his hands in his pockets. He sighed. "I suppose I can arrange for a few visits if Mr Pence allows."

Sahira sat cross-legged by the bars, feeling the pieces of herself settle into their old pattern. She was wrong about not having a home: where these animals were, that was her place. "The Company is giving him my money."

Mr Cops picked a stray strand of hay from his shabby trousers. "They're doing *what*? But I don't understand. It was to come to you. I made that clear."

"Mr Godstow arranged for the fee for the tigers to go directly to the orphanage. I'm never going to see a penny." Even though she was a child, she knew this would be the case. She shrugged at Mr Cops's seeming outrage.

"From what I understand, it's a charitable institution. They're not supposed to charge you to stay there," Mr Cops continued.

"It's the only way they could be persuaded to take me. It isn't a good place, Mr Cops, you must've realized that." Sahira touched the bump on her head, hoping for sympathy. "Can I not stay here instead?"

Mr Cops gazed at Sahira, then at the tigers, both of whom had settled down near her, much more contented now she was there.

"I'm sorry, Miss Clive, I simply can't do that. You're a little girl. You can't move in with the keepers over the stable, and my wife won't be impressed if I announce I'm taking in a stray. Mrs Cops is in the family way. Our first child." He blushed and rubbed his whiskery cheeks. "I'm afraid you have to stay at the orphanage, but I'll see what I can do about Mr Pence, concerning the money."

Sahira was sceptical he could have any influence over that man. Mr Pence was sitting in a nice little bower he had built himself, bringing home to his nest all the shiny coin he could. He would not be impressed by a raven from the Tower squawking at him. "What can you do to change his mind?"

Mr Cops smiled and tapped his nose. "You catch more flies with honey than vinegar."

Sahira frowned. "I'm not sure that's true. Flies actually quite like the sweeter vinegars. We used them as traps in the jungle."

He chuckled. "Lass, you'd best not take things so literally. It's a saying. I mean that we need to find the right bait. It's a lesson you could do with learning, if your fight with those boys was anything to judge by."

"They started it, sir." It wouldn't do for him to think she was a troublemaker.

"I'm sure they did, but you shouldn't be too quick to resort to fighting back, especially against a foe who is bigger or more numerous than you."

"They were trying to steal my boots!" The outrage still stung. The tigers' ears pricked at this sudden change in tone.

"Then you need to offer them something they want more."

"Like what?" Sahira was conscious that she had nothing but a trunk of clothes left to her and she couldn't see either of the Newtons being interested in her animal-trimmed dresses. Nor, on point of principle, did she want to give them anything. They would strip her of everything she owned if she gave in the once.

"Tickets to the menagerie would be a start, now wouldn't it? It's a perk of being an unofficial tiger tamer, 'cause that's what you'll be." He smiled.

Sahira jumped up. "So you'll let me come back? Every day?"

He clicked his tongue, a sound of scepticism. "I'm not sure about that – it will depend on Mr Pence. And there's your education to think of. But you've shown me that the tigers need you. If you sleep at the orphanage and come here as often as you can be spared, then I'll be much obliged."

Surely she could be spared all the time – there was nothing new that Mrs Pence could teach her, unless it was how to spoil all her enjoyment in poetry. Sahira's parents had given her a complete education. "Thank you, thank you! You won't regret it, I promise you." Sahira felt as if she could have danced around the menagerie with him, but he didn't look the sort to kick up his heels unless he'd made too free with the ale, and maybe not even then.

"Now, if the tigers will let you go for a moment, there's a question I want to ask you about the python."

"Of course!" Sahira bade farewell to Rama and Sita, reassuring them she'd be back and cautioning Sita against refusing her food. She hoped it was enough for now.

In the course of the next few hours before the menagerie closed, Sahira met the other notable inhabitants that filled the yards. Mr Cops had built an aviary where birds were able to fly – a huge improvement on the cages in which they used to be kept. He explained how he had taken the previously unthought-of approach among keepers of researching the best methods for making captive animals happy. Only the lack of space was stopping his dreams of making a good home for all the creatures from being fulfilled. She recognized quite a few birds from her country, among them the parrots that had travelled with her from Calcutta. It was by no means a replacement for the jungle but at least the sounds and smells were familiar and the birds could flap and flutter short distances from perch to perch. There was also a monkey room where visitors could meet the various simian species in relative warmth and comfort – not Sahira's favourite place as she knew just how dangerous those creatures were. They might look fetching but if upset or mishandled they had a vicious bite. One young man she knew in India had got such an injury from a rabid monkey and gone mad soon after. It worried Sahira that Londoners seemed to think monkeys were playthings, but her invitation to return was not secure so she had to keep such views to herself for the moment.

Most visible to the visitors, though, was a mischievous African zebra who was tame enough to wander among them. This was Sahira's first time seeing one up close and she marvelled at his black and white stripes – the equine equivalent of a tiger's pelt. He had the unfortunate habit of stealing anything that the people left untended: bonnets, sandwiches, newspapers, and, most particularly, ale, for which he had developed a taste. When she met him, he had his nose in a pint pot left on a bench by the beer stall.

"This zebra needs someone to keep an eye on him," she suggested.

"Can't spare a keeper," said Mr Cops regretfully, pulling the stubborn creature away by his halter.

And that prompted another idea, but Sahira didn't want to spring all of her suggestions at once. Like any animal, Mr Cops needed to be coaxed in the direction she wanted him to go. All the better if he went because he thought it his idea, rather than hers.

"So where is the python?" she asked, thinking that there wasn't much daylight left and she would have to return to the orphanage soon.

"I've put him in a basket near the stove at my house. The wife's keeping an eye on him. Come." Mr Cops took her to his house, which was built into the wall of Lion Tower and was named, logically enough, "Lion House". He called out a cheerful "How do?" to his wife as they entered. Mrs Cops bustled out of the backroom where, from the evidence of her needles and ball of white wool stuffed in her apron pocket, she had been knitting for the new baby.

"Is this the little Indian girl?" she asked, looking dubiously at Sahira's auburn hair. Having this gingery brown colouring made it hard for anyone to imagine the jet-black hair of her mother.

"Yes, ma'am." Sahira bowed, hands together.

Mrs Cops laughed and clapped her hands. "Ah, I see it now. Alfred says you have a way with animals. I hope you do, because I refuse to house that snake on the stove much longer. I know the lid is fastened but it gives me the shivers just thinking about it in there. I had a nightmare about him swallowing me up in one gulp last night."

"That was the fault of the pickled herring you served for dinner, dear, not the python." Mr Cops gave her a kiss and a pat on the shoulder, not taking her fears too seriously.

Sahira realized then that being married to the animal-mad keeper must be no easy thing. Her parents had been blessed that they were both equally keen on animal collecting. "I'll do my best, Mrs Cops, to get the snake better and on its way to its cage."

Mrs Cops gave her a grateful look. "That's all we can ask. I'll put together a spot of supper while you make your inspection."

Mr Cops lifted the lid on the python. Sahira knew immediately what was the matter. In fact, she was a little surprised that the experienced keeper had not seen this before. The scales around the snake's eyes had turned bluish white and the body had lost its healthy sheen.

"It don't look good, does it?" Mr Cops said regretfully. "Do you think it's the cold? March in London must be like the dead of winter from where he comes from."

"We don't really have winter like yours near the Equator but I don't think that's the problem."

"What is?" Mr Cops stroked the diamond patterned scales. "Is it dying of old age?"

"Only the skin. Your python is shedding, Mr Cops. In a few days, it'll emerge as good as new. You just have to let it get on with the process."

He sat back on his heels. "I should've thought of that! But it was a new creature to me and I assumed he was sick, like the tiger."

"I don't think either of them is really sick. I would say they are both adjusting." Sahira knew only too well how they felt. Fitting in with this new London life felt a little like sloughing off her old ways, revealing a new and vulnerable skin. She could cope for a while but then she would remember the loss of her parents. It was like walking along contentedly in the jungle, and then suddenly plunging through the camouflage of branches into a tribesman's pit. In Sahira's case, it was filled with grief-sharpened spikes at the bottom. She knuckled the tears from her eyes, hoping the keeper wouldn't notice her weakness.

Mr Cops replaced the lid. "Moulting. That's good. I'll leave it here then. I'll just tell the wife to work around it for a day or two."

Sahira recalled poor Mrs Cops's nightmares. "I'm sure the snake will manage quite happily in a quiet cage somewhere."

"No, no, I want to keep an eye on him. He's doing well enough here so I won't move him again."

After a generous supper of bread and cheese, Mr Cops looked out the window at the darkening skies as his wife cleared the dishes.

"I'd better arrange for you to be escorted back to the orphanage by one of my keepers, lass."

"I'd be most obliged, Mr Cops. I'm not yet certain of the way, but I promise I'll learn. I don't need special treatment."

"I'm sure you will learn but I like to look after everyone under my care. I'll send Joseph Croney with you – he's no use for aught else around here at the moment." He stepped out and rang a bell by the door to his house.

"How's that, sir?" Sahira asked, wondering if there was another employment opportunity in the Tower if one of the keepers was slacking.

Mr Cops shook his head. "Poor lad's not been the same since January. He was victim of a serious leopard attack."

"Oh my word!" Sahira hugged her arms to herself protectively, knowing far too well what that would've been like.

"He was cleaning out their den but neglected to secure the gate to where they were being kept. The male broke in and leaped on his back."

"Yes, of course." Sahira nodded knowingly. "It's how they subdue prey when hunting. They must have seen him as encroaching on their territory. He's lucky to be alive."

Mr Cops gave her a sidelong look. "Indeed. The beast held on with its teeth. Only the swift action of two of my men saved Croney's life. They beat the creature off with a rifle butt – couldn't risk shooting it in case they hit him."

Sahira leaned forward, eager to hear the rest of the tale. "What happened next?"

"He was rushed to the doctors and they stopped the blood loss before it was fatal. He's only just emerged from Guy's Hospital but I'm afraid he's a changed man," Mr Cops said despondently.

"He was never that keen on the animals to start with," murmured Mrs Cops. "You made a mistake there."

Mr Cops humphed. "You aren't to mind anything he says, Miss Clive; the experience of almost being leopard supper has sent him half-mad."

"You know you should let him go," said Mrs Cops, lips pursed in a thin line.

"What's a man to do though, Mary? I can't send him away – no one will employ him now. I have to watch him, keep him away from the bigger animals. What else is there for him?" Mr Cops said, clearly exasperated. Sahira sensed it was not the first time they'd had this conversation.

When Croney arrived in response to the bell, Sahira saw why people might be reluctant to bring him into their household. The unfortunate man was an alarming sight, his face bearing the puncture scars of leopard's teeth and scars from its claws. Perhaps it was not the scars, though, but his unpleasant expression, looking at everyone and everything with bitter resentment, that limited his employment opportunities? Escort duty didn't appear to be Croney's favourite choice of occupation either. He muttered darkly about having better things to do on a Saturday night as he set off northward through the busy streets to Whitechapel.

Sahira remembered the honey and vinegar advice Mr Cops had given her earlier. "I'm sorry to be a bother. I much appreciate your kindness in seeing me back to the orphanage."

He scowled at her, pale blue eyes blazing through the puffy red scarring on his face. "Not kind. 'Tis orders. You're the child who likes them devil tigers, aren't you?"

"My father caught them and I travelled with them from India. Yes, I do like them."

"We shouldn't have them near people," Croney said gruffly. "They should stay in the jungle." Sahira noticed now that he had difficulty with his left leg. They would make an odd sight, both of them limping along.

Look people, she wanted to explain to the curious onlookers, *the true cost of daring to handle God's most dangerous creatures.* They were both veterans of that peculiar kind of profession.

And, given the chance, she would add that you couldn't blame the animals for following their instinct. She certainly bore the elephant that had crushed her leg no grudge.

Sahira hoped she could sweeten Croney's attitude to her tigers and persuade him to see they were there through necessity rather than by choice. "You might have a point, sir, about it being best to leave them in the jungle. We would have left them in the wild but they were stealing goats from a village and people feared it might be their children next. So they had to come here, you see?"

"Hah! Told you." Croney waved in the general direction of the Tower behind them. "Not right having them here. Their souls are wide open to evil. They're possessed. You can tell that by looking in their eyes."

"I don't think so." Sahira had often read fury in the eyes of a captive tiger, but not anything evil. They weren't creatures with any concept of right and wrong, so how could they be judged by human standards?

"I know so." He pointed to his scars as if that settled the matter.

Sahira decided she would only make an enemy if she tried to debate the question further. They limped on in silence until he left her at the door of the orphanage without so much as a nod in farewell.

CHAPTER 7

S ahira was the object of much envy that night in the girls' dormitory.
"You really saw the tigers?" asked Emily, hugging her knees to herself as she sat on her narrow bed. She twirled the end of her white-blonde plait. "Cor, what was that like, eh?"

Sahira combed her hair out, hanging her head upside down to get to the tangles at the back. "It was wonderful. They're called Rama and Sita."

"Rama and Sita?" Emily asked, clearly keen to know more.

"My father named them. After a famous couple from an old story they tell in India – a prince and his beautiful wife."

"And you're to go back to see them again?" asked Ann, struggling to tame her curls into a braid for sleeping.

"Come here," beckoned Emily. She expertly divided Ann's hair and made a stubby plait at the back of her head. Behind the three girls, in the places nearer the door, the younger ones were already in bed. The eldest were allowed an extra fifteen minutes before they too had to turn in. Matron was already nodding off in her armchair in her little office. This was the closest the three could come to a private moment in the orphanage.

"Oh, what would I give to see so many wonderful animals!" sighed Emily.

"You've never been?" asked Sahira. "But the menagerie is only a short walk away."

"It costs so much to get in, especially if you're a family with five children. We were never able to spare the coin." She grimaced, recalling something unpleasant. "And Dad liked his gin too much to put anything by for us."

It seemed remarkable to Sahira that Emily's parents, when they were alive, had placed their own pleasures first. *Was this how English families behaved?* she wondered. Her parents had spent so much of their time teaching her and taking her exploring; she hadn't wanted for anything. Maybe she had a chance to give something back?

"Mr Cops said I could have tickets for my friends." Sahira had already promised herself that she would not give the passes to the Newtons. Mr Cops was wrong: bullies shouldn't be bought off. They had far too much they didn't deserve already. "If he comes through on his promise, I'll make sure you're first on the list. You two – and Ned."

"Really?" the girls squealed excitedly in unison. "That would be the best thing that's happened in a long time," Emily said. "And it's sweet the way you notice the boot boy. He's been so much happier since you arrived." Emily sprang up from the bed and hugged Sahira. She was always much more impulsive than the quiet and careful Ann, Sahira had learned. "And thank you. By the way, while you were gone, Ann and I salvaged what we could from your green dress." She pulled out a length of elephant ribbon from her pocket. "The material was badly ripped but it might do for a petticoat if you don't mind the colour."

Sahira took the ribbon and ran it through her fingers, elephant following elephant like you sometimes see them, trunk entwined with tail of the one in front. "What's wrong with green?" she asked quizzically.

"It's just that petticoats are usually white," Emily said matter-of-factly.

"Why?" Sahira asked.

Emily frowned. "Now you ask, I don't know!"

"Green is a perfectly nice colour and white shows the dirt so quickly," Sahira said.

"Then you can make yourself one when it gets back from the wash," Emily offered.

"Yes, maybe I will," Sahira smiled. "Thank you for rescuing it. That gown was one of my favourites."

Ann eyed Sahira's locked trunk with interest. Sahira kept it shut, not because she feared any of the girls would steal, but she had no faith in Matron, the Newtons, or even Mr and Mrs Pence. "Do you have any more in there?" Ann asked.

"Oh yes," Sahira replied.

"So what will be your Sunday best now?" Ann's curiosity was getting the better of her.

"What do you think Mr Pence will think of peacocks?" Sahira asked, a twinkle in her eye.

Emily and Ann both burst out laughing. "Oh, I can't wait to see his face!" said Emily.

Ann slipped under her covers. "Sahira, I've been meaning to ask, is it your habit to sleep on the floor?" She asked the question delicately, probably fearing to upset Sahira's foreign sensibilities.

"No, of course not, but Matron told me a girl had died in that bed. I didn't want to sleep on the same mattress." Sahira wrapped herself in her blanket, preparing for another uncomfortable night. Jeoffry circled three times and settled down beside her.

Emily and Ann exchanged a look. "That's true – it was hers," said Emily. "But she died in the workhouse hospital. Mr Pence doesn't like the bother of nursing us when we fall ill and sends us off to that institution. No one ever comes back."

Sahira felt terrible being pleased that a girl had died elsewhere. "I'm sorry – that's so sad."

Ann shrugged, but her eyes sparkled with tears. "We all miss her; she was so full of life and mischief when she was here, but it's common enough to get sick. We just have to hope we end up in a better place than this in the next life."

Sahira picked the blanket from the floor and spread it on the bed. "That isn't hard to imagine. In God's house are many mansions, so my father told me. And none of them look like Mr Pence's orphanage." She said a quick prayer for the soul of her predecessor, shooed the cat over to make room, and prepared for the first comfortable night she had spent for months.

Sahira didn't so much dream as daydream in that space between sleeping and waking when the world was quiet and the sun only just contemplating rising. Jeoffry had already left to start his day down in the kitchen, bothering Ned for scraps, so she felt lonely. Thinking of the elephant dress, Sahira let the creatures wander through her imagination, all those she had seen, from the rich man's painted one, wearing a silken howdah and jewelled harness, to the poor farmer's beast of burden decorated with mud. She missed them. Shire horses were well enough but they were no substitute for the gentle giants of Indian streets, carrying loads to market or logs for buildings. There were none in the menagerie at present but they weren't unknown in England.

"Are you awake, Sahira?" Emily rolled over to face her.

"I am now," replied Sahira with a smile.

"You've a funny expression – distant, like you're somewhere else."

Sahira sighed. "I wish I were."

"What are you thinking about?" whispered Ann from the next bed over.

"Elephants," Sahira said wistfully.

Ann laughed softly. "It is Sunday morning before six and you are thinking of elephants! Of course you are!"

"I've never seen one," said Emily. "Doubt I ever will."

"Oh, but you might." Sahira sat up, blanket draped over her shoulders like a cloak. "My father told me a story about the first elephant ever seen in London, not counting the ones the Romans might have used in warfare. It came here hundreds of years ago."

"Romans?" Emily exclaimed, a note of uncertainty in her voice.

Sahira realized she was in danger of digressing. "That's another tale. This elephant, the very first one we know about, was a present from the King of France to Henry III, the monarch who also got the leopards-who-may-have-been-lions." That made Sahira wonder: had word gone out among European monarchs that the English king liked exotic beasts or were they all laughing behind their hands at giving this less than successful ruler yet another thing to worry about?

"Leopards-who-may-have-been-lions?" asked Emily.

"They used the same word for both so to this day no one knows what he was given. Funny, isn't it?" Sahira added.

"What about the elephant?" asked Emily, keen for Sahira to continue her story.

"Just imagine the elephant walking slowly into the Tower, large ears flapping," Sahira mimed the actions as she spoke, "trunk raised in awe at its new home in the menagerie. So solemn, so wise, it probably did not much enjoy its new life in damp, drizzly England."

"How do you know this?" Emily's question betrayed a mixture of surprise and doubt.

"Oh, that's simple. Because a monk drew a picture of it in his book of animals revealing it to be an African rather than one of the more familiar Indian elephants."

"I'm not familiar with either," muttered Emily to Ann.

Sahira found that hard to imagine, but the girls came from such a different world to her. "My father saw the illustration in a college library when he was a student in Cambridge."

"Ooo, Cambridge, is it?" Emily's tone was gently mocking. "I told you she spoke like a toff, Ann."

"Is that being a toff?" Sahira shook herself, remembering she was mid-story. She could return to that subject later. "Anyway, he said it was one of the reasons he became an expert in animals. You can tell the breed, he said, from the big ears. He thought it impressively accurate for a time when they still thought unicorns and griffins were real."

"They aren't?" asked Ann. Sahira wasn't sure if she was joking.

"No. But what I want to know is, what was the elephant's story? How did it get from the plains of Africa to end up in a small pen in a city at the other end of the world? No one knows the tale and the elephant died a few years later of drinking too much wine. Clearly, the keepers had no idea what to feed it."

"What are you supposed to feed elephants?" asked Ann.

"Not wine – though it was surprising how long that idea stuck with animal handlers here. My father said that there were to be many more drunken elephant catastrophes to follow until someone put two and two together. He told me that zoologists like him were only just beginning to treat animal diets scientifically – that was why the creatures he caught and shipped survived when so many others didn't." Sahira stopped talking, only realizing now that all the girls in the dormitory were listening to her story.

"Do you like elephants, Sahira?" asked a little girl down the far end of the room. "They sound scary."

"They are excellent and strong." Sahira reached under the covers and rubbed her aching leg. "Though I count myself lucky that I was trod on by an Indian rather than an African one."

The bell rang in the hallway, signalling that it was time to get up. Sahira was already out of bed, digging through the contents of her trunk. She shook out her peacock dress. Compared with this gown, the green elephant one was a study in restraint. A peacock with fanned tail was embroidered on back and front in silver thread on royal blue. Her mother had thought it a perfectly vulgar article, but her father had encouraged Sahira, making the argument that she would only be young once and had time to develop a more sober taste.

"My love, Sahira is going to be mixing with the proud memsahibs when she goes to school in England. Why not give her a few fine feathers?" He had intended to send his daughter to a boarding school in Bath but that plan had been buried with him in the Atlantic. He had always claimed he was as poor as a church mouse (why these mice were particularly poor he had not explained), yet he was convinced his father would foot the bill once he met his granddaughter.

"If you can charm the old fellow, Sahira," her father had said as they leaned on the rail watching the brown coast of Africa slip by, *"you'll do much to heal the breach made by my marriage."*

The peacocks hadn't been part of that plan – a simple white dress with only a trim of swallows had been chosen for the first family visit. She was to keep the peacock one in reserve, like an army's big siege guns, he explained.

Sahira's mother had shaken her head, saying he was too optimistic.

Father had refused to be daunted. *"We'll turn up unannounced. The old man is too much of a gentleman to turn ladies away."* But they had not had a chance to turn up at all; only news of her parents' death was sent to Fenton Park. Would Lord Chalmers even grieve? There was certainly no sign as yet that he cared what had happened to his kin.

Ammi, Baba. Sahira swallowed, but the lump would not leave her throat.

A cool hand touched her shoulder. "Are you all right, Sahira?" asked Ann.

She was sure she would never be completely all right again. "I was just thinking of something my father said."

Ann nodded in understanding. Every girl here had a similar loss to mourn and knew well how grief could take you unawares. She picked up the dress that Sahira had draped on her knees.

"Oh my! This is very fine – like something for a princess in a play!" exclaimed Emily, coming to join Ann.

Sahira's spirits lifted at her friends' expression. "Do you think this will vex Mr Pence?"

"Without a doubt," said Emily. "It's far more fancy than your green one."

"Have you ever seen a peacock?" asked Ann.

"Many of them – noisy, annoying creatures they can be too. And that's just what I intend to be." Sahira took the dress from Ann and stepped in. Emily deftly did up the row of mother-of-pearl buttons at the back.

Ann stepped back to admire the effect. "You look too fine for this orphanage."

Emily nodded in agreement.

"All of us are." Sahira gave them a rueful smile.

Ann's face clouded in doubt. "Perhaps you should keep it hidden and wear something less challenging this time?"

"And spoil the surprise? The Pences and Newtons are doubtless hoping they've destroyed all my finery."

"True. It would be a shame to miss out on twisting their tails," said Ann.

Sahira smoothed down the fabric. "What do you think would happen if I turned up on my grandfather's doorstep, as my father had planned?"

"You have a grandfather?" asked Emily.

"One I've never met, but he's a rich and important man – a lord, actually. Would he take me in dressed like this?" Sahira held out her skirts.

Emily poked Sahira in the ribs. "That – or send you on stage. I've not seen finer costumes even in Covent Garden." She clasped her hands to her chest. "Wouldn't it be divine to be an actress, to have a hundred costume changes and the public eating out of the palm of your hand?"

"Sounds most unsanitary," Sahira suggested.

Emily laughed. "I meant like Fanny Kemble."

"Who?"

"You don't know who Miss Kemble is?" Emily exclaimed. "She's only the theatre's darling and my heroine. She saved Covent Garden from ruin and she writes plays. She is my idea of the complete lady."

Sahira wasn't much interested in theatre, finding real animals so much more interesting than the activities of pretend people, but she could clearly see that Emily was as enamoured of that life. "Then you must follow in her footsteps if you can."

"From this place?" Emily collapsed on the bed. "I can't see the Pences allowing me anywhere near the stage door."

"They won't always rule your life. You will have choices once you leave here, won't you?" Sahira pulled the laces tight on her blue boots then spun in a circle. "How do I look?"

"Wonderful. You put the two of us in the shade," said Ann generously, though she looked very pretty in her pale yellow muslin. Patched and mended to be sure, but it suited her colouring. "Let's go to breakfast and see what everyone else thinks."

What Mr Pence thought was expressed in a mouthful of porridge spat out on the table. Sahira processed to the head of the girls' table, Ann and Emily flanking her like handmaidens.

"Eleanor Clive, what on earth are you wearing?" Mr Pence thundered.

"My Sunday best, sir," she answered.

"I've never seen anything so outlandish."

Truth about her origins had not served her well so far, so Sahira decided to spin a tale that would be believed, something with the flavour of the Arabian Nights. "I'm not surprised, sir. These are the peacocks of the illustrious house of Golconda. Only a princess of the blood is allowed to wear them."

"Is that silver thread?" marvelled Mrs Pence, her eyes narrowed on the skirt. No doubt she was calculating its value in the second-hand market.

"As befits a princess. A powerful curse lies on anyone who dares touch the peacocks if they aren't of royal blood." Sahira knew that stories had been circulating in England for years about the treasure of the Golconda mines near Sahira's city of Hyderabad, the only known source of diamonds in the world. They were reputed to be unlucky to any man who acquired them by dishonest means; Sahira was hoping that logic would extend to other Golcondan riches.

"Princess? She can't be a princess, not livin' 'ere," scoffed Alf Newton. The twins were staring with malice plain in their eyes.

Sahira couldn't fault Alf's logic but ignored them, which she knew they would hate. "May I take my seat, sir?"

Mr Pence nodded curtly and bent close to his wife. They embarked on a whispered argument. Sahira was very pleased she had a stout lock to her trunk and kept the key with her at all times.

"Have I made a mistake?" Sahira asked her friends from behind her hand.

Emily grinned and shook her head.

Ann looked more doubtful. "You've certainly set the fox among the hens."

As Sahira walked back from church in file with her friends, a large carriage, what Emily called an "omnibus", trundled by. Morose-looking horses had the difficult task of pulling it.

"Omnibuses are new to London," Emily explained.

"Where are people going in them on a Sunday?" asked Sahira.

"That lot? They're likely to be heading to one of the tea gardens, out in Sadler's Wells maybe. If only we could join them," Emily said wistfully.

It was beginning to worry Sahira how horses were treated in London; she was yet to see a happy, healthy specimen. Then an advertisement on the back of the 'bus caught her eye:

REGENT'S PARK ZOOLOGICAL GARDENS
– LONDON'S NEWEST ATTRACTION

She nudged Emily, who had been looking at the bills posted outside a closed theatre. "Where is Regent's Park?"

"Across town. About four or five miles from here, I'd guess."

"Have you been there?" asked Sahira earnestly.

Emily laughed and shook her head. "Sahira, if I can't afford the Tower menagerie, what hope would there be for me to visit a zoological garden in a park where only the toffs go?"

"I don't know." Sahira shrugged her shoulders in defeat. "I don't understand this city."

"Only the very richest live there. As for the zoological garden, the papers say that it's only open to those who know one of the founders, or people they approve."

Sahira liked the idea of a zoological garden – it sounded more like the menageries she knew in India. "You mean someone like my grandfather?"

"I expect so, if he really is a lord." Emily winked. Sahira couldn't blame Emily for doubting that claim. She had already admitted to her friends that being a princess was a fiction. "I don't know much about it myself," Emily continued, "but the newspapers say that several members of the government are involved, including the Prime Minister and the Home Secretary, as well as men of science and exploration."

Sahira was ashamed to admit she did not know who the Prime Minister or the Home Secretary were – or even know very clearly what they did. India had been run by lots of local rulers who were coming increasingly under the sway of the East India Company. In Hyderabad they had a Nizam, his viziers, and a Resident representing Company interests – was this odd English system anything like that?

Emily sighed. "I can see you want to ask a question. Go on."

"What is a prime minister?"

She rolled her eyes. "The man who runs the government on behalf of the King."

"Ah, he's the chief vizier. Go on."

"It's the Duke of Wellington at the moment. You must've heard of him?"

"Oh yes. He led the British army in India before he beat Emperor Napoleon at Waterloo. People still talk about him in Hyderabad – they say he was a good leader, but ruthless."

Emily nodded. "He hasn't changed. He's very traditional and stern. My dad didn't like him much. Dad was what is called a radical because he thought all men should have the vote, but Old Beaky…"

"Who?" Sahira asked, marvelling at yet another strange English turn of phrase.

"It's what we call the duke because he has a big nose. Anyway, Old Beaky is set against any change. He thinks nothing can improve on how the country is run at the moment by men of property."

"He's a man of property then?" asked Sahira.

"How ever did you guess?" Emily said archly. "Then there's the Home Secretary – that's Robert Peel. You might've heard of him."

Sahira shook her head.

"He's the man who created the police force last year. We nicknamed them Bobbies after him, but quite a few around here don't like them. They call them Peelers."

"People like Tommy and Alf?"

"Exactly." Emily nudged her. "See: you do understand London."

Only when thinking of it like a jungle, Sahira decided. The beasts at the top – the lions like Wellington – did not want to give any territory to other creatures, defending the pride of the privileged. Hyenas like the Newtons liked it most when the jungle was lawless and the lion sleeping in his den. Having the lion employ – Sahira tried to think of a suitable comparison to policemen – *elephants* to drive off the hyenas from the grazing population was doubtless an unwelcome shock to the scavengers.

"So you think my chances of going to the zoological gardens are not good?" she asked as the omnibus turned out of sight.

Emily linked arms with her. "I'm afraid so. But you have the tigers in the Tower – which is more than most of us can claim."

Yes, thought Sahira. *At least I have them.*

PART 3
TYGER, TYGER

CHAPTER 8

Sahira heard nothing more about returning to the menagerie that day and went to bed quite despondent. Only the knowledge that the tigress needed her gave Sahira hope Mr Cops wouldn't forget his promise.

The next morning, she received a summons before breakfast to report to Mr Pence's study. The menagerie keeper was waiting there, cap in hand. He smiled and nodded to Sahira, which she took as a sign that negotiations had gone well.

"Eleanor Clive," said Mr Pence, standing behind his desk. "Mr Cops has requested you help him with your father's animals at the menagerie. You will accompany him this morning, but on other days you will go after morning lessons. Understood?"

"Yes, sir," Sahira replied, trying hard to restrain her excitement.

"And I'll pay her wage direct to you, Mr Pence," Mr Cops stated, giving Sahira a warning look not to object.

Mr Pence opened his accounts book with a sigh. "I would far rather you hand over the fee for the tigers as agreed with Mr Godstow of the Company."

"Well now, that would be a fine thing indeed," agreed Mr Cops, "but my lawyer has advised that I have to wait until Captain Clive's estate is settled. As the order was placed with the captain personally, not with the Company, then my man thinks that the payment should go to the heirs, not to an unconnected person like yourself. I might find myself in court otherwise."

"But Miss Clive owes me for her board and lodging," Mr Pence objected.

"Which I'm sure her wage will more than cover as I'll be paying her the same as my keepers. Don't say she costs more than a man with a wife and family to feed – a little thing like her?"

"You'd be surprised."

"I dare say I would." The two men locked gazes, a power struggle going on between them.

"Very well." Mr Pence nodded, giving the victory to Mr Cops this time. "Run along with the keeper, Eleanor, and mind your manners."

She bobbed a curtsey. "Be with you in a moment," she said to Mr Cops, as excitement bubbled through her. She dashed upstairs to her trunk and took out several items from the bottom. Closing the lid and double-checking the fastening, she hurried downstairs, bundle tucked under an arm. Mr Cops was waiting in the bare corridor outside the dining room.

"Do you want to stop for breakfast?" he asked, gesturing inside. "If you're quick, I can wait."

Sahira waved to Ann and Emily who were already seated. "Oh no. I'm not hungry." Who could be hungry with tigers to visit? "How is Sita?"

"Pining for you again, but Mr Pence refused flatly to let you come on a Sunday. He said you were to concentrate on your prayers."

Mr Pence no more cared for prayers than a crocodile. He hadn't even come to church with the orphans, which Sahira hadn't minded as it meant she had been free to talk to Emily on the way back. "I'll soon sort Sita out, don't you worry, Mr Cops," said Sahira eagerly as they turned out of Duck Street.

"I'm sure you will, lass." He paused at a bakery and bought a warm buttered roll. "Can't have you wasting away too."

It tasted delicious, still hot from the oven. "Thank you so much for handling Mr Pence."

"Slippery customer, that one. Reminds me of that boa constrictor. Can't say I like him much." Mr Cops shook his head.

"If you can keep the tiger money away from him, it gives me hope that I won't always be penniless."

"It's a shame to sacrifice your wages to him, but I decided the prospect of a bird in the hand was better than two in the bush."

Sahira tried to work out what he meant but couldn't see it. Bushes were better for birds than hands as a rule. "Pardon?"

"If I hinted that the money was tied up in the courts then he would rapidly work out he wouldn't see a shilling for years. The law in this country moves with all the haste of a sloth."

"The money isn't tied up, is it?" Sahira asked.

"No, but don't tell him. You're the only heir so I reckon I can place it on account for you somewhere without falling foul of the law. It won't be much, so don't get big ideas."

"But it's better than nothing."

"Aye, it's better than that."

On arrival at the menagerie Sahira requested a quiet place to change out of her orphanage uniform and into the old clothes she had brought with her. Left alone in a storeroom, she slipped into what she thought of as her animal hunting gear: thick cotton baggy trousers and tunic. She tied up her hair in a strip of cloth and tucked it in, turban style as her mother had so often done for her. That memory brought a pang of grief. She let it ripple through her before emerging. She found Mr Cops waiting with two other keepers.

"Who's the little Indian lad?" asked one. "I thought you wanted us to show Captain Clive's daughter the animals."

Mr Cops recovered quickly from his surprise. "Why, Ben, it is the girl, can't you see? Miss Clive, Ben Poulter and Mike Kerry. My right hand – and left hand – men." He gestured to each in turn.

"That last would be you, Mike; you're the one who's left-handed," teased Ben.

Sahira bowed to them both. At a glance, she judged them both as capable, like the seasoned guides her father employed to take them into the jungle – short and stocky with work-roughened hands. "I hope you don't mind me wearing my Indian clothes, Mr Cops? I don't want to ruin the gown the orphanage has given me." And the fact that Sahira infinitely preferred them didn't influence her decision, of course.

Mr Cops tugged on a side whisker. "Can't say that it's a problem for me. Adds a certain exotic flavour if the visitors catch sight of you, and they'll probably take that more in their stride than if they see a girl in a dress. In fact, I think it is just the thing."

"Thank you." Sahira gave an exaggerated bow.

"In any case, Miss Clive, we've got bigger fish to fry today. The Constable of the Tower is making an inspection at noon so perhaps we should err on the side of caution and you should keep out of sight then, eh? Ben, Mike, show Miss Clive where we store the animal feed." He checked his pocket watch. "Hurry along now."

Delighted to have got away with returning to her usual garb, Sahira hugged her arms to herself and followed the two keepers about their tasks. "Please, call me Sahira. And what's this about frying fish?"

Having accompanied the keepers on the rounds to feed the animals, Ben and Mike left Sahira mending a perch in the aviary while they swept up for the inspection. It apparently wouldn't do for any noble foot to get mired in dung. She was enjoying the birdsong when she heard the special visitors approach, the tramp of feet and the hubbub sending many of the singers into hiding.

"So, Cops, I heard you've just taken delivery of a consignment of animals from India." The man that spoke was strong and commanding. He had a captain's voice, heard on a ship's deck even if a storm were howling.

She peeked through the foliage. A tall silver-haired gentleman with a prominent nose strode across the yard followed by a flock of black-jacketed underlings. One was taking notes of everything the man said.

"Yes, your grace." Mr Cops had his hat in his hand, a sign he considered the visitor far above his touch. "Would you like to see the tigers?"

"I believe I expressed a wish that the number of animals in the menagerie be reduced, not increased – reduced with a view to its eventual closure," said the man with the booming voice.

Closure? He couldn't shut down the menagerie, could he? wondered Sahira.

"You have your responsibilities, sir, but I also have mine in the ancient position of His Majesty's Keeper of the Lions," countered Mr Cops. "If we don't keep up gate receipts, sir, then I can't feed the animals. New attractions bring in more visitors."

At the rear of the visiting party came a man in a fine maroon jacket and cream waistcoat, with a boy of around Sahira's age by his side. The boy had curly dark hair and alert eyes, darting every which way to take in the sights. They appeared to be on the fringes of the group, enjoying the displays rather than participating in the discussion between Mr Cops and the tall gentleman.

"Need I remind you that the Tower is primarily a garrison, not an amusement?" drawled the old man. "As Constable, I cannot have your animals getting in the way of my soldiers."

"But, your grace, the menagerie has existed since Henry III's day," pleaded Mr Cops.

"I always thought him a weak king. Not one of his better decisions. This is the nineteenth century, man, not the fourteenth! We need a modern army, fit for purpose in the modern world." He spoke as one who would not be swayed.

"But the menagerie has been supported and enjoyed by all kings and queens through the centuries since its founding. Indeed, King George is most fond of it." Sahira wanted to cheer Mr Cops. He was trumping the Constable's wishes with the highest authority in the land.

"Humph!" The gentleman in that snort gave the impression that he disapproved of many of the things the present king enjoyed.

"Sir, sir, Prime Minister! A note from the palace." A young pink-faced underling ran to catch up with the group, a letter in hand.

The old man was the Duke of Wellington? marvelled Sahira. He certainly fitted Emily's description and Mr Cops had addressed him as "your grace", the right form of address for a duke. Was he both Constable of the Tower and Prime Minister? Could they not find enough men to share out the jobs more evenly? Surely the duke had better things to do – like running the country – rather than spending his time complaining about the number of animals in a menagerie?

The duke had moved to one side to take the note. Sahira studied him from behind the potted palm tree. She had to admit that it was quite exciting to be in the presence of such a great man, one whose name would long outlive any others of her time. This was the hero who had beaten Napoleon; the same man who, decades before that, began his illustrious career by defeating the infamous Tipu Sultan of Mysore, one of the last of India's rulers to resist the East India Company's power. Sahira wasn't sure what to think of Wellington after learning about the ruthlessness with which the duke had crushed rebellion in India. Her father had said the Company's ambitions had long outgrown its original purpose of promoting trade between the two countries; it was now the only form of government left in much of India.

And here the duke was, trying to take over the control of Mr Cops's little kingdom just because he thought the animals got in the way of the garrison! Hero though he was for the majority, Sahira decided that she didn't like him.

Wellington passed the letter to the man in the maroon jacket. "Peel, we had better return to parliament. The news about the King's health is grave."

The gentleman scanned the contents, then pulled a face at the boy. "I'm sorry, Bobby; I'll have to cut short our excursion."

"May I not stay, Father?" asked the boy. "I won't be any trouble and I really want to see the tigers."

Mr Cops approached. "I'd be happy to see the lad gets home safely, sir."

"All right, Cops. I'll leave the carriage for him. May I ride with you, your grace?" Peel asked.

"Of course, Peel. I've been wanting a word about your London police force. I've had a few complaints," said the duke sternly.

"Teething troubles, only to be expected," Peel replied, his voice wavering slightly.

The two politicians went off together, their minds back where they should be – on managing the complicated matter of running the nation. That left Bobby with Mr Cops. Sahira could hear him firing all kinds of questions at the keeper about the upkeep involved in housing tigers.

"Do they only eat fresh meat? I've heard they prefer to live alone, is that true? Is their skin striped or is that only the fur that grows out of it?"

Mr Cops tried as best he could to answer the barrage until he spotted Sahira.

"Young man, let me ask your questions of my tiger expert here." He beckoned her forward. "Can you satisfy the lad's curiosity?"

She bowed. "I will try."

The boy's attention was now on her. "Oh, how perfect: a real Indian! And you speak English!"

She resisted a smirk. If Mr Cops wanted her to play the part of a native tiger expert to win friends for the menagerie, then she would fulfil the role to the best of her ability. "Yes indeed, *sahib*."

"Sahir…" Mr Cops swallowed the last syllable of her name. "Take Master Peel here to see Rama and Sita. I'll join you in a moment."

Bobby Peel kept up his flow of questions as Sahira led him to the tiger cage. He had clearly been wondering about many things, from the number of cubs in each litter to how long a tiger's whiskers were. He diligently noted her replies in a little notebook.

"Wait a moment: I'll just put that in my nature diary." He flicked through the pages too quickly for her to read but there were many entries. "I love animals. I want to be a naturalist when I grow up and study them. Do you think a tiger cub would make a good pet?"

"Do you want to reach adulthood with both hands or only one?" she replied.

"I take that is a 'no' then?" He sighed and scribbled something down. "Your English is very good – almost as good as mine."

Sahira decided to be charitable and assume he meant that as a compliment, but she couldn't resist adding, "I imagine my Hindustani and Persian are somewhat better than yours."

He chuckled. "Oh, you are splendid! My friends would enjoy meeting you. They'll think me a top chap for inviting you to one of our parties. Will you bring some of your animals to my house and meet them? They're great fellows, all our age. My brothers will like to see your animals too, though Will might squeak a bit. He's only just out of the nursery. Do come. We play cricket in the square. Do you know how to play?" Bobby asked, gesticulating excitedly.

Sahira shook her head, feeling as if she were caught in a stampede.

He nodded sagely. "No, I suppose you wouldn't. No matter: we can teach you. We always recruit from the younger servants to make up a decent team on each side. The tigers might be a bit too much for our house – Mother wouldn't approve – but can you bring some snakes and a monkey or two?"

He appeared to be taking her agreement for granted. Sahira tried to be diplomatic with her refusal. "You'll have to ask Mr Cops. I doubt he'd allow me."

Bobby waved that away. "Oh, he will. My father is Home Secretary, a very important man in the government. Your master will want to keep him happy."

That might be true but Sahira didn't like the boy's assumption that he could order her about in his father's name. "All the same, I can't come."

His dark eyes flashed. He was not a boy used to being turned down and certainly not by one of her station in life. "That's preposterous! Don't tell me you have something better to do? Father will pay you for your time."

"I cannot come, Master Peel, because it would be quite inappropriate."

He frowned. "Let me be the judge of that."

"I'm afraid not. You see, sir, I'm not who you think." She unwound the turban, letting her hair fall free, and bobbed a curtsey. "Sahira Eleanor Clive, daughter of Captain Clive of the East India Company." It was worth exposing her true identity just to see the look on Bobby's face. "I doubt your friends will vote you top chap if they find out they're expected to play cricket with a girl. Now, if that's quite settled, let me introduce you to my tigers."

If Sahira thought her revelation would dampen Bobby's interest, she was sadly mistaken. After getting over the initial shock, he turned his questions on her. In desperation, she went out the main gate to the wharf along the Thames in hopes of shaking him off among the fishermen and boatmen, but to no avail. He was like a clinging vine caught on her tunic. How long had she been in the country? Why did she have tanned skin and reddish brown hair – had she been out in the sun a long time or was that her normal colour? Was her mother really an Indian lady or had she made that up, because she didn't look very Indian now he had a closer look at her?

Sahira stopped him there. "What does an Indian look like?"

He waved that away as if it were self-explanatory. "Well, dark hair and skin, but not as dark as an African, and not curly."

"Then you've not met many people from India, have you? Some, mainly in the north, are as fair skinned as you with pale blue and green eyes; the ones in the south can have skin as dark as a coffee bean. Some have curly hair; some straight. I see as much variety among the people there as I see on the streets of London."

That did silence him for a moment. But then he started up again. "I will amend my notes. I like learning new things – thank you. So, when you grow up, will you be the wife of a man with many wives, or just the one?"

Sahira found his question impertinent. "I'm as much English as I'm Indian. I'm to stay here now."

"Ah, so just one husband." He noted that down.

She put a hand over the page, tempted to rip it from him and throw it in the nearby river. "Stop that! I am not a menagerie animal to be studied."

Bobby bit his lip; it was finally getting through to him that Sahira was upset by his questions. "Am I being too curious? My mother always says I am like a runaway steam train."

"A what?"

"Oh, I'll show you. They are quite the most marvellous things ever invented." Diverted on to a new enthusiasm, he rifled through his notebook and showed her a drawing of a strange cylinder-shaped vehicle with a pipe at the front. "They're opening a railway line for passengers from Liverpool to Manchester soon and Father says we can go and see it if I'm good."

"But what does it do?" Of all creatures she had seen, it looked most like her beloved elephants.

"It uses steam to drive the wheels and the vehicle rockets along a track at twenty to thirty miles an hour! Can you imagine it?"

She couldn't. "A cheetah can run faster."

"Oh much." Bobby nodded. "But not with a load of cargo and passengers. It's the beginning of a new age. We won't recognize the world very soon."

Sahira didn't recognize this one already so wasn't as pleased by that prospect as Bobby Peel appeared to be.

He must have read her expression correctly so tried another tactic to convert her to his point of view. "Just think – if you could have a boat powered by steam, you could go home to India without worrying about winds and tides. You could get there in weeks – not months! Wouldn't you want to be able to come and go as you liked?"

But Sahira had nothing to go back to – no one to wait for her at the end of that journey. She kicked a pebble into the Thames.

"I'm as out of place as the Tower's polar bear." She was speaking mainly to herself but Bobby overheard.

"What polar bear?" Bobby paged through his notebook, scanning the pages for some reference to the bear in question.

Perhaps telling him this tale would get him off the subject of his unsettling ideas of the future? Sahira thought. "He's my favourite character in the Tower stories my father told me." She sat down on an upturned basket. "Did you know that Henry III kept in the Tower a polar bear, as well as three leopards-who-might-have-been-lions, and an elephant?"

Bobby looked up, glued to her words. "Is that true?"

"Oh yes. A present from King Håkon of Norway."

"Fancy that: a polar bear! I've never seen one."

"Nor have I, but I've seen a picture in a book." She used her hands to illustrate her idea of a polar bear. "They are huge and white and live up in the snowy north. They are very fierce creatures so being its keeper was a position for a brave – or desperate – man."

Bobby was quite caught up now in the story, hugging his knees to his chest as he perched on a basket next to her. "But they kept it in a cage surely – like your tigers?"

"Ah – no. It used to spend its days right here." She gestured to the wharf. "The city fathers complained about how expensive it was to feed the bear so they came up with another solution: let the bear feed itself from the fish in the Thames."

Bobby looked doubtfully at the muddy waters.

"You have to remember that the Thames was a cleaner river and the city very small. It was full of fish – especially fine salmon, just what a polar bear most likes to eat when he can't get seal. Tethered by a chain, he used to swim from the bank, or just dip in his paw," she mimicked his action, "and up would flip a glistening fish." Her hand was now a fish. "Then with a chomp of his great jaws," she clapped under Bobby's nose, "he would gulp it down and laze happily in the sun."

Bobby laughed. "Oh that is marvellous! You simply must come to tea with my friends and tell your stories." He looked her up and down with a quizzical expression. "But perhaps you could wear a dress?"

CHAPTER 9

Still buoyed up by the excitement of spending a day with the menagerie animals – especially her dear tigers – Sahira arrived back at the orphanage. Bounding through the halls, she was in too much of a hurry to worry about the cold looks she attracted. She didn't blame the others: she understood that she already was singled out by her heritage and now here she was, disappearing each day to a place of marvels. What was time in a stuffy classroom compared to helping with the animals?

On reaching the dormitory, Sahira's mood was brought rapidly down to earth. It was plain that someone had attempted to break into her trunk. The brass around the lock was covered in telltale scratches and the catch unfastened as the lock picks had done their job. Only the excellent work of the carpenter in Hyderabad had prevented the would-be thief from getting inside. As with many mysteries in India, the trunk was not as simple as it seemed to an outsider. Not only was it secured by a conventional lock, a deterrent to idle interest, but there was a second wooden bolt that had to be released by sliding part of the decorative edging of dancing monkeys aside. None of this would withstand an axe or a chisel, so Sahira resolved to remove the trunk to the Tower and beg a corner of a storeroom from Mr Cops. After all, if the King kept his Crown Jewels there, then her little Indian trunk should surely be safe?

Sahira found Ann and Emily in the nursery playing with their baby brother and sisters. Ann had two little curly-headed girls on her knee; Emily was building a castle out of blocks for a rosy-cheeked boy with hair the colour of treacle. This was part of their life Sahira had not yet seen and she now understood why they both felt so lucky to be in the orphanage. It was her turn to feel envious – this time of anyone who had a family.

"Sahira! How were the tigers?" asked Emily, her cheeks flushed. Sahira hoped Emily wasn't embarrassed to be caught playing with her little brother; she thought it a charming scene. The little boy knocked down the tower Emily had so painstakingly built him. He gurgled and clapped his hands.

"They're better now they've seen me." Sahira sat cross-legged and began to construct a temple for the little boy to demolish.

"So what happened? It has to be more interesting than what we did: sewing and yet more sewing," said Ann, while her sisters stared at their visitor with wide-eyed fascination.

"Not much," Sahira balanced two bricks against each other to form a precarious archway. They fell down before the little boy could reach them but that didn't matter: he laughed anyway. "I cleaned out a few cages, talked to some of the other keepers… oh, and I met the Prime Minister."

"What!" exclaimed Ann and Emily in unison.

"Not that I was introduced. I happened to see him taking a tour with his followers."

"Oh my – even so," said Ann enviously.

"But I did get introduced to the Home Secretary's son and have been invited to his house with my snakes to play cricket," added Sahira, delighted by their reaction.

"Oh, but you can't!" said Ann.

Sahira tried to maintain a straight face. "Why not?"

"You don't have any snakes," said Emily matter-of-factly.

"I'm sure I could borrow some."

"But only boys play cricket." Ann imparted this as if it were a great secret.

"He thought I was one – a boy, that is."

"Oh, Sahira, I don't think…" Poor Ann always worried that Sahira was going to get into trouble.

She grinned. "Don't fret: I set him right. But I'm still invited to tea."

"Will you go?" Ann asked.

She shrugged. "I don't know. He was a bit annoying really."

Their conversation was interrupted by a crash and a scream from far below, swiftly followed by the sobbing of a child. Ann and Emily fell silent, listening. Their brother and sisters clung to them.

"What's going on?" Sahira whispered.

Ann exchanged a look with Emily. "It's Cook. She's been on one of her little trips down Gin Lane."

Sahira must have looked confused because Ann explained further. "Emily means she's been blind drunk for a day now. Gets her wages on a Saturday and spends most of Sunday drinking them. Today is hangover day and we all suffer, but most especially Ned."

"You stupid boy!" shrieked Cook down in the depths of the house. "You've made me drop the supper and now it's not even fit for the pigs!"

They didn't hear Ned's reply but they could imagine his "it weren't me, M'um" and cries as she went after him with her wicked wooden spoon.

"Can't we do anything?" Sahira asked.

Ann shook her head.

Emily hugged her brother. "What do you think we could do? We're just orphans."

But Sahira didn't feel "just" an orphan, whatever that meant. She had spent the day with tigers. "I'm going down there."

Ann caught hold of her skirts. "We can't change things. You have to accept it. Bad things happen in this place."

Sahira felt she had already closed her eyes on too many abuses. "But they shouldn't." She tugged herself free. "Stay upstairs if you must, but Ned is my friend."

"No, no, I'll come too," Ann relented, setting her sisters down on the rug. "Stay here, darlings; I'll see you later for your bedtime story."

Emily silently followed her lead and the three girls hurried down the stairs. All of the other orphans had gone into hiding, apart from the Newtons, who were leaning over the bannister and listening in to the commotion in the kitchen below with great hilarity.

"What do you think? Booted out this time for certain?" asked Alf.

"Nah. A shilling he just gets a beating," replied Tommy.

"Done." The brothers shook on it.

Sahira swept past them. They were both such toads. Actually, now she thought about it, toads were nice creatures and didn't deserve the comparison; the Newtons were worse than ticks. Yes, that suited them – bloodsucking, disease-bearing pests. She burst into the kitchen to find Ned cowering in a corner while Cook loomed over him, a huge spoon in hand. Before anyone could stop her, Cook brought it down on Ned's back.

"You're nothing but f-filth! Nobody wants you, nobody loves you. You should be glateful – grateful – I give you this roof over your head!" she spluttered.

Sahira wrenched the spoon from Cook's hand before it could descend for another blow and threw it across the room. Cook wove on her feet, not quite sure what had become of her weapon. She looked at her empty palm in surprise.

"Cook, you are a disgrace," Sahira told her smartly, just as her mother used to dress down the servants if they displeased her. "You are drunk. Sit down and have a cup of tea. You need to sober up." Ann moved quickly to pour her a cup from the teapot that stood warming on the stove.

The cook gaped at the girls like the fish lying ready for gutting on the table.

"Ned, can you stand?" Sahira helped him to his feet. He was shaking.

"Oh, Sahira, you're going to be in so much trouble!" he protested.

She gave Cook a dismissive look. "She won't remember. We had a porter who was like this. Used to get roaring drunk one day, cause trouble, and then be as innocent as a lamb the next."

The woman was now sobbing into her cup, telling Ann how hard done by she was, ending up here in a filthy orphanage when she had dreamed of a house and family of her own, a handsome man to call husband, none of these ungrateful children and holier-than-thou teachers. Ann rolled her eyes at Sahira over Cook's head.

"Let me look at those bruises," said Sahira. Ned had marks all over his arms where he had tried to shield his head. "This has to stop."

"But I've nowhere else to go," he said in the saddest voice she had ever had the misfortune to hear.

"Don't take any notice of all her horrible words about you not being loved. You have friends." Jeoffry came in, having decided the storm had blown over, and curled up next to Ned. "We'll help you."

"I don't need 'elp," he said unconvincingly. His attempt to muster his pride was heartbreaking.

"Then you won't mind if I say that I need someone to help me carry my trunk to the Tower tomorrow. Would you give me a hand?"

Emily touched her arm. "What are you planning, Sahira?"

"Someone tried to open my Indian trunk today and failed. Tomorrow they might hack it to pieces. Ned is going to help me carry it to safety."

Emily gasped. "Do you know who did it?"

"The Newtons, I suppose." Sahira shrugged.

Emily bit her lip, glancing over her shoulder in fear of being overheard. "Matron did have her eye on your dresses."

"Can she pick locks?" Sahira asked doubtfully. "Doesn't seem like her style. Couldn't she just demand I hand them over?"

"What Emily is saying," explained Ann, one arm patting Cook reassuringly, "is that it is unlikely even the Newtons would risk entering the girls' dormitory. They obviously shouldn't be there and even Matron would shoo them out."

"Then maybe someone did it for them? Or they sneaked in when she was dozing in her chair? The main point is that my trunk isn't safe."

"I thought we were trying to save Ned?" asked Emily.

"We are doing both." She turned back to the boy. "So, Ned, will you help me tomorrow?"

He nodded, no doubt a little confused as to how that would rescue him.

Sahira washed her hands at the pump, then wiped them on a linen towel. "That's settled. Let's see if we can salvage anything for supper before we have a riot upstairs."

The next morning after lessons, Ned and Sahira struggled downstairs with the trunk.

"Where are you going with that?" asked Matron, though she didn't stir herself to get out of her armchair.

Sahira pushed a strand of hair out of her eyes. "I'm taking it to the menders. The lock's broken. I can't get at my clothes."

"That's a shame," she said, voice envious. "You have such nice ones. Never seen an orphan come here with so many fine gowns." She nibbled the sweet biscuit she had chosen to accompany her pre-dinner sherry. "Then I've never met a real Hindoo princess before neither."

They bumped the trunk down the stairs. It was heavier than Sahira remembered and she wondered if they would be able to make it all the way to the menagerie, just the two of them. Ned must have been thinking the same thing.

"Sahira, do you have any money?" he asked.

She remembered the coin the lightermen had given her. "A little. A shilling."

"That'll do." Ned slipped off into the crowd and returned a few moments later with a tradesman who had an empty wheelbarrow. Having seen Ned beaten down in the kitchen, Sahira realized she had underestimated how capable he was on the streets where he had lived all his life. "Barty will take it to the Tower. You won't need me."

Sahira grabbed Ned firmly by the elbow. "Oh yes I do. I have big plans for you, Ned."

He tugged free and levelled his gaze at her. "I've worked it out, you know."

"Worked what out?"

"You pity me."

"Ned, what are you talking about?"

"See someone worse off than you – there can't be that many of those – and you 'ave to 'elp." He straightened up and brushed off his threadbare jacket. "You don't 'ave to do that. I've been looking after myself since I was born. I don't need saving. You'll just make things worse for me."

"I won't," Sahira pleaded.

"You will. You might not have noticed but you're 'ardly the favourite in the orphanage. Being your friend won't 'elp me; it'll just give them another excuse to bully me."

"I… I…" Did he not want to be friends? "I didn't think about that."

"I 'preciate what you're trying to do, but it won't wash. I 'ave to look after myself. Always 'ave and always will." Ned turned to walk away. "Off you go, Barty. Drop it at Lion Gate with the keepers. See you later, Sahira."

"Right you are, Ned," said Barty.

Sahira watched the man wheel her prized possessions toward the Tower. She wanted to go with him but she wanted Ned more.

"You don't want to be friends with me any longer?" Sahira called.

Ned grimaced. "That's not what I'm sayin'. But you shouldn't treat me like you know best when you don't."

Sahira understood that she had hurt his pride with her managing ways. Her mother had always accused her of jumping in with two feet when a cautious testing of the waters was better. "I'm sorry, Ned."

He gave her a nod. "That's all right. I know you're only tryin' to 'elp."

A little crushed by his assessment, Sahira still didn't want to give up completely on what she had thought a brilliant idea. "Wait – will you come with me anyway? I really did have a good plan. It involved a zebra."

He hesitated, his curiosity clearly getting the better of him. "A zebra? Like the animal at the end of the alphabet?" He had obviously been peeking at the infants' reading books.

"Exactly like that," Sahira replied.

She saw a change wash over him. "I'll come with you to see the zebra. But I don't need 'elp, remember?"

"Oh yes, I remember. But I know a zebra who does."

Ned's eyes were wide as they toured the menagerie. He had never been before so each animal was a revelation. Forking straw into the camel's manger, Joseph Croney growled at them to stop dawdling, but there was too much to see for grumpy words to spoil Ned's pleasure.

"What's that?" Ned asked, tugging the sleeve of Sahira's work tunic. "A big dog?"

"A wolf."

"Could it kill me?"

"Maybe, if you were foolish enough to go in there with it. Mostly it preys on smaller creatures, like lambs and goats." The wolf opened its eyes; they were the colour of a yellow diamond Sahira had once seen on a nobleman's turban. The wolf's pelt had two tones: light and dark. Grey fur lay on top, with a creamy underside to muzzle, throat, and belly. It blinked once then rolled over, supremely bored by his admirers. "He'd normally have miles of territory that he patrols. Stuck in here, I think he's got lazy."

Sahira towed Ned along to the tigers a few cages further on. "And here," she said with a flourish, "are the jewels in the crown: Rama and Sita!"

"Oh my word!" Ned stared at the tigers, who had come to the bars to greet them. "These are your friends?"

Sahira pulled him back as he was swaying toward them like an iron filing to a magnet. "I'm not sure human terms work on tigers, but as far as they can feel affection for me, they do. But I have no illusions. In other circumstances," she bent down to his ear, "I could be supper!"

Ned gasped then chuckled with horrified delight.

"But these aren't why I brought you here. I want you to see the zebra." She led him out beyond the yards where most of the animals were penned, to the little green where the zebra strolled. Being only Tuesday, there weren't many visitors so it was looking quite disconsolate at the empty ale stall.

"Hey, boy!" Sahira called, holding out a handful of carrot tops she had begged off Mrs Cops.

The zebra's ears perked up and he trotted over, giving his series of little yips that meant he was pleased to see them. Sahira expected zebras to make sounds more like a donkey but normally he let out little barks more like some species of monkey she knew. The braying, according to Mr Cops, was reserved for when he was feeling amorous and then he had to be kept in his stable for the safety of visiting mares.

"Here, you feed him. Keep your hand flat." She placed the feathery leaves on Ned's palm.

"Oh, 'e's splendid. What's 'is name?" asked Ned as the zebra lipped up the treat and mashed the leaves between strong yellow teeth.

"I've only heard him called 'the zebra'. I think you can call him what you like," Sahira said.

"What name could do 'im justice?" Ned wondered aloud.

"Stripey?" His twitching skin was fascinating, the stripes running up into the bristling mane.

Ned gave her a friendly push. "Don't be silly: your tigers are named after 'eroic characters from a famous story. There must be something suitable for a zebra."

She searched her memory for her father's favourite Bible tales. "Nebuchadnezzar, the Babylonian king? He went mad and ate grass like a wild beast at one point."

Ned gave her a nod. "That sounds grand: Nebuchadnezzar the Zebra."

"Morning, Sahira." Mr Cops approached across the lawn. "Who's this you've brought with you?"

"A friend from the orphanage, Mr Cops. Ned, this is Mr Cops: he's the Keeper of the King's Lions."

Ned gave one of his excellent little bows. "Pleased to meet you, sir."

Mr Cops gave him a nod of approval. "Met the zebra, I see?"

Nebuchadnezzar was now nosing Ned's pockets in hopes of more treats. Ned pushed him firmly away. "Yes, sir."

"He's a pest, that one. For ever stealing the visitors' sandwiches and I'm afraid to say he likes his drink rather too much. Have you ever seen a drunk zebra?"

"No, sir." Ned chuckled.

"It's not a pretty sight, I can tell you." Mr Cops shook his head.

This seemed the perfect cue for Sahira to mention her plan. "I suppose you can't spare the men to watch him?"

Mr Cops pushed his hat further back on his head, a little defensive. "Of course not. I can't nanny all my animals – there're over a hundred of them!"

"But you want to keep the zebra?" Sahira prodded.

"I do. Sahira, out with it. I know you are leading up to something." He twirled a finger in the air like he was reeling something in.

"So," she said carefully, wondering how this would go. It seemed such an obviously good idea to her, but often adults didn't take the logical path even if it were pointed out to them – like when he turned her away the first day. "If you had a boy to lead the zebra about, one who wouldn't cost much to feed and house, someone like Ned here, then your problem would be solved?"

"I can't just go taking in boy-visitors to be a keeper."

"Oh, but you can, sir," blurted out Ned, who seemed to have forgotten all about not needing Sahira's help to improve his lot. "I belong to no one and no one wants me. Nebuchadnezzar and I will suit each other very well."

"Neb-who?" Mr Cops asked, brow furrowed in confusion.

"We named the zebra – christened him if you like," Sahira explained. "It's quite shocking how so many of the animals lack names. Ned doesn't want to be called 'boy', nor I 'girl', so why would the zebra want to be called just 'Zebra'?"

Mr Cops cast his eyes to heaven. "I knew the moment I saw you standing outside the Tower with the tigers that you would be trouble."

Sahira folded her arms. "I like to think I help solve problems rather than cause them."

"You really have no one, lad?" asked Mr Cops.

"No, sir." Ned was looking so eager that surely Mr Cops wouldn't be able to harden his heart. "I'm boot boy at the orphanage but Mr Pence is trying to get rid of me."

The mention of Mr Pence settled the matter. Mr Cops had clearly taken against the gentleman. "Right then, I'll take you on trial. You keep… what did you call him?"

"Nebuchadnezzar," Ned offered.

"*Nebuchadnezzar* under control. No more sandwich stealing, no more getting drunk on visitors' ale. Nebbie, old boy, this lad is going to keep you on the straight and narrow!"

Ned gave a little whoop of joy and ran his hand down the zebra's back. "Can I ride 'im?"

Mr Cops laughed and shook his head. "He's never been ridden, but I wager Sahira will have you riding in the Derby next if given her way."

CHAPTER 10

Mr Cops had no qualms about offering Ned a bed over the stables, quite the opposite to his attitude toward Sahira when she had asked the same favour. She tried not to mind that she wasn't allowed the freedom of a boy. But, of course, she did. It would have been the same in India, she reminded herself, so she knew she was fighting the world by finding that unfair.

Walking back alone to Whitechapel as the shadows lengthened, Sahira tried to keep alert as she had in the bazaar at Calcutta. With a little imagination she could transport herself there: bakers tossing flatbreads between expert hands; baskets of cashew nuts, dates, and lemons; the little pyramids of spices laid out like a colourful range of Himalayas; swirls of muslins, plain and patterned, like sunset clouds above them; bolts of silk wrapped like Cleopatra in her rug, only to be unfurled when a rich customer requested; knives for sharpening; old pans for mending; fish and meat herded down one smelly end where the ground was splattered with guts and entrails. Compared with that, the London market she was walking through now appeared to have had all the colour leeched from it: dark greens, blood reds, greys, black, off-whites, and sticky browns – the same colours as the unappetizing dishes at the orphanage.

She missed turmeric, ginger, cinnamon, cardamon. All that was offered here was mustard, salt, and pepper.

The journey gave Sahira time to begin to regret her earlier actions. By finding a new home for Ned, she had done herself out of an ally at the orphanage. Added to that, she hadn't considered the likely reaction of Mr Pence and Cook to her theft of their boot boy. She guessed that they would take the view that it was fine for them to threaten him with dismissal, but for someone else to rescue him, that was another matter entirely.

"What have you done with my Ned?" screeched Cook on Sahira's return. She must have been watching for her from the area basement and dashed upstairs to intercept her in the hallway. Sahira could tell from the state of the dining room that supper was not ready and the house in a Cook-inspired uproar.

Sahira took off her shawl and hung it on a peg by the front door where the orphans placed their outdoor clothes. *Pretend nothing unusual has happened and maybe Cook will go away.* "He's taken a new job."

Strong fingers, toned on kneading bread, pinched Sahira's ear. "What do you mean, you dirty daggle-tail?" Reflexively, Sahira grabbed Cook's wrist and dug in her nails. She howled, released Sahira's ear, and shook her hand. "You little witch!"

"It's not my fault, Cook. Mr Cops of the menagerie has taken him in. It's nothing to do with me," Sahira pleaded. She wasn't in the habit of lying but she dared not think about what pain Cook would inflict next if she told the truth.

Cook threw up her hands. "But who's going to do the work in the kitchen now?"

Sahira wanted to say Cook would have to pay someone to work for her – and treat them a lot better than she did Ned if she wanted to keep them – but she swallowed her words. Now was not the time to wave the red flag before the bull.

"Mr Pence!" roared Cook. You've got to come!" Sahira tried to slip away but Cook blocked her exit upstairs. "Oh no you don't!"

Mr Pence emerged from his study, cane in hand ready to administer quick, painful reprimands to whoever had bothered her. "What is it, Cook? Don't you know I am entertaining an important guest?"

"This… this savage…" she pointed a trembling finger at Sahira, who stood quietly, hands folded meekly in front of her. "She's spirited Ned away and left me high and dry in the kitchen. Says he's got a new job – at the Tower, of all places."

Mr Pence squeezed his cane in his hands. "Has she now? Eleanor Clive, did you take Ned with you to the Tower this afternoon?"

She was cornered. "Yes, sir." Sahira's heart pounded with fear. This was not good.

"On whose authority?"

She looked up, startled. "Authority? I hadn't realized Ned needed permission."

Mr Pence cast his eyes to the ceiling. "Your own, I suppose, as an Indian *princess*?"

Sahira sensed a trap. "No, sir. I... I just didn't know Ned had to ask to come with me – to see the zebra."

Mr Pence flicked his fingers at his staff member. "Cook, get one of the other orphans to help you – take the whole pack of them for all I care. They laze around the house too much as it is. Eleanor, into the study."

Sahira hesitated, glancing longingly up to the girls' dormitory, which had become something of a haven for her in this place. She could see faces clustered around the bannisters as the others watched from the shadows. The expression on Ann's and Emily's faces was fearful but the Newtons were gloating.

"Now!" barked Mr Pence.

Sahira trailed after him into his private domain. The last time she had been here was to sign the register. This tome lay open on the desk. In front of it sat a man in a crisp dark suit. He had a crop of bushy white hair like a parakeet's crown of feathers and his smile was about as friendly as the bird's hooked beak.

"Mr Rummage, this is the girl," announced Mr Pence. "As you might have heard, I regret to say that her troublemaking skills are well developed. And as you have revealed, she is also mendacious." He turned on Sahira. "That means, girl, that you lie."

She knew full well what it meant. "I didn't lie. Ned does have a new position."

"Not about the boot boy – you lied about who you really are. Mr Rummage is Lord Chalmers's man of business from the firm Rummage, Rummage and Battledore, sent here by his lordship."

A wild burst of hope flamed inside Sahira. Perhaps in the nick of time, the lawyer had come to rescue her from this place and offer her a home? Maybe her English family wanted her after all? "You've come to fetch me, sir?"

Mr Rummage waved away the hand that she had stretched toward him. "I am under orders to look at you, girl, and report back. That is all."

"Oh." Sahira dropped her hands and laced them tightly behind her back. She should have known better. If the family had wanted her, surely they would have come themselves?

Mr Pence took his stance behind the desk. "Mr Rummage has set me straight about a number of things. He claims that your mother was no princess, just a Muslim woman your father took into his household."

"I never said she was a princess – that was the story given you by the man from the Company."

"I distinctly remember you making such a claim in front of many witnesses on that absurd display of your peacock gown."

He had her there. She hung her head. "That was just a story."

"Stories are lies. What is more, Mr Rummage says Lord Chalmers doubts that any valid marriage took place between your father and the Indian woman."

"But it did!" Sahira burst out.

"Silence! I'm talking about a failure to conduct a proper British ceremony. My cousin, Mrs Bingham, reported the rumours in Company circles that your father had become a Muslim and betrayed his nation by casting his lot in with the natives. He even dared criticize the Governor General."

He probably had criticized the Governor, but what was that to do with her legitimacy? "My father was Christian, my mother Muslim. My parents were married – twice," Sahira replied, but her voice was weaker than she wished. The ceremony had taken place in a Christian church and in a Muslim ceremony a week later – or so her parents had always told her. Mother was a lady of high birth; she would never have lived with an Englishman without the status and respect marriage gave her.

But knowing how strong-willed her mother was, Sahira didn't doubt that she would have considered a Muslim ceremony sufficient.

"I'm sending to India for confirmation," said Mr Rummage. "However, that is immaterial. Even if the girl is the product of a legal marriage, Lord Chalmers could not accept her. Just look at the child! She is too dark. Had she a lighter skin, we might have passed her off as European, but one glance and anyone would know her shameful origins."

"I'm afraid you're right, sir," agreed Mr Pence with barely hidden glee.

"If Captain Clive had been in his right wits when he left, he would have made arrangements for her to stay behind as other officers have done for their Indian children."

Sahira could feel the flush of shame creep up her neck to her cheeks. But what had she to be ashamed of? She forced herself to lift her chin and meet Mr Rummage's eyes with her own. She knew that her amber-coloured irises, so like the tigers' according to Father, had the effect of unnerving people. "I'm a legitimate daughter and my father expected me to be treated as such."

Mr Rummage cleared his throat, fingering his watch chain that lay across his waistcoat. "Regrettably, Captain Clive has passed so we have no idea of his intentions. He might have been planning to put you and your mother away on his return. He had written asking for his father's help."

"Put us away?" Sahira's temper got the better of her. "You do not know my father if you think he would allow that. No, he loved us. He even thought his father might be brought to care for me too if he met me. He wanted to ask for help, yes, but it was to pay for my schooling as Lord Chalmers does for his other grandchildren." She could feel tears threatening but she hoped the heat of her anger would dry them up before they fell. "Where is Lord Chalmers? Why can't I see my... my grandfather?" She almost choked on the words. She was beginning to hate her closest relative in this country for his cowardice in not facing her himself but sending this grey little man to do his dirty work.

"Control yourself, Eleanor!" snapped Mr Pence. "You have chalked up punishment enough by your actions today without adding rudeness to a guest to the list!"

"I'm not the one calling someone an illegitimate child!" Sahira exclaimed.

"Eleanor Clive!" Mr Pence threatened.

She squeezed her eyes shut, breathing through her nose to calm down as her mother had taught. Elegance and good manners are the mark of an un-Issa, her mother's family.

The lawyer stood up. "I was told to offer you a choice. Your passage back to India, steerage class, will be paid if you return to your family there and never disturb Lord Chalmers again, nor lay claim to any blood relationship."

Sahira swayed on her feet. They were planning to send her back to a country where she had no home with nothing but her passage paid? She had no illusions that there were as many prejudices against someone of mixed blood in India as there were in England. Her mother had agreed to come to this country and place her daughter at school here, knowing that no man of her class in Hyderabad would marry Sahira; whereas she had hoped an Englishman, liberal-minded like Captain Clive, might eventually fall for Sahira when she had learned to fit in. The hope was that her grandfather's status might make many overlook her birth.

But that only counted if Lord Chalmers recognized her as part of his family.

"My other choice?" she stammered.

"You stay here in the orphanage. I will monitor your progress and send occasional reports to your grandfather. He does not wish you ill; he just does not want you around, tarnishing the good name of his family. When you are of age, I will organize a suitable situation for you," Mr Rummage said.

"I don't know what you mean," Sahira said. *Suitable for whom?* she wondered.

"Marriage to one of his lordship's tenants perhaps, on one of his Irish estates." The lawyer leafed through a notebook as if searching for a name. "Yes, that would do. They are desperate enough there to think the connection a boon."

Sahira's response was immediate: "No, thank you."

"What?" Mr Rummage asked, incredulous.

Sahira regained her composure. "No. I don't like either option. You can tell my grandfather that he needn't concern himself about me. I'll make my own way without his aid."

This reply wrong-footed the lawyer. "Child, you surely don't understand!"

"Eleanor, do you know what you are saying?" Mr Pence chimed in.

"Yes, sir. I surely do. You offer to send me back to a place thousands of miles away where I have no one anymore. My mother has no close relatives alive and I know well that the journey is dangerous and the destination hostile to someone like me. Or you say, 'sit here and be quiet and if you're good you might marry an Irishman', a complete stranger – one that only wants to wed me to curry favour with the grandfather who despises my existence? So no, thank you."

"You can't just refuse!" Mr Rummage exclaimed.

"Why? Is slavery legal then?" Sahira countered.

"You're a minor," Mr Rummage scoffed. "Children can't decide such things for themselves."

Sahira felt her resolve strengthening. "But my grandfather doesn't claim me so has no guardianship over me. Unless you are telling me he is willing to acknowledge me before the courts?"

The man swallowed. "No, no, I don't think that would be my recommendation. It is imperative the connection is not made public for the sake of his granddaughters."

"*I* am his granddaughter."

"I mean his English ones on the marriage market. A whiff of scandal and they might lose their chance at making the best matches."

"And that's more important than me?"

The lawyer turned to the orphanage director, who had a very self-satisfied grin on his face. "Mr Pence, I see what you are dealing with. I didn't expect such impertinence from one of only twelve years."

Sahira had had to grow up fast since being orphaned. "What have I done? I've only refused what you offered, as is my right, surely?"

He ignored her. "I will give her three months to reconsider her answer and return in the autumn to discover if experience has curbed her pride." He placed a bag of coins on the desk. It fell over, spilling golden guineas on the blotter. "Until then, I'm instructed to pay for her place here."

Sahira reached out to hand the bag back. "I'm already earning my place. I don't need my grandfather's charity."

But Mr Pence was too quick for her and had pocketed the amount. "Understood, Mr Rummage. I will work on making sure she knows the reality of her situation."

Mr Rummage got up and offered his hand to the orphanage owner. "I'm relieved to be entrusting her to safe harbour. Goodbye. Eleanor, I hope you learn the error of your ways before it's too late." He gave her a nod and walked out, leaving her alone with Mr Pence.

Girl and orphanage owner stared at each other a moment, the animosity between them so strong it was like the stench of the fish market in the air.

"Hold out your hand," Mr Pence demanded, bending the cane between his fists.

"Why?" She tucked her hands behind her back, though she knew that was futile. He had wanted to hit her ever since she arrived.

"You need to be disciplined."

Could she avoid this punishment, come up with a clever story to divert his attention? Her mind had gone blank. There was no escape she could conjure up in the next few moments. She held out her hand, determined that it wouldn't shake. She didn't quite succeed.

"You have earned six strokes for taking Ned away without permission, and six for being rude to a visitor. When I have finished, you will thank me for the correction and go to bed with no supper, understood?"

Sahira didn't reply, just gazed at him, wishing her stare had the power to kill or she had claws to rake across his hateful face.

He poked the end of the cane in her chest, one prod to go with each word. "Do. You. Understand?"

"I understand. Sir," she hissed.

She didn't close her eyes as he administered the strokes. He insisted on making six on one palm and six on the other so that both hands would be sore. Sahira vowed not to make a sound, even though her eyes were watering and her breath ragged.

"Now thank me," he demanded.

She cursed him in Hindustani, wishing his nose rot off and his teeth fall out. That earned her an extra stroke.

"Thank me!" He looked like a rabid dog, mouth flecked with foam.

"Thank you for teaching me what you think is correction," she said hoarsely.

He knew she was defying him but he couldn't quite pinpoint how. "Hands out!" He made the last stroke across both palms, his hardest strike of all. "Remember this. Do not do anything to earn such again or you'll go straight to the workhouse after Mr Rummage gives up on you. Dismissed."

Sahira was already on the way out as he gave the order for her to leave. Shoulders straight, she marched through the crowd of eavesdroppers.

"Fourteen!" mocked Alf. "My, my, Indian Clive, you must really have got on his wick."

Tommy hooked the back of her dress. "Give us your boots, or it'll be much more than fourteen puny little pats from a cane that you have to worry about."

She told them in Hindustani to go jump in the Ganges River, and marched upstairs.

CHAPTER 11

Sahira half-expected Mr Pence to say she was forbidden to return to the menagerie but she had not factored in his desire to carry on receiving her wages. No one tried to stop her as she went out after morning lessons. She ran with her halting stride all the way to the Tower, desperate to put as much distance between herself and the orphanage as she could. She changed quickly and painfully, swollen fingers clumsy on the strings and buttons, then went in search of the tigers.

She kneeled before the bars, rather too close if truth be told. She could feel the warm breath of Sita huffing on her skin as she crouched before her.

"Sita, I really, really… h… hate London." She'd been holding in her tears since her beating but now she let go. Her crying was messy – chest wracked with sobs, nose running, mouth a grimace of misery – but it didn't matter as there were only the tigers to see. She wanted to run away with them.

The tigress grunted, circled, and took a place so that her back was pressed against the bars. Swiping a sleeve across her face, Sahira tentatively reached out and stroked the fur, something she'd never dared do before. The rough silk soothed her. Rama sat proudly beside his mate, watching them both, perhaps guarding his girls. It was hard to say what was going through his mind. He must blame Sahira for bringing him here, yet he seemed to like her as much as a tiger could like anyone.

The door banged open and Ned ran in. Sita got up and prowled further off, as if embarrassed to have been caught comforting a human cub.

"Sahira! I'm so pleased you've come. I missed you this morning. This is just the most wonderful place I've ever been! Nebbie has stolen three half pints of ale already. He's so funny, such a clown!"

She tucked her hands under her arms and hoped he couldn't see the tear stains across her face. "You're supposed to be stopping him doing that."

"Oh, I do, but I let him have the occasional sip – he so likes it. Good morning, tigers!" He waved enthusiastically at her friends. If there hadn't been bars between them, Rama would have put an end to such familiarity with a leap. As it was, he turned his back on Ned, tail a-twitch with disdain. Ned just laughed.

Sahira got up, shaking off the pins and needles in her calf muscles. She gave her eyes a stealthy wipe with her sleeve before facing Ned. "So it's working out well for you?"

"Like a dream." Ned took a second glance at her. "Are you feeling all right, Sahira? You look sad. Have you been crying?"

She couldn't deal with anyone's sympathy at the moment, not unless they had four paws and whiskers. "I'm fine," she lied. "Tell me what's going on here."

"The big news is that the old lion is sickening." He pulled Sahira along to the cage next to the tigers. A great lion lay stretched out on the straw, bald patches on his fur showing he was in bad condition. "Poor old George. Mr Cops says it is mainly old age getting to him."

A rattle and a curse announced the arrival of Joseph Croney with a barrow of dung. "We should shoot the blighter."

Ned stuck his tongue out at the keeper's back. "No, we shouldn't. And anyway, there's an old London story that the top lion represents the King. If the lion is in a bad way, it means bad news for its namesake."

Sahira's father had always laughed at such tales but her ayahs had been careful not to attract bad luck, saying humans would never know the mind of the gods on such matters. "Does it hold true?"

Croney gave a harsh laugh. "Mr Cops just swaps the names around when one dies – no point offending the royal family. This old George here will be succeeded by the cub William if he kicks the bucket – and William will then be George, get it?"

"But the King is ill – the real one, I mean. Mr Cops might need William as William," Sahira said.

"How do you know that?" asked Ned.

"The Prime Minister told me." She tried one of her usual grins but her face wasn't cooperating.

Ned took a closer look at her. "Sahira, there's something the matter. What is it?"

"There you are!" boomed Mr Cops. Croney hurried off to spread his doom and gloom somewhere else. The lion looked up wearily then settled back to his sick bed. "The aviary won't clean itself, ladies and gentlemen. Sahira, here's a broom. Ned, what about Nebbie?"

Ned brushed straw off his knees. "I left him tied up by the ale stall. The barkeep said he'd watch him."

Mr Cops raised a brow.

Ned realized the foolishness of what he had said. "I'd better get back. Quickly."

"You do that, lad." Mr Cops watched him dart out and chuckled. "Sharper than a case of knives, that boy." He turned back to Sahira. She couldn't get her fingers to wrap around the broom handle without wincing. Alert to the silent injuries of his animals, the keeper diagnosed the problem at a glance. "Show me."

Ashamed, Sahira held out swollen palms.

"Mr Pence did this?" he asked.

She nodded, gulping against a renewed wash of tears.

"For bringing the boy here, I suppose?"

She couldn't bear to tell him the whole story. "Yes," she replied simply.

He took the broom. "Go see my wife and tell her I sent you – ask her to do what she can for that. You need to cool the skin to reduce the swelling. It should've been done immediately but I suppose he considers it part of the punishment." He sighed, removed his hat, and scratched his head. "That man! I wouldn't entrust him with my horse, let alone a child. Run along now."

Relieved not to have to wield a rake or broom with sore hands, Sahira knocked shyly on the door of Lion House. Mrs Cops answered and smiled at her visitor in recognition.

"Have you come to see how Pithy is doing?" She stood back to let Sahira inside.

"You don't mind the snake now?" Sahira mustered a smile.

"Can't say I like him, but he is awfully fascinating, peeling off his skin like that as if he were a piece of fruit."

Sahira stepped across the threshold and went into the kitchen. Mrs Cops lifted off the lid of the basket to show a freshly shining python coiled up inside, lying on the papery remains of his old scales.

"I think he's done with his shedding," Sahira said. "He can go to his cage now."

"I'll tell Fred." She put the lid back on, making sure it was secure.

"Actually, I'm not here for the snake, Mrs Cops. Your husband said you might be able to help me with this?" Sahira held out her hands.

"Oh, you poor love! Who did that to you?" She swooped down on the girl and gathered her to her apron, tight as a drum with the baby inside her.

Her unexpected tenderness broke the dam again. It seemed permissible to let go in front of another woman, a motherly one at that. Sahira wasn't crying just for the beating but for everything: losing her parents, being adrift in a strange land, being rejected by her family. So many hurts queued up inside, they jostled to escape.

Mrs Cops let her sob out the story in incoherent gasps, interjecting her "poor love" and "what a horrible man" at suitable intervals. By the end, the front of Mrs Cops's apron was damp with Sahira's tears. She let the girl wind down, then guided her gently into a chair. "Sit there. This demands a cool wrap and some tea and cake." She bound Sahira's hands in strips of cloth soaked in icy well water, then set about boiling a kettle. "Nothing seems so bad when you have a cup of tea and something sweet to lift the spirits. Not that I'm making light of your loss, sweetheart, but your parents would be pleased that you survived. They would be wishing you happy too."

"I don't think I'm ever going to be happy again," Sahira admitted.

She stroked the girl's tear-stained cheek. "You say that, but people come back from the most terrible setbacks. Life finds a way. Just give yourself a chance to grieve and heal." She put a piece of ginger cake down next to her. "Try this. Made with treacle to my mother's own recipe. Guaranteed to mend a broken heart."

Sahira took a bite, trying without success to keep fresh tears back. She had always prided herself on being strong. She'd not cried when her parents died. Mrs Tailor had encouraged her to weep but instead she had just felt numb. Now she couldn't seem to stop. This was the second time she'd cried that morning – more times than she'd cried for months.

"I'd say you were due a good cry," Mrs Cops said, pouring a cup of tea. "Tell me about your parents – stories of the good times. When I think of my own parents, God bless them, I always try to remember the best days we had, not the sadness of their passing."

It was a relief to talk about them rather than just remember them on her own as she'd been doing constantly since they died. No one in London knew them so she'd not had a chance to share her memories. "There was the time that Ammi – that's my mother – found a mongoose in her dressing table drawer curled up on her pearls. She did shriek so."

"I don't blame her! I don't suppose someone put it there on purpose?"

"Might've." Sahira found a genuine smile on her lips. "Baba was rearing it to help with our snake problem. It was only a baby one. Baba and I teased her for days. She was normally so brave about animals, like the time she killed a cobra with a stick when she found it in my cradle."

"Oh my goodness!" exclaimed Mrs Cops.

The misery inside melted away as Sahira spun tales for Mrs Cops of their rambles in the jungle, of the elephants bathing in the Ganges, and the temples lost under vines. "And the butterflies! You've never seen anything like it, Mrs Cops. Some are as big as dinner plates and the colour of sapphires."

"And to think you gave up all that to come here. You must find us quite a disappointment." She blew the steam away from the surface of the tea in her cup.

"It wasn't supposed to be for ever. Baba wanted me to be educated in England as girls aren't usually put through school in Hyderabad.

He then hoped I'd return to join them in India, and perhaps marry a young clerk from the East India Company, someone who shared our love for animals. He said I shouldn't be alone but it was hard to find a place for me: I belonged to two worlds, neither of which wanted me. He said that it was his only regret about his marriage – that Ammi and he had put me in this position."

"You have no brothers or sisters?" Mrs Cops served her a second slice of ginger cake.

"There was one little brother who died as a baby. After that there were no more. I don't think my parents could bear the idea of losing another one. The climate of India is terribly cruel to little ones. But in the end, it was *me* who lost *them*, wasn't it?" Sahira was feeling sad again, but it was a nicer kind of sadness, a pure feeling of missing with less anger mixed in, calm like the sky after the monsoon had swept through. "I have no one now but the tigers."

"You will make a new family for yourself, Sahira. You've already started by making so many new friendships." She patted the girl's narrow shoulder. "Hands any better?"

Sahira unwrapped the cloth and peeked. "Yes."

"I'll get some cold water for you to dip them in. Sit in Fred's chair by the fire. No work outside for you today, young lady. You can occupy your time as our python expert, keeping watch over his moulting."

Sahira's hands returned to their usual size the next day with only a little soreness to remind her of the beating. They hurt most when she clenched them or tried to hold a needle or chalk in her lessons. At the menagerie, Mr Cops handed her a pair of his wife's old gloves before she set about any work, and that helped. She was soon back to her old self, or as close as she could come. She couldn't shake off the feeling of being more vulnerable than she had realized. She had never been beaten before, her parents preferring other methods of discipline that appealed to her sense of right and wrong rather than brute force. It was a rude awakening to find out that there were adults who had that power over her and she couldn't do anything about it. Her respect for Ned grew. How he had retained his cheerful nature despite a lifetime of such treatment was a marvel. He had to be very resilient.

Sahira told him so one sunny afternoon while she rested with him on the lawn, Nebbie standing quietly nearby in the zebra equivalent of a snooze.

"You speak funny, you know?" observed Ned. "Long words, like the vicar uses."

"What long words?" she asked, watching the clouds form their dance of shapes, sheep becoming dragon, shifting to crocodile.

"Resi-something. Where did you learn that?"

"I don't know. My father, I suppose. He loved the Bible and other books and used to read to me all the time – Shakespeare, Dryden, Pope, Wordsworth. He enjoyed novels too. I think his favourites were the ones by Sir Walter Scott – Scottish mountains and derring-do."

"He read to you? Why did he do that?" Ned asked.

Once again Sahira was reminded that Ned had never known such care from an adult. "It was fun. And it helped me learn. Even Mrs Pence reads to us when we're sewing, though that's because she's trying to make us good."

"You are good." Ned plucked a blade of grass and tickled her under the chin.

She batted his hand away. "Pest. I'll read to you if you like. I miss proper stories. Mrs Pence's taste is limited to 'improving works'."

"I don't have any books," he admitted.

"I'll see if I can get hold of some. There might be a few battered ones that no one will miss from the orphanage."

"Don't let them catch you or they'll accuse you of stealing – and that's a hanging offence, or you might get transported to Australia. No story is worth that." He was deadly serious.

"Don't worry, I have lots of stories lodged in my memory too."

"Miss Clive?" A shadow fell across her face. Ned and Sahira scrambled to their feet. It was Bobby Peel, back again, this time with a thin gentleman in tow. The man must have been in his early twenties and was dressed in a black swallow-tailed jacket. He had a keen light in his eyes, warning Sahira that he was not to be dismissed despite his slight stature. "Miss Clive, this is my tutor, Mr Evesham."

Confused by being in her work clothes, Sahira bowed Indian style before switching to a curtsey. Mr Evesham smiled.

"Can I pet the zebra?" Bobby asked Ned.

"Go ahead, sir." Ned waggled his eyebrows at Sahira, silently asking how she knew the rich boy.

She shrugged, lost for an explanation. She hadn't expected him to remember her.

"So, Miss Clive, when can you come to tea?" Bobby asked her over his shoulder as if they were just picking up their old conversation after a second's lapse rather than several days. "Mr Evesham, is Friday convenient for us? At my birthday party?"

"Yes, that will be excellent." The tutor's voice was a soft baritone with the lilt of a Welshman.

"Can you bring the zebra?" Bobby was serious.

Sahira opened her mouth to refuse, but Ned jumped in first. "I'm the new zebra keeper. How far away do you live, sir?"

"In the West End, Upper Grosvenor Street," Bobby replied.

Ned shook his head in a show of not very convincing doubt. "That's a fair way to walk."

"Can he manage it?" Bobby nodded to his tutor who slipped several coins into Ned's hand.

"Oh, I think so." Ned grinned, pocketing his tip.

"I'll send a footman to escort you both. A zebra walking across London might attract quite a crowd. Miss Clive, would you like me to send a carriage for you?"

Once again, Bobby had taken her consent for granted. "I'm not sure I'm free, Master Peel."

"You are, Sahira. I checked the duty roster. Not much happening on Friday," said Ned, the traitor.

"You are the daughter of Captain Richard Clive, aren't you?" asked Bobby, thoughts taking another track.

"Yes," replied Sahira.

"Hmm, thought so. I'll see if I can arrange it," Bobby said.

"Arrange what? And I still haven't said I'll come," Sahira protested.

"She'll come," said Ned, "but she has a poorly leg because an elephant trod on her. The carriage is a good idea."

"Ned!" she exclaimed. Was no secret safe around him?

"An elephant? African or Indian?" asked Bobby, getting out his notebook.

Sahira growled just as Bobby's tutor laid a restraining hand on his sleeve.

"Ah yes, sorry." He tucked it away.

Screams from the first yard tore the air. Visitors were running out of the predator enclosure, but many others were heading toward the trouble. Under the shrieks came the angry roars of the tigers. Abandoning Bobby and his tutor, Sahira ran as fast as she could to Rama and Sita, taking the keepers' route around the back. If someone was hurting them, there'd be trouble!

When she arrived at their cage, she found it empty. Not so the old lion's den. Her tigers were rolling in a knot of orange and black, interlaced with tawny, as they wrestled the poor old king. On the bridge over the yard, men were laying bets on the outcome but anyone could see the lion was outclassed and outnumbered.

"Stop!" Sahira shouted, but she had no chance against the fighting instinct of big cats. Grabbing the broom, she rattled the bars with the wooden end. Rama had the lion's throat in his jaws.

"Get back, Sahira!" warned Mr Cops. He turned a hose kept for washing out the pens on the creatures, ordering his men to pump the water up from the well. The force blasted Sita off the lion and she skulked back to her den. Rama was not so easily dislodged. Ben Poulter and Mike Kerry entered the cage, one armed with a whip and rake, the other with a rifle.

"Don't shoot!" Sahira begged.

Mike cracked his whip and Rama dropped the lion to snarl at him. His muzzle was red.

"Rama, back in your den! Please!" she called.

Tail whipping in displeasure, Rama circled. For one terrible moment she thought he might attack Ben. So did the keeper because he levelled the gun to his shoulder.

"Rama, I beg you!" cried Sahira.

With a final roar, he backed into his den, flinching from the whip's crack. Mike slammed the door closed.

"Who left this door unlocked?" shouted Mr Cops, rushing to the lion.

"Not me," said Mike.

"Who was on lion duty today?"

"Me," said Ben, raising a shaking hand. "But it was closed, I swear it, when I left him."

Mr Cops turned to the poor lion. Sahira crouched as close as she could on the other side of the bars.

"Is he going to make it?" she asked.

Mr Cops shook his head. "Ben, clear the place of visitors. Give me your gun. Sahira, you'd better leave too. You won't want to see this."

Her eyes glazed with tears. "You… you won't do anything to the tigers, will you? Please, Mr Cops?"

His eyes flicked up to hers, understanding in their depths. "The tigers were just following their nature – I can't punish them for that. No, the one who'll catch it is the stupid person responsible for leaving that door unlatched. Run along now."

Sahira stumbled along the corridor that ran behind the pens. She collided with Joseph Croney, who was listening from the safety of the stairs.

"The lion's a goner?" he asked eagerly.

She nodded, wiping the back of her hand across her eyes.

"All right then." He went back to his barrow, whistling.

A gunshot ripped through the menagerie. The ravens of the Tower fluttered their clipped wings and cawed in distress.

The lion king was dead. Long live the King.

CHAPTER 12

Sahira was relieved that Mr Cops did not blame her tigers. The only punishment they received was to be in lockdown until their bloodlust subsided and Rama had stopped his snarling and pacing. Poor old George though: he was carried off to the anatomist's house for dissection. Exotic animals were much sought after by those who studied the creatures, and the menagerie could always do with the extra coin. As predicted by Croney, into his place was ushered young William, now to be known as George, and no one was to mention the fate of his predecessor to Buckingham Palace.

That was the plan. What actually happened was someone in the menagerie leaked the story to the press and the papers carried the sad tale of the demise of one of the Tower's favourite creatures. They even illustrated the confrontation so no one, not even those who couldn't read, would be unaware of the disaster.

The next few days in the menagerie, Mr Cops walked around with a scowl.

"He's worried the duke will use it as an excuse to close us down," said Ben as Sahira stood beside him, washing out the animal feed bowls by the pump. "You heard what the duke said on his last visit?"

She nodded.

"And now there's that old story about the lions representing the king of the day. That's a dangerous one, what with all these revolutions across Europe. Some hothead might make it a reason to try it here. They might claim the people are the tigers or some such story."

Sahira could see how someone might try to turn it into an omen. "But it was an accident!"

Ben shook his head. "Was it? I swear I shut the door properly. I don't make mistakes about that – not when my life, and the lives of the animals, are at stake."

Sahira could vouch from her own observation that he was not a careless keeper. "Who do you suspect?" She had her own ideas but she wondered if Ben thought the same.

"Can't say for certain but I know someone who's had a spring in their step since it happened." He looked across at Joseph Croney, who was repainting the door to the aviary. He didn't seem to mind the birds and Sahira noticed that Mr Cops had kept him well away from the larger animals since old George was killed. They all suspected him but no one could come right out with their accusation.

"Hadn't you better leave these bowls and spruce up?" asked Ben as the Tower clock struck the hour. "Don't you have a carriage coming for you?"

Sahira rolled her eyes. "I still haven't said if I'm going. I don't like to be bullied into something by any boy. I have enough people telling me what to do at the orphanage."

"Sahira, you've got more pride than any number of lions! It don't matter what you think with the likes of Mr Peel or any of the high-ups. If there's a carriage coming, they expect you to be in it."

"It seems they teach their children the same thing too."

"Oh, that Bobby's all right for a toff. And the menagerie needs all the friends it can get." Ben nodded over to the White Tower, where the Constable had his apartment.

Sahira felt that horrible twist of fear in her chest again. "The duke is really going to shut it down, after centuries, in the face of tradition?"

Ben shrugged. "He's going to give it a good go, I'd say. Times are changing and we have competition now from the new zoological gardens in Regent's Park. Only the old King stands between us and closure – and you've seen what happens to a king when tigers like the duke get them in a corner."

Deciding she could agree to the outing with honour if she were doing it for the menagerie, Sahira changed in the storeroom where she had stowed her trunk. She decided that she wouldn't waste any of the more flamboyant gowns on the boys and settled on a quiet forest green one with a border of tree frogs. She combed her hair and tied it back in a black ribbon, the only scrap of clothing she had of the right colour to show that she was in mourning. She rubbed the worst of the dirt off the scuffed toes of her boots, wondering where in London she could get blue polish, and then presented herself to Mrs Cops for a final inspection.

Removing a strand of straw from the hem, she gave Sahira a nod. "Tree frogs! How original. You look very fine, Sahira. Have a lovely time. I'm sure the food will be very superior to anything you've tried so far in England."

"Aren't you going to tell me to behave?" asked Sahira.

Mrs Cops kissed the top of Sahira's head. "I'm sure you'll do us credit."

It was lovely to hear that she was representing the menagerie and considered part of their team. Sahira went outside to take the baskets of animals Mr Cops had prepared for the excursion. He'd chosen well: a quiet little marmoset who clung to his sleeve, a tortoise, some harmless snakes, and a parrot in a cage that could whistle sea shanties.

"Put the cover over him if he starts on his rude words," he cautioned. "When I got it from Jamrach's shop on Ratcliffe Highway, his visitors had already made it unfit for most drawing rooms. I reckon the boys won't mind though."

"They'll probably think it great sport," Sahira agreed, taking the ring of the cage from him. "What's his name?"

"Napoleon," Mr Cops replied.

Hearing its name, the parrot fluffed its jewel blue and red feathers and screeched: "*Vive la France!*"

Sahira chuckled. "I would've thought this was one animal in the menagerie the duke would approve of, seeing how he caged his namesake."

Mr Cops tweaked the black ribbon. "You're a wit, aren't you?"

"At least half a one."

He guffawed at that. Sahira smiled back. She remembered that she liked making people laugh, her parents especially.

The Peels' carriage arrived as promised, the coachman looking none too pleased to be ferrying a girl and various beasts across town. Sahira looked longingly up at the box where he sat high above the crowds and wondered if she dared. The marmoset, now transferred to her shoulder, chattered in her ear. She had a pretty white face and golden-coloured fur. Her chittering seemed to say that she liked Sahira's hair well enough and was happy to sit there rather than in the basket Mr Cops had provided. No one could resist her charm for long and even the snooty driver was seen to smile as she wrapped her hands around the end of the ribbon and waved it like a fan, experimenting with the unfamiliar material.

"Might I – might we – travel alongside you?" Sahira asked, finally braving the request she had been contemplating. "I promise we won't be any trouble and Tiny likes to see what's going on." So did Tiny's minder.

The coachman ruffled the capes of his enormous coat. The layers were to keep the rain off in bad weather. For all anyone knew, under that mound of cloth, the man himself could be but a skinny creature, like a crab in a too-big-for-him shell.

"All right then, Miss," he replied. "No fussing or you're in the carriage."

"Thank you!" Accepting the driver's hand, Sahira scrambled up alongside him and now shared his view over the two glossy backs of his matched pair. They shone like guardsmen's toecaps. "My, they are fine horses!"

"My master only has the best," agreed the driver. He clicked his tongue and twitched the reins. The horses woke up from their daydreams and set off for the West End.

Sahira searched for a topic of conversation that would not vex him. "Did you by any chance see a zebra on your travels?"

"Lawks, yes! Attracting quite a crowd it was. Young Master Bobby sent all the available footmen to help escort it across town." Now he had settled to having her alongside him, the coachman, who she learned was called Jenks, proved talkative. "The young lad leading it though was making quite a few pennies for himself by letting little ones sit on its back. I don't reckon they'll be there before us even with their head start."

As they made their way west through the choked streets of the city Sahira saw no sign of Ned or the zebra, but there was plenty else for Tiny and her to look at: churches with spires; bow windows of glittering jewellers and dusty counting houses; a column marking the spot where the Great Fire of London broke out; canny street sellers hustling the passers-by; lush gardens hidden behind walls; men in white wigs and black cloaks flocking like starlings to a seed tray.

Seeing her interest, the coachman nodded to a fine gateway. "Them's the Temple gardens where the barristers live. You don't want to go through them doors. The lawyers will bleed you dry of every penny."

Thanking God that her tiger money had escaped that fate, she turned her back on them. Mr Rummage, her grandfather's lawyer, was probably inside that secret garden.

The further west they went, the lighter and cleaner the streets became. Roads opened up to display fine mansions set around garden squares, young lords and ladies playing under the watchful eye of their nurses. None of these had the hungry look of the children on the streets around the orphanage. It was as though in four miles she had travelled further than she had on the voyage from India. Now she began to understand where Britain got its wealth and power if it could afford to house its privileged like this. Only the very richest in Hyderabad had anything approaching this level of comfort and here there were many families all nestled together, golden chicks in a silk-lined nest.

Jenks didn't pull up outside the Peels' house but took the carriage around to the mews at the back. "Easier to unload the creatures," he explained gruffly.

Sahira wondered if that was the real reason. Maybe Jenks thought his master might notice that he'd let her ride with him? Or perhaps he was ashamed to be seen as the driver for the particular circus she carried with her? Whatever the case, the carriage arrived at the same time as Ned, who led Nebuchadnezzar into the same stable yard. Ned was grinning fit to burst his buttons.

"We made at least twelve shillings!" he gabbled as soon as Sahira jumped down. A footman came to help her with the baskets.

"Eat snails!" shrieked Napoleon the Parrot. He then set off on a rendition of "Black-eyed Susan", whistling the opening lines over and over.

That soon could become very annoying but Sahira didn't want to spoil his fun by drawing the cover over his cage.

Leaving Nebbie behind near the water trough, Ned and Sahira were shepherded up to a room on the third floor that had been fitted out as a schoolroom. Through an open door further down the corridor there was a nursery for younger children, furnished with a splendid rocking horse and shelves of tin soldiers lined up in regiments. Clearly the Peel children lacked for nothing.

"What do we do now?" Sahira asked the footman as he left them to make themselves at home.

"Master Peel and his friends will be along very soon. They wanted to see the animals before tea and my lady suggested you keep the creatures away from the cakes."

"Very wise." Sahira checked the window was closed, then opened the cage so Napoleon could stretch his wings. He immediately deposited his calling card on the nearest desk. "You might want to tell the servants there'll be a mess to clear up."

The footman tapped his forehead to acknowledge the warning and went downstairs, no doubt to regale the servants' hall with tales of the zebra's trek across town.

A thunder on the stairs announced the boys' arrival. They burst into the room like puppies spilling from a basket, shaggy hair, bright eyes; their tails would have been wagging if they had them.

"Miss Clive, Ned, you came! And in a dress! Not you Ned, of course: I mean Miss Clive." Bobby bounced across to them. He slapped Ned on the shoulder and hesitated in front of Sahira before settling for a bow. She curtseyed, holding out her skirts. "Tree frogs, splendid! Did you know you can eat any kind of frog as long as you don't eat the skin? That's where the poison lies."

"Eat snails!" shrieked Napoleon on cue.

Bobby immediately turned his attention from the natural history lessons to be taught by the skirt trim to the parrot. "What a marvellous bird. What's he called?"

Sahira wondered what to do about the boys milling about, jumping and hooting. They would spook many of the animals she had hoped to show them, apart from the indomitable Napoleon, who doubtless would shriek his insults even over the guns at Waterloo.

"Would you mind taking seats?" she asked politely.

Her words were ignored as the boys competed to feed the parrot.

"Please?" she pleaded.

Fortunately, the tutor, Mr Evesham, at that moment arrived at a sedate pace, in conversation with an older boy. Taking stock of the situation, he let out an impressive whistle. Like soldiers called to muster, the boys stopped in their tracks and stood to attention.

"Lads, there is a lady present and she asked you to do something." They looked at each other sheepishly.

"Slugs and snails and puppy dog tails!" squawked the parrot.

"Quite. Greet her like young gentlemen rather than a rabble," Mr Evesham instructed.

They executed passable bows.

"Now fall in!" he commanded.

The boys scrambled for the best seats at the desks.

"Introduce your friends, Master Peel," said Mr Evesham.

Blushing, Bobby got back to his feet and ran through their names rapidly. When he came to the older boy at the door, he paused. "And this is John Bracewell, your cousin, Miss Clive."

John gave Sahira a deep bow.

Shocked, she put a hand to her chest, fearing her heart would leap its way right out of her ribcage. Bobby had hinted he was arranging something, but she hadn't expected this. He could have warned her! "My cousin?"

"Isn't it splendid he came?" Bobby said excitedly, clearly oblivious to the awkwardness of the situation.

"My mother and your father were brother and sister," said John. He had to be about fifteen with thick light brown hair worn in fashionable curls on top, short at the sides. That, matched with a pair of lively green eyes, made him quite handsome. Sahira mustered a wobbly curtsey. Bobby had put them both on the spot. "I was sad to hear of Uncle Richard's passing, as was my mother."

He approached and she now saw that he was wearing a black armband.

"Thank you," she whispered, afraid that if she tried to speak further she would do something unforgivably sentimental, like weep.

"We are much obliged to you for bringing your animals to show us," continued John. "I always loved tales of your father's exploits in the jungles. Perhaps you can tell us more about the ones here today?" In the gentlest way, he was hinting that she should get on with the show and not make a spectacle of the family scandal.

Clearing her throat, she began.

"Let me introduce you first to our parrot. His name is Napoleon," she said, happy for the distraction.

"Curse Old Beaky!" the bird shrieked.

The boys laughed.

"As you can see, he shares the patriotic feelings of his namesake and I'm sad to say he's been taught all the wrong things to say by the people who had him before the menagerie."

"Where did he come from?" asked a red-headed boy.

"Jamrach's," replied Sahira.

The lad nodded sagely. "My uncle bought a wombat from there. It makes a fearful mess of his library."

Sahira paused, wondering if she should mention that wombats were best not housed in a library, but decided to let it go and instead continue with her explanation of the diet and habitat of a parrot in the wild and how the Tower kept him in the aviary with the other birds.

"Don't they kill each other?" asked a little boy at the front, one of the younger Peels from the nursery.

"On the whole, jungle birds live well side by side, not like the meat eaters or birds of prey." She fed Napoleon a nut which he took after calling her a trollop. The boys sniggered at the insult and he called them blackguards, which pleased them no end. She left him to his peanut and turned to the basket of snakes. She got through the explanation of these creatures with some credit, all the while distracted by wondering what her cousin thought of her.

Cousin.

Sahira knew already that her father's sister, Janet, had married and had a family but she had never been able to picture these relations who lived thousands of miles away. She should have paid more attention because she couldn't even remember whom her aunt had wed. A Mr Bracewell, obviously, but was he the sort to share Lord Chalmers's prejudices, or might he allow Sahira to meet her aunt?

Some excited whispering caught her attention.

"She's got a monkey in her hair!" a boy exclaimed.

She had forgotten Tiny, so light was her weight. Leaving the snakes wrapped around the arms of the most venturesome boys, she coaxed the monkey out so they could admire her.

"This is a marmoset. She's shy but she might go to you if you sit quietly," Sahira said.

That promise worked like a treat. The boys became as still as statues. Mr Evesham passed behind her.

"Couldn't have done it better myself," he murmured, giving her a wink.

Tiny behaved well, accepting transference onto Bobby's shoulder. She proceeded to tug his earlobe.

"I think she's telling you not to forget to wash behind them," Sahira suggested, making the audience giggle again.

When the wonders of the baskets had been admired sufficiently, Ned led them downstairs to meet the zebra. Sahira stayed behind to pack up, wagering that there would be several rides given in the mews if Ned had his way. She had to hope he remembered that Nebbie was not used to being ridden. Zebras weren't bred for it like horses.

But something was off. Sahira counted the snakes twice, realizing she'd lost track of one of them. A hand appeared in front of her, a milk snake dangling from it.

"Is this what you are looking for?" asked her cousin.

"Thank you," she said, relieved. She put it back with the others. "Not to be mixed up with the coral snake that looks very similar. A coral snake is deadly."

"As I've just had it wrapped round my arm, I'm pleased you know the difference." He smiled at her quizzically. "Why are you here, Miss Clive?"

"What do you mean?" she asked. Was he going to tell her off for bringing the family into disrepute with an animal show?

"Why aren't you at Fenton Park – or at school? In fact, where are you living?"

So he didn't know. "I'm…" How to explain? She had to tell the truth. "I'm in an orphanage. Lord Chalmers doesn't wish to acknowledge the connection."

"An orphanage?" He stuck his hands in his pockets and whistled. "I doubt he knows anything about it. Grandfather had a stroke three months ago; then came the news of your father's death, which set back his recovery. He's rarely conscious and makes scant sense when he is. Step-Grandmother thinks he's lost his wits."

"Step-Grandmother?" This was the first Sahira had heard of her.

"His second wife." John flushed slightly and looked over her head. "A young lady he married swiftly after Grandmama died ten years ago. She doesn't take much interest in his children apart from the heir, I'm afraid. She only worries about her own offspring."

That was like many species in the wild, favouring their own and driving off rivals. "Do you think it was her who told the lawyer to say I wasn't welcome?"

"Unlikely," John replied. "She's not callous, just self-absorbed. That might have been our Great-Aunt Dorothy, Grandfather's sister. She's as mean as… what did you call it… a coral snake?"

Sahira nodded. It didn't matter which of the family it was who barred her from Fenton Park: the result was the same. Still, it turned the anger she felt toward Lord Chalmers to pity to know he wasn't behind the rejection and remained seriously ill.

"Mother will ask me how you are. What should I tell her? Do they treat you well at the orphanage?" he asked.

Sahira massaged her aching palms. "It's –" *horrible* "– well enough, I suppose. They let me work at the Tower menagerie."

John gave her a quick grin. "That will make Mother howl. She has very set ideas about proper female behaviour. My poor sisters can't step out of doors without chaperones to watch their every move. They're all launched on the marriage market and no shade may fall on their good name."

That put an end to the fleeting idea of appealing to him to live under his roof. Doing that would mean having to leave the tigers and that wasn't possible. In any case, Sahira knew from Mr Rummage that she was likely to be regarded as "shade". Better the orphanage than that.

"She'll want to see you once I tell her our paths crossed," he continued. "Where should she call on you?"

Sahira thought of herself wandering the Tower in her tunic and trousers or dressed neatly in orphan grey. "Duck Street, Whitechapel. I am there until midday; then I go to work in the menagerie."

He shook his head in disbelief. "Really? They let a girl work there? I thought you'd just made that up."

Was he disapproving? "How else do you think I met Bobby? My tigers need me, Master Bracewell."

"I'm sure they do. And call me John, or Cousin, if you prefer."

"I'm Sahira. I'd like to have someone I can call Cousin. I'm woefully short of relatives who will acknowledge me."

"We Bracewells will – at least I think so." A little frown appeared on his forehead as he gave it serious thought, perhaps for the first time. "Father can be a little stuffy and traditional but he knows how much Mother loved her brother."

"What does your father do?" asked Sahira.

"He's an engineer working on the new railway." He paused. "Mother is considered to have married down, you know?"

She shook her head. "I'm not familiar with the caste system here."

He smiled wryly. "You will be. That's how I met Bobby. My father thinks he's splendid, the son he wished he had." He looked wistful for a moment.

"I'm sure he thinks no such thing."

John gave her an over-bright smile. "I'm too artistic for him. I'd prefer to spend my days painting rather than making technical drawings. He thinks I'm out of step with the new modern age of machines and industry because I prefer wild landscapes and ocean views. According to him, I'm too romantic."

A smile spread across Sahira's face. "You're like Wordsworth: you like to see into the life of things."

"That's from 'Tintern Abbey' – one of my favourite poems! I didn't know you'd be familiar with the English poets!" John helped her carry the baskets downstairs. "I love poetry – so does Mother."

Finally, Sahira was beginning to feel like they might be related. "So do I – and so did my father."

John cast a look at her sideways. "You know, Sahira, I think I'm going to enjoy having you as a cousin. The rest of the Clives are brutes but finally they've produced someone cultured!"

"I hope your father allows us to remain acquainted," she said cautiously.

"He must. I'll argue my case well, I promise."

Sahira wanted desperately to believe him, but knew from experience not to hope too much.

CHAPTER 13

After Sahira had deposited baskets of animals at the Tower and changed into the dove-grey gown, the coachman delivered her back to the orphanage. Jenks had become quite friendly over the two journeys, particularly after Tiny decided his capes were the perfect habitat from which to peek out at the passing streets.

"This your home, Miss?" he asked dubiously as the carriage pulled up outside Mr Pence's establishment.

"Not my home – never that," she said as she climbed down. She could still feel the quiet touch of the marmoset's fingers on her neck and she had the memory of meeting her cousin to warm her. This had definitely been her best day since her arrival in England.

"But you live here?" Jenks gestured to the foreboding building in front of them.

"Unfortunately, yes," she admitted.

Jenks sniffed as if to say he didn't think much of that.

"Thank you for driving me today," Sahira said.

He touched his whip to his hat. "It's been a pleasure, Miss." He cracked the whip in the air – he had explained that, like the best drivers, he rarely used it on the horses and then only to tickle them awake. Anyone who hurt a horse or drove it too hard should be roasted, according to Jenks. Sahira liked Jenks. Sensing a bag of oats in their near future, the pair trotted off away from this dank part of town, back to their stable.

Sahira looked up at the sooty brickwork and sighed. Only the thought that she would see Ann, Emily, and Jeoffry stopped her from bolting into the night.

"Where have you been all day, Clive? We've been waiting for you," sneered Tommy. He was lounging on the area steps and had been spying on her as she descended from the carriage.

"Having tea with the Home Secretary's son," she replied straight-faced. Mr Evesham had presided over the lively party given for Bobby's friends with all the calm of a first class admiral. Nelson would have faced the enemy's ships at Trafalgar with similar dignity. It had been Bobby's birthday and there had been a grand cake.

Sahira hurried inside before Tommy could think of a comeback on her remark. She let the front door bang behind her.

"Report, Eleanor Clive," called Mr Pence from his study.

Tucking her hands behind her back, she entered. Hard as it would be, she resolved not to let Mr Pence rile her.

"You've missed supper," said Mr Pence.

"Yes, sir." She was still so full of cake she had no regrets on that count.

"Why are you late?" he demanded.

"I had an engagement in the West End, sir."

"*An engagement in the West End,*" he parroted, with less charm than Napoleon. "What do people in that part of town want with *you?*"

Sahira decided not to mention Bobby or her cousin. It was best that Mr Pence knew as little of her business as possible. "I took some animals to a party, sir." She fixed her gaze slightly to the left of his head so she didn't have to look at him.

"Did they pay you?"

So that was why he was so interested. "Sir?" Sahira didn't want to admit it to him but Mr Evesham had presented her with a generous tip, managing it in such a way that it felt as if she had done him the favour of accepting it.

"Turn out your pockets," he said.

She knew better than to defy him this time. Sahira put the five shillings on the desk, keeping a couple back.

"I'll add these to your account." He swept them up and put them in the top drawer of his desk. "You may go."

He hadn't asked to which house she had gone. For all he knew it could have been a gambling den or a thieves' hideout. She bobbed a minuscule curtsey, just enough to escape without further punishment, and left.

Sahira found Ann and Emily sitting together in a corner of the dormitory, not their usual spot by the beds but the one near Matron's room. A third girl was with them, one Sahira didn't recognize. A hefty lass with a mass of pert brown ringlets and tweezered eyebrows that really didn't suit her, she looked too old for the orphanage, at least sixteen. There was something about her that put Sahira immediately on her guard.

"Hello, I'm Sahira," she said carefully, pulling up a footstool to join them.

The girl sniffed and turned away. "Does anyone smell that? What a stink!"

So that's how it was. Her first impression had been correct. Sahira decided to ignore her. "Emily, did you have a good day?"

Her fair-headed friend wouldn't meet her eyes, acting as if she weren't there. "I can't smell anything, Joanna."

"It smells of animals and... what's that little extra? Yes, the stench of a foreigner," Joanna sneered.

Sahira looked to Ann for an explanation but she gave a minute shake of her head.

"Do you know where I can get some blue boots? My brothers told me that they'd seen some here," continued Joanna. "And dresses sewn with pearls."

The penny dropped. The Newtons had moved in their sister – if that's what she really was – to take control of the one part of the orphanage that had so far slipped through their fingers. Sahira was sickeningly disappointed in her friends though: how had they allowed themselves to be turned against her so quickly? She rose, giving up on them for the night. Maybe tomorrow they would explain themselves. She didn't want her one happy day in England spoiled.

She moved over to her bed. A piece of coal flew through the air and hit her on the back.

"Get it away from there!" shrieked Joanna.

"Get what from where?" asked Ann confusedly.

"There's a rat near my bed. It's not touching my bedclothes, not after I had them changed and those soiled ones thrown out."

Sahira was momentarily lost for words.

"She… Sahira can share my bed," offered Ann.

"But then you'll be dirty and we'd have to throw you out too! I'm not sleeping in here with her and that's final."

"Then don't sleep in here!" Sahira snapped.

"And now the rat squeaks," she mocked.

Some of the younger girls watching this battle – ones who should have known better – sniggered.

"Matron!" called the new girl, mock panic in her voice. "Matron!"

Matron lumbered in from her office, cap askew. "What's the matter, Joanna dear?"

"I can't sleep with that savage in the same room as me."

Matron squinted at her, eyes having trouble focusing. "What savage is that?" she asked.

"The one who smells of dung. That one." She pointed at Sahira.

"Oh, but that's just Ellie," Matron replied.

"I'm not sharing with her. My father won't like it. In fact he demands she be got rid of: he doesn't like his children mixing with foreigners," she spat.

It was obvious what had happened while Sahira had been at the menagerie. "So your brothers went bleating to him, did they, and sent you in to do their dirty work?" The injustice of it infuriated Sahira, sending her temper rocketing until it burst into unwisely blunt words. "Matron, this is an orphanage, not a private club for Harry Newton's children, and my place here is paid. Why are you even listening to her?"

Joanna folded her arms. "Harry. Newton," she said, loading the words with menace.

"Ellie dear, why don't you run along and find somewhere else to sleep?" said Matron with a weak smile.

"Where?" Sahira asked flatly. "This is the girls' dormitory."

Matron's gaze skittered away as she fumbled her apron strings. "You'll find somewhere, I'm sure."

Right. So Matron had all the backbone of a jellyfish.

The few things that she'd dared leave here had been bundled in a corner. She scooped them up in a blanket and walked out. There was no point trying to sleep in there while Joanna was in occupation. That would only end with the theft of her boots and a sharp kick in the middle of the night. Territorial disputes were often bloody; Sahira knew that retreat was a good strategy when you stood on weak ground.

Sahira made her way down to the kitchen. Cook had already left for the day and Jeoffry was curled up on the hearth. This would do. It was where Ned had taken refuge so had to be fairly safe. He was a worldly wise boy and wouldn't have slept anywhere near the Newtons. Sahira sat in Cook's chair, drew her knees to her chest, and dropped her forehead forward. Her life, she reflected, was becoming like one of the French fairy tales Father had read her, even down to sleeping among the ashes. Unfortunately, there didn't seem to be a prince and a ball just around the corner, only a sick old lord, a pair of caged tigers, and a few faint-hearted friends who wouldn't even stand up for her in front of an obvious bully.

Sahira got up before Cook arrived, washed under the kitchen pump, and took a slice of bread out into the yard. She decided to stay outside as long as possible. She wouldn't bother with breakfast because, if they behaved as usual, the Newtons would have planned another round of humiliations. Pigeons pecked around her ankles, uncomplicated, loyal friends. She shared out the crust.

Ann crept out to see her just as the house stirred.

"I'm so sorry, Sahira," she whispered, sitting next to her. "If it makes it any better, neither Emily or I slept a wink last night. We feel awful."

Sahira shrugged, still wary of her.

"She... she threatened our brothers and sisters – the little ones in the nursery. She says she's got the nurses in her pocket. A little something in their milk, they'd sicken and we'd never see them alive again. So many children die, no one would question it."

"And you believed her?" Sahira asked hoarsely.

Ann wiped a tear from her eye. "I have to. I can't risk them. The Newtons are ruthless. Look, just give them those silly boots and have done with it! Then we can be friends again."

"You think?" Ann was naive if she believed it would stop there. "This isn't my fault, Ann. Don't make it into something I've done."

Ann's shoulders slumped.

Sahira knew she couldn't ask Ann to choose their friendship over her sisters, nor Emily her brother. What would she have done if the choice had been between them and her tigers? Maybe she would have shown the same cowardice. It is so much harder to take risks when the people you love are threatened.

Sahira felt something good drain out of life, like so many things had of late. "Thanks for being my friend while you could. Don't worry about me. I'll manage."

"I am still your friend, even if not much of one right now," she said, her voice wavering.

"No, Ann, I don't think you are – and it's not really your fault. It's the fault of this place. It's a kind of cage and it forces all of us to act against our nature. We're all like wolves chewing off their own paws to escape a trap."

Sahira didn't say any more. Her words had been punishment enough for someone who was essentially decent and kind. What more was there to say? Ann hadn't chosen to put her over others. After a few minutes, Ann got up and left, touching Sahira's shoulder with the lightest of farewells.

Jeoffry came into the courtyard with Ann's departure and jumped up on her lap. She stroked his soft fur. Animals were so much easier to love.

Hearing the noise of the day starting inside the building, the rattle of crockery and voices of the monitors marshalling the orphans in line for porridge, Sahira remained where she was. Even Jeoffry eventually abandoned her as he smelled something more tempting next door. She thumped her head against the bricks and stared up at the little patch of cloudy sky. The treatment meted out by the orphanage ended any duty she had toward obeying its rules. The ones who were supposed to protect her were weak or greedy and the Newtons cruel; in fact, the entire situation was so unfair! She couldn't sit meekly sewing for Mrs Pence if they wouldn't even provide her with a bed. She had to escape.

As the others gathered for breakfast, she slipped out the tradesmen's entrance in the kitchen and up the steps to the pavement. Her heart raced: being caught now would probably end in another beating in Mr Pence's study, and in her frame of mind she'd probably try to snap his cane. How that would go – one smallish girl against a grown man – was pretty clear. Fortunately, no one tried to stop her. It was too early to report to the menagerie without explaining her truancy. She wandered aimlessly for a while but there was no park or place of refuge open to someone like her. Searching for something to occupy the morning, she decided to settle her curiosity about the shop Mr Cops had mentioned the day before: the animal emporium on the Ratcliffe Highway just north of the docks. Jamrach and Sons – the family were well known for their ability to get you any creature you desire. Her father had often supplied their orders and she remembered seeing Mr Jamrach's decisive handwriting on letters he had received. Sahira knew now that she had to make plans for her own future, as no one else seemed prepared to step forward. Might there not be a role for her as an animal collector? She may be too young now, but in a few years, who knew where she might be? If she were good at her trade, men like Jamrach would ignore her gender, wouldn't they?

"'Ere, Missy, want to see some kittens?" Lost in her thoughts, Sahira had strayed off the main road. An ox of a man got in her way. He wasn't carrying a basket but his old coat sagged at the pockets with something much heavier.

"No, thank you," she replied sharply, kicking herself for her beginner's mistake.

"I've lovely ones, down there." He grabbed at the back of her skirt and pointed to dank alley. "Bound for the river in a sack if a nice little lady won't save them."

Did he really have some that needed rescuing? "How old?"

"Oh, just a few days. Cute as buttons." He stood too closely, leaning into her when he spoke.

"What colour are their eyes?" she asked.

He paused a moment. "All sorts – blue, green..."

Sahira would never have gone down the alley with him – her parents had taught her better than that – but at least now she wouldn't have any real cats on her conscience. Kittens didn't open their eyes for at least a week. "You're a liar." She ripped her skirt free and ran. Glancing behind, she saw him hesitate as to whether he could catch her, then give up to wait for some easier prey.

That had been too close for comfort. The encounter reminded her that she should keep her wits about her and not let her own preoccupations become a distraction. She was in one of the most dangerous parts of London and she didn't know this jungle like she did the ones at home. Having avoided one snake, she shouldn't tumble into a nest of red ants. After that scare, she chose the people she asked for directions with care, women with young children in the main, who were too busy shepherding their flock to plan anything that would harm her. They all knew the shop and one even knew the exact address. Counting the numbers as she went down the broad highway that ran east–west north of the river, she arrived outside Jamrach's shop as the shutters opened for the day. She would have found it by the smell alone. On dry land, she had never seen so many animals crammed into such a small space.

The assistant came out to hang up cages of singing birds, using a long pole to loop them around hooks placed for the purpose.

"Do you need a hand?" Sahira asked.

Smoothing back the lock of oily black hair that had flopped over his eyes, he gave her an assessing look. He could only have been a few years older but his gaze said he could tell a person's spending power to the last ha'penny from the cut of their clothes.

"What's one of Pence's orphans doing so far from home, eh?" So he had recognized the uniform.

"Would you believe me if I said I was on an errand?" she ventured.

He wiped his nose on his sleeve – a charming habit. "Nah, but at least you know I know where you live. Any funny business and I'll be down on you like a crate of elephants."

"That would have to be one very big crate." She picked up a cage and gave him her sunniest smile. "Where does this one go?"

"You bring them to me, I hang them," he said gruffly.

After the bird cages, Sahira helped him carry out hutches, home to some patient rabbits.

"We can leave these on the street," her new acquaintance explained, warming to her as she showed no signs of "funny business". "There ain't much value in a bunny and it brings in the children. Special breeds we keep out back."

"Do rabbits make good pets?" she asked, crouching down in front of the wire mesh.

He gave her a curious look. "Don't you know? Most people with a bit of space round here have a rabbit or two – some for eating, some keep them as a pet."

"I'm not that familiar with rabbits," Sahira admitted.

Studying her more closely, he finally noticed she was a little different from his usual customer. "Been abroad?"

"I lived in India until last autumn."

"You've not had a pet?"

"We travelled and collected animals. None of them were our pets. I don't count our working animals, horses, mongooses and so on." Sahira offered the nearest rabbit a green leaf from the supply put aside for the purpose. It nibbled the lettuce thoughtfully.

The assistant was interested now. "What kind of creatures have you collected?"

"Snakes, birds, tigers: the usual kind of thing," she replied matter-of-factly.

"My eyes, harken to her: 'the usual kind of thing'!" He chuckled. "Oh, you're priceless. I wager Mr Jamrach would like to meet you. He'll be in any time now. You hang around and tell him your tales and there'll be a shillin' in it for you. Bring in anything special with you? He's always in the market for exotic creatures."

The assistant, who now confided that he was called Bartholomew Langland, or Tolly, allowed Sahira to wander the shop as he served the first customers of the day. Leaving him to help a gentleman select a chinchilla from a little enclosure in the main shop, she found a way out to the yard at the back where the larger animals were kept. She didn't like what she saw: they were far too cramped. One young mountain lion was in a cage that barely allowed her to stand. A macaque looked through the bars with a blank expression like a hermit in a forest cave. A brown bear sat chained in one corner, staring at his paws. He showed no interest when she approached, reminding her of a prisoner condemned to the gallows who knew his life was at an end. If she could have conjured up keys and a flying carpet like Aladdin's genie, she would have taken them all out of here and magicked them back to their homes; instead, she could only make sure they had fresh water and food within reach.

A raised voice echoed in the shop. A flutter of expectation ran through the caged animals. The bear roused, went up on his back feet, and growled. The monkey shrieked. Birds squawked and bashed against bars. The mountain lion snarled.

"What are you doing, Tolly, you nincompoop? Letting Cops's Indian girl into our shop!" roared a man who had to be Mr Jamrach himself.

Sahira couldn't make out Tolly's reply but it had to be some kind of excuse. Was there a back exit?

"Nonsense, she doesn't have anything to sell us. He's sent her to spy on us. I'll soon send her on her way with a flea in her ear! Where is she?"

Cornered in the yard between cages and bear, Sahira had no choice but stand her ground. She turned to face the door as Mr Jamrach stormed out into the yard.

"Right." He pushed up his sleeves. "I'll show you how Jamrach treats spies!"

PART 4
INVISIBLE WORM

CHAPTER 14

Sahira backed away, more scared of an irate Jamrach than the gloomy bear. "I'm not a spy!" she exclaimed.

"Likely story. Get away from Bruno." He grabbed a broom.

"Not while you're threatening me." She tried to judge the length of chain and reach of paw. Bruno lurched forward, testing both. Fortunately he was aiming for Jamrach, not her, because Sahira was well within striking range. She skittered sideways into the far corner. Now the bear acted as a barrier between her and the irate shopkeeper. Jamrach couldn't reach her even with the broom without getting within the bear's range.

Jamrach must have worked out the same thing himself. He stood with the broom held like a pike in front of him. "You can't stay there all day, girl."

"I can give it a good try," she retorted.

"You've got a hiding coming your way." He raised the broom.

"And that's supposed to tempt me out?"

His bushy red whiskers twitched. "I'll strike a bargain with you. I'll let you pass if you tell me what Cops wants with me now."

"I don't know. I came here on my own," she admitted.

"Don't believe you. I'm not selling him any more creatures. He'll have to keep that menagerie of his open without any more help from me. You tell him that. But first, you need to be taught a lesson about spying!"

Sahira thought quickly. There was only one way she knew to deter a dangerous man from a violent course of action. "Will you lay your weapon aside, sir, if I prove that I can tell you the tale of each and every animal you have in your shop?"

"What foolishness is this?" This didn't stop him but it did put a hitch in his stride.

"Not foolishness. I can tell you how Ali al-Zaibaq turned into a bear, just like that one there. And how the carpenter tricked the lion cub into a cage, which must be how she got to be in one so small." Sahira pointed to the mountain lion pacing overhead. "Not to mention Abu Muhammad the Sluggard and his monkey who earned him a fortune." The macaque looked unimpressed but Jamrach was listening.

"Earned him a fortune, eh?" He still hadn't put down the broom but at least now it was at parade rest rather than pointing at her. The bear shuffled back into his normal spot by the wall. "A teller of tales, are you? Then you can tell Cops he has to leave me alone. I can't afford the powerful enemies he's making. If they decide I can't keep shop here, then I'm ruined – and they could do that as easy as…" He snapped his fingers.

If the enemy in question was the Duke of Wellington, then he was right. The Prime Minister could invent some excuse like public safety and Jamrach would be forced out of business. "Don't worry, Mr Jamrach, Mr Cops doesn't need you. He's got my animals now – my tigers." Sahira started to edge out of the corner, hoping the bear and the shopkeeper had both given up on their more militant mood.

"*Your* animals?" He picked up the broom again.

She bobbed a curtsey. "I'm Captain Clive's daughter."

"So that's who you are! When I heard Cops had a new assistant, I wondered where she came from. I thought the circus, maybe, when you started on your marvellous tales." His brow wrinkled as he remembered the rest of the news. "I'm sorry about your father. He was a good man. Reliable."

"Yes, he was. And he taught me the same skills. I'm going to collect animals when I'm older," said Sahira.

Jamrach chuckled and returned the broom to its place against the wall. "You are, are you?"

Nothing ventured, nothing gained. "Will you buy from me if I enter the business? In a few years' time, I mean?"

He gave the small girl a mocking look. "Oh yes: I'll buy any exotic animals you collect, titch."

"That's a deal," she replied.

Doubt flickered across his face. He realized she was serious. "Only if they are in good condition, mind. And they've got to be rare. No more blooming parrots."

"No parrots, good condition, rare: got it. Now may I go?" she asked.

He bowed and let her pass. "Why do I think I might regret this morning's work?"

"Oh you won't regret it, sir. I promise," she said brightly.

"Oh, by the way, you mentioned tigers," he called after her.

"What of them?" She turned back to face him.

"Just, I've a very special order from a good client. He wants that pair and will pay well. Tell Cops that."

"What does your customer want them for?" she asked warily.

"Never you mind. Can I trust you with the message?" he continued.

Sahira nodded stiffly. She would do it, but he hadn't put a time on when she had to pass on the message.

"Then run along before I change my mind about that hiding," Jamrach waved her off.

Holding the hope in her heart that she might one day earn her own living pursuing her father's profession, Sahira said goodbye to Tolly in her passage through the shop and returned to the streets in a happier frame of mind. She had a place to go to now too: the morning was wearing away so the menagerie was expecting her. No one at the orphanage would be looking for her – who would care if she disappeared into the city? If she could only fool Mr Cops and the other keepers that she was still returning there each night, then this pleasant state of affairs could continue indefinitely. Life in London would finally be bearable.

As long as she found a place to spend the night.

She decided she would spend it with family.

That evening, as the time came for her to leave for the day, Sahira made a great show of bidding farewell to friends among the animals as well as the keepers.

"Give my regards to Cook!" said Ned cheekily as he led the zebra to his stable.

"Will do – when I next see her," replied Sahira. "Goodnight, Ben, goodnight, Mike."

With everyone busy settling down for the night, Sahira crept into the area next to the tigers where the fresh straw was stored. Rama got up, stretched his back legs, and came to inspect her.

"Don't mind me," she whispered, burrowing into the heap. She knew Mr Cops did a final round to check all was well just before bedtime.

Rama found nothing worrisome about a cub making a nest for herself so he settled back next to Sita. How he must be fretting with no place to run or hunt, thought Sahira regretfully. He was trapped – and she, for the first time since arriving, felt free.

"I'll sort out something better for you, I promise," she murmured. *Would the zoological gardens be better than this?* she wondered. "Gardens" sounded hopeful. The very first animals lived in the Garden of Eden, didn't they? She'd always imagined that as a vast place, as big as a country, so they could all fit inside. Rama would prefer a forest but in its absence that might do.

Sahira was dozing when she heard the squeak of Mr Cops' lantern swinging on its ring.

"How do, beasties," he said softly. "All well, eh?" He held the light up to each cage. Sahira didn't dare breathe. "You all right, George?" he asked the newly promoted lion. "How do you fancy the name William again? Seems like we're getting a new king soon." He walked onward to the tigers. Sahira had an awful moment when she feared he might step on her but his boots stopped an inch from her toes. She peered through stalks of straw at him, hoping – praying – he wouldn't glance down. "Looking after her, are you, Rama?"

The tiger had raised his head from his mate's side and was watching Mr Cops with his fathomless stare.

Sahira held very still.

"She's a good girl, isn't she? Full of life – too much for her own good, I dare say."

Rama opened his jaws, displaying sharp white canines.

"I'm glad you agree. Shame she had to stay at that awful place, ain't it? Not right for one like her. That snake will find a way of making her life as miserable as possible, bleeding hypocrite," Mr Cops said angrily.

He wasn't talking about Sita but about her!

Mr Cops leaned companionably on the stout staff he carried, used for parting argumentative animals. "I'd like to let you have a go at him, but that wouldn't end well, would it? They'd have the troops out in a jiffy for a London tiger hunt. The duke would like that, having served in India and all. Have us shut down before the ink was dry on the order."

Rama sneezed. Mr Cops took that for agreement. "Well then, I'll leave you and your lovely lady to sleep. Sorry you missed your turn in the yard today. I'll see what I can do tomorrow. Sleep tight."

The door slammed and the key turned, locking them in for the night.

With a sigh of relief, Sahira emerged from her hiding place. She was touched that Mr Cops spared her a thought in her absence. Her father would have liked Mr Cops, she decided. For once that didn't make her feel sad. With Rama and Sita's comforting presence, she could think of her parents without being overwhelmed by grief.

Sahira's stomach rumbled. She'd stolen some sunflower seeds from the birds – that would have to do for supper.

Sita got up. She was restless. Tigers were more active at night than during the day so it was the hour when the tigers would most resent their confinement, particularly after having been cooped up without a run in the yard. Sahira looked at the door that gave on to the only open space the tigers were allowed to go in. Dare she? There was no one to see. Mr Cops should be tucked up in bed by now, the other keepers in their quarters. It was only fair that the tigers get as much freedom as she could possibly grant them.

Her decision was made even before she really knew it. Going to the outer gate, she opened it. It creaked horribly on its hinges. Heart in her mouth, she paused, but there was no shout of alarm. Everyone was out of earshot. The tigers were both standing expectantly by their gate. The exit for the tigers was lifted from inside the keepers' area.

Sahira tried to raise the grate to allow them into a short tunnel to the outside. It proved heavier than she expected. Two keepers normally did this.

Rama paced fretfully, irritated by the delay.

"Sorry, sorry," Sahira murmured as the gate slid back down again. She looked around for something to help her and saw a spade. Her dad, a scientifically minded man, had told her of the advantage of a lever. If she could wedge that under the gate and push the other side off a fulcrum, then maybe she could lift this on her own like lifting a heavier child on a seesaw. What could she use as a fulcrum? She found a small water barrel that would do the trick. The tigers watched with interest as she set about testing her theory. She had a few false starts as the spade or the barrel refused to cooperate, but finally she succeeded in lifting the gate. Rama and Sita streaked through as if sensing she couldn't hold it long. As soon as the tops of their tails were clear, she let it slide back down.

And how exactly are you going to get them back in? Sahira asked herself.

Too late now for regrets. She postponed worrying about that until later.

The moon was out. The tigers chased each other in circles around the small crescent-shaped yard. The other animals raised an envious rumble. George Junior gave his lion cough – a carrying sound – and the tigers roared a challenge. Sahira thought it might have been a taunt.

"Please, don't summon the keeper," she murmured.

But, of course, her plea had no more effect than a drop of water on a forest fire. Fortunately, Sita and Rama were too caught up in their play to worry about the caged lion. They were now tumbling each other, pretending to fight but claws remained sheathed. Sahira wished she could join them but knew better than to be lured into a belief that she was in any way welcome. She was human – she would die from one play-fight like that. Instead she climbed up an internal stair to the bridge that spanned the enclosure. Usually the public stood here to marvel at the creatures exercising in the yard. Many a bonnet and glove had been dropped here accidentally on purpose just to see what the animals would do with them (destroy them was the obvious answer). Sahira sat with her legs dangling over the drop. If Rama really wanted, she supposed he could leap and catch a blue boot in his jaw, but he ignored her. *Which was as it should be,* she told herself. In the tigers' lives she was a servant, like the humblest handmaiden to the Nizam and his favourite wife. She was allowed to admire and feel the privilege of her position.

With a full moon overhead, the tigers were transformed. Dulled down were their orange stripes, but their white fur shone silver and their black so deep that they seemed to have taken the night into themselves. With a little imagination, Sahira could supply the forest canopy, the lake choked with lotus blossoms, the scent of night blooms on the air. The barred entrances to the cages became caverns, the bridge a fallen trunk across a ravine, the cries of distant streets the murmur of a waterfall. They were home! She stood up and lifted her hands to the sky, to pluck down the moon itself. The tigers paused beneath her, heads raised to the stars, and roared.

"What's that?" A male voice came from over the wall.

"It's them wild animals," replied a second. "Loud tonight though. Lord, we'd better hope they've not escaped." He laughed, signalling he wasn't really worried.

Not keepers, Sahira realized. These were soldiers returning late to their barracks in the Tower.

"Don't know how you can sleep with them so close. Keeps me awake it does," the first soldier countered.

"You get used to it in a week or two. Besides, it won't be for long now. The duke's got plans for this area. It's to be our new parade ground," the other said.

Their voices were fading. "And the animals?" asked the new recruit.

The old soldier chuckled. "Well, they won't be on parade with us, will they?"

CHAPTER 15

Despite Sahira's best efforts, Rama and Sita refused to return to their cage. She couldn't both hold up the gate and coax them in so gave in to the inevitable, leaving the tigers at play as dawn broke. Time was running out. She waited by the gate where the food for the animals was delivered and sneaked out as the first cart was unloaded, immediately losing herself in the crowds on the wharf. She hoped none of her friends would get the blame, but then, Mr Cops had seen them in their pen late at night so would know that it hadn't been negligence on the part of the keepers shutting up for the evening.

Would his suspicions turn to her?

He'd seen her "leave" and besides, the gate was too heavy for a girl, wasn't it? Mr Cops did not look the sort to think much about levers.

"Sahira! What on earth are you doing 'ere?" Sahira jumped, taken completely by surprise. Ned had found her. She'd foolishly strayed near the baker's stall, enticed by the smell of bread she couldn't afford, and not realized that Ned would be sent out to fetch the fresh loaves for the keepers' breakfast. Of course, that was exactly the kind of errand they would give their youngest recruit.

"I'm... er... taking in the sights of London," she said lamely. "Got the morning off."

He put his hands on his hips and scowled. Though he was an inch shorter, he still somehow gave the impression he was looking down his snub nose at her. "You're bamming me."

"*Bamming* you?"

"Telling porkies, trying to pull the wool over me eyes, straight up lying!" He was angry now. "I thought we were friends?"

"We are." If she lost him, she'd be down to just a couple of tigers as the only ones on her side.

"Then tell me the truth. Why are you 'ere so early?" His eyes shone with sudden realization. "It were you, weren't it? You let Sita and Rama out! Were you trying to 'elp them escape?"

That guess was so wild she had to laugh. "No. There's no escape for us, not really." Sadness roosted in her heart.

"But it were you? Mr Cops thinks 'e's going mad, thinks he forgot to shut them away or somethink."

Sahira folded her arms across her chest. She was cold. Did this country never warm up properly? "It was me. I spent the night in the menagerie last night."

"Cor." His brow furrowed. "But why? What about Mr Pence?"

Sahira was surprised to find tears prick her eyes as she recalled Emily and Ann's betrayal. She'd been trying hard not to think about that. "I…" The words got stuck.

"Sahira, are you… are you crying?" Ned sounded shocked.

She swiped the back of her hand across her eyes and answered angrily: "No, of course not."

He tugged her elbow, pulling her to one side out of the main thoroughfare. "Tell me what's 'appened."

"Nothing," she said weakly.

"So you just made yourself 'omeless for a lark? Sahira, I wasn't born yesterday. Don't you trust me?"

"Of course I do!"

"Then tell me," he said sternly.

So Sahira did, explaining about the Newtons' sister, losing her bed, and the rest.

"Joanna Newton? She's a barmaid at the Anchor, must be about eighteen now. I bet it's 'er." Ned looked down at her feet and smiled bleakly. "They really must want those boots – this 'as to be about savin' their pride now. Good for you to keep 'em. And Mr Pence just let you go?"

"I didn't ask permission. It seemed if the orphanage wasn't going to give me a bed, I had no place being there. I don't want to get packed off to the workhouse –"

Ned shuddered and crossed himself. "That you don't."

"So… so I suppose I'm homeless, like you say."

"What about that fancy cousin of yours?" Ned ventured.

She'd had the same thought: John might help. "I don't know where he lives."

"You can ask Master Bobby," he suggested, as though it were as easy as that.

"I can hardly go walking up to the Peels' house, knock on the door, and ask. I'd be turned away."

"You don't 'ave to do that. Send 'im a note. I'll see it gets delivered," he said.

There was a chink of light, even if it meant relying on the charity of relations who would probably prefer not to recognize she existed. She wouldn't spoil things for their daughters; if they just let her live somewhere quietly where she could visit her tigers, that would be enough. Sahira hugged Ned.

"Thank you," she said.

After a second's hesitation, he hugged her back. "You're welcome." He looked a little embarrassed to be caught showing affection in the middle of the street – a tough kid didn't do that. "Come on, I'll sneak you back into the menagerie and see you get some breakfast. I've got to buy it first though."

Sahira trailed after him, watching with some expert appreciation at his haggling over the price of the loaves. She'd been very good at bargaining in the bazaars of the towns she visited with her parents. Her father often gave her the task, as he looked too foreign and her mother was too well born for the cut and thrust of negotiating. Ned was a gifted dealmaker, coming away with an extra loaf, one of yesterday's so only a little stale. He passed this to Sahira.

"It won't be missed," he said.

"How do you fancy coming with me on animal-collecting expeditions when we're older?" Sahira asked, ripping a bit of crust off.

"Is that like a proper job?" Ned replied, juggling an armful of bread.

"It's what my father did – and what I'm going to do when I can. I've already got Mr Jamrach to agree to be a customer as long as I don't send him 'bloomin' parrots'." Spirits lifted by having a friend to talk to and something to eat, Sahira no longer felt so overwhelmed.

Ned chuckled. "I'd like that. I'd like to see where Nebbie comes from, maybe find him a lady zebra and then we'd have little zebras. Wouldn't that be grand?"

"Then we'd have to go to Africa." She swallowed, remembering how her parents had died soon after the ship left Cape Town. *Concentrate, Sahira: no bad memories, not now, only good.* "I saw zebras when our ship called into port – and elephants – ones with huge ears and tusks, much bigger than the kind I know."

Planning their first trip – which would bag them at least a pride of lions, they decided – the two friends slipped back into the Tower.

Sahira spent the next few days following the same routine: sneaking a breakfast with Ned at dawn, wandering the local streets to avoid Mr Cops until noon, then a happy afternoon going about her duties. Just as she had expected, no message came from the orphanage; nobody cared two hoots, as Ned put it, as to what had become of her.

"Why two hoots and not one – or three?" she asked Ned seriously as they shared the bread on her third day of freedom.

He shrugged. "It's just a saying, Sahira."

"And is it 'hoots' like an owl or like the horn on the mail coach?" she pressed.

"You're really givin' this too much thought."

She frowned at him. "But how am I to understand this place if I don't understand the things you say?"

"I don't understand 'alf the things I say, so why should you be any different? Now 'urry up. The keeper will be 'ere shortly."

Sahira brushed the crumbs from her lap. She wore her orphanage uniform while wandering the streets so as to blend in, her Indian work clothes being too distinctive. "I will. I'll see you later."

"This won't last, you know," Ned said glumly, walking alongside her to the exit. "'E'll catch us one day."

"Don't be a crocodile of despair, Ned," she jested.

"A what?

"Snapping at my happiness. I finally like London." Sahira smiled.

"What's a crocodile like?"

"Big jaws, fierce, meat eater, like a huge lizard but lives in rivers," she explained.

"Cor, I'd like to see a crocodile." He gazed at her in wonder.

"Maybe you will, when we go animal collecting together." She turned to wave goodbye, then left Ned at the gate.

She headed east, intending to explore the area around the docks. It shouldn't be too dangerous at this time of day, not like at night. The troublemakers were normally still sleeping and she could watch the ships being unloaded. Among the sailors would be men from India. If she could catch them at the right moment, maybe they'd tell her news and stories from home?

Turning into the docks where she had landed, she recognized the carter who had carried her tigers to the tower, as well as his excellent elephant-sized horses. She didn't want the man to see her; fortunately he was busy with his current load, which gave her a chance to make her acquaintance with the shire horses. They tossed their heads to at her unfamiliar, tigerish smell, but then relaxed when she made no sudden moves. Soon they were accepting strokes and pats to their huge necks. She had to stretch on tiptoes to reach.

"There she is!" The cry came from behind her, startling the horses. The nearest one tossed his head, sending Sahira stumbling to the ground.

"Grab 'er, someone!" It was the Newton twins. Sahira's heart raced, beating like the hooves of a fleeing antelope. Where could she go? "That one – in blue boots!"

The carter looked around. "Here, what you doing with my horses?"

Sahira scrambled to her feet and ran. Why had they not just come for her at the menagerie? Why were the Newtons hunting her on the street? That made no sense. But she knew one thing: she couldn't let them catch her. She headed back to the Tower, going at her top speed with her limping gait. Mr Cops would at least protect her from the twins and she had a head start. That is, until the Newtons changed the game on her.

"Stop, thief!" yelled Tommy. That brought all the bystanders in on their side. Sahira did not have just two pursuers now, but a pack of stallholders, sailors, and even beggars who sensed a reward for capturing her. Her hip sang with pain.

"Get Blue Boots!" shouted Alf, hurdling a newspaper stand.

Sahira darted in and out of the carts making their way from the docks. The carters lashed out at her with their long whips. One caught her cheek, drawing blood in a thin line of fire, another the back of her legs. She stumbled again, her injured leg protesting.

That was enough to snare her. A sailor darted out of a doorway and tackled – a big man smelling of garlic and beer. Sahira went down underneath him, squashed like a bug under a rolled newspaper.

"Got her!" crowed Alf. He hauled Sahira to her feet, his grip cruel on her neck.

"Thanks, mate," said Tommy, tossing the sailor a penny.

"Vot she steal?" asked the sailor in broken English.

"Never you mind. She's wanted at the Thieves' Court." Tommy stared him down.

"Thieves' Court?" The man was obviously questioning what he'd done. "You all right, *devushka*?"

"No – no, I'm not!" exclaimed Sahira, seeing the slightest of chances to escape in his change of heart.

But a second sailor took the man by the elbow. "The Russian's just arrived," the Londoner said to the twins. "Don' know nothink about your dad." He tugged at the big man. "Leave it, Vlad."

Vlad took a step forward. "But…"

"Really, leave it. Not our business." The sailor towed the reluctant Russian back to the inn whence they had come.

Tommy cracked his knuckles. "Right, let's go." He shoved Sahira between the shoulders.

"Tommy, it's almost time for me to go to work at the Tower. I'll come back to the orphanage later," she said desperately. "I promise."

"Didn't you 'ear, mutton'ead? You're not going to the orphanage. Our dad wants a word."

A prisoner under escort, Sahira was marched further into crooked streets leading to the Thieves' Court.

Harry Newton held his court out in the backyard of one of the many gin palaces in the East End. Though dragged here unwillingly, Sahira could see why the poor might voluntarily spend their last coins on the fiery spirit that they called Mother's Ruin. In contrast to the shabby housing around it, this gin palace was a glittering jewel of plate glass and mirrors, with a touch of luxury in the padded velvet seats – if you overlooked the stains. A barmaid with a flushed face and low-cut blouse idly wiped the bar; she looked away when she saw Sahira with the twins. Men and women were slumped over their bottles despite the early hour, lost in their own worlds. A shot of gin might give them a holiday from the misery around them, until their money ran out. And they certainly wouldn't be coming to Sahira's aid, even if she screamed at the top of her lungs. This was Harry Newton's world.

"Dad, we found her," said Tommy with what sounded like real happiness, not his usual sneer. He shoved her into a brick courtyard in front of a man seated on a bench, smoking a clay pipe. Built like a dockyard worker, Harry Newton was lounging in his shirt sleeves enjoying the sunshine that struck the spot where he was resting. A few of his men stood around him, seemingly relaxed but clearly on the watch. Their eyes never stopped flitting from predator to prey. Sahira thought of the wild red dogs in India, the most vicious of animals. They worked in packs and dominated the lesser creatures around them. Harry Newton, with his gap-toothed grin and reddish-brown hair, was the alpha dog.

He took his pipe out of his mouth and tapped it on the side of his boot. Ash fell to the floor in a little glowing pile. "You did, son? That was quick."

"She was down at the docks – prob'ly looking to ship 'ome," said Alf, not wanting to miss out on the praise.

"You both did well. So this is the one they want? Doesn't look like a Hindoo princess to me. Sure it's her? We won't get the reward unless it's the right one."

"I promise, Dad. We know 'er, don't we?" The boys were fawning on their father like puppies, seeking his approval.

"Pence can't complain then. 'E only asked me this mornin' to find her and I deliver – as usual." Harry Newton grinned at his boys. "Let's take 'er back. I fancy a stroll."

"We wants 'er boots first." Tommy gave her a wicked smile. "You goin' to fight us again, mutton'ead?"

Sahira was too exhausted and too scared to try anything in the centre of Harry Newton's little kingdom. So she did nothing as they pushed her to sit on a bench and untied the laces. With a sharp tug, her feet were bared. Tommy knotted the boots together and hung them around his neck as a trophy of victory. As they were flaunted before her eyes, she remembered seeing the leather for her beloved boots for the first time on a stall in the bazaar, shining in the sunshine next to a sunset-red pair of shoes and slippers made of canary yellow leather. She'd known at once that the blue had to be hers so had tugged her father's hand and pointed. He'd ordered a pair of stout boots made in her size immediately. Sahira swallowed against the memory of her father's words: *So my little girl is going to walk the London pavements in sky boots, is she?*

"Is she always this quiet?" asked Harry, studying her.

"Nah, she tells stories and makes stuff up all the time," said Tommy, taking a swig from a cup that stood near a jug of ale at his father's elbow.

"'Ere, you little tyke, that's mine!" growled Harry, clipping his son around the ear. "Don't you get ideas." He held out the cup to Alf. "There you go. Must be 'ot work, chasing this little 'eathen around the docks."

Alf took the cup and grinned at his brother as he drained it to the bottom.

"Tells stories, doesn't she? That don't sound too bad to me," said Harry.

"She's got precious stuff in a trunk, pearls and things, but she's 'idden it," said Tommy. "We sent someone to crack it but it's got a special lock and they couldn't get in."

Harry came to stand before her and kicked the sole of her foot. "What 'ave you done with it?"

Sahira hugged her arms to her sides.

"We know. She took it to the Tower – paid a barrow boy to take it," said Tommy.

"Everybody pays me a tax when they arrive and you," Harry stabbed a finger at Sahira, "owe me. Where's the trunk?"

Sahira said nothing. Harry's hand shot out and slapped her hard. She reeled back on the bench.

"Tell me!" he shouted.

"I put it in the tiger cage!" hissed Sahira. How she wished she could scratch and bite them!

Harry turned to his sons. "I 'eard they 'ad tigers at the Tower. Is that likely?"

"She works with 'em – at least that's what she claims. She could be lyin'," said Tommy.

Rubbing his palm, which stung from the blow he'd given her, Harry gave a sound of disgust. "We'll take 'er back now and get the reward. You get that trunk from 'er and bring it to me, all right?" Harry hauled her up by the elbow. "Right, quick march. I ain't got all day."

"I have no shoes," she said, shaking with useless rage. She refused to think it was fear.

"And that's my problem? You're lucky I left you with toes," he hissed.

Sahira had gone barefoot at home often enough but never on the cold, muddy streets of London. She had to watch every footfall to avoid cuts or stepping in muck. As the reality of her new life settled on her – the flicker of hope she'd harboured snuffed out by the hands of the Newtons – she felt like all the fight had gone out of her. It must be how Rama and Sita felt now that the bars around them had closed in, with even their friend Sahira doing nothing to free them. Maybe this was her punishment? She was lucky they hadn't taken a swipe at her first for imprisoning them.

But she knew they didn't blame her, even though they could. Thinking of the joy she felt seeing the tigers playing in the moonlight, Sahira hugged the memory to herself, the only warm spot in her chilled body.

After a brisk ten-minute walk where no allowance was made for her weak leg or bare feet, Harry Newton rapped on the door of the orphanage. Mrs Pence answered.

"Ma'am, I bring good news," he boomed, entering past her without pausing for an invitation. "Your lost sheep 'as been found, the coin you swept London for 'as turned up, the prodigal 'as returned."

Tommy and Alf pushed Sahira inside. She stood shivering in the entryway.

"Mr Newton, if you'd just wait –" began Mrs Pence, casting an anxious look toward her husband's study.

Harry bent close to her ear, his smile a ghastly thing to behold. "'Arry Newton does not wait, ma'am. I wants me reward." He marched straight into Mr Pence's room. "'Ere she is, Pence, right as rain, as promised."

"Who is this man?" asked a female voice, refined, not like the women who worked in the orphanage.

Sahira marvelled at the transformation that came over Harry Newton. His bluff manner vanished and he became obsequious. "My lady. Apologies, I did not know Mr Pence was occupied with so fair a guest."

"Cheek," muttered the woman. "But you've found my niece?"

The word penetrated Sahira's blankness. *Niece?* Then this had to be John's mother – her father's sister. She looked up from the floor of the entryway to find a woman staring at her from the door to Mr Pence's study. With elaborate ringlets pinned around her ears and a blue satin carriage dress with puffy sleeves, she was clearly from the upper classes. No wonder Harry Newton had immediately changed his tune.

"Sahira? Why has the child no shoes – and what's happened to her face?" She directed that question to Harry. Sahira felt a little flicker of hope that she would finally have an adult in her family who cared about her.

"She is a savage, ain't she? She don't like wearing 'em," said Harry, lying happily with the flair of long practice. "My boys were looking after 'em for her. Tommy!" he beckoned.

Scowling, Tommy unlooped the boots from his neck and shoved them at Sahira. She hugged them tightly to her chest, gaze swimming in tears.

"Sahira, I'm your Aunt Bracewell." The lady held out a hand. Sahira didn't know what to do with that so stayed rooted to the spot, embarrassed to be at a loss. She felt like she was failing some test she didn't understand. Her aunt dropped her hand. "Do you speak English? John gave me the impression you did."

Sahira nodded.

"But you were raised in India – and you now work with my late brother's animals?"

She nodded again.

"How old are you?" she asked, her voice gentle.

"She's twelve," said Mr Pence. "Raised a heathen, I'm afraid. We've been trying to tame her but as you saw, she's too wild for a decent home – running away at the first opportunity. But she's young yet – might be a chance to reform her if she's brought up strictly."

"Sahira, a word, please." Her aunt held out her hand, this time in a gesture that indicated Sahira should take it in hers. "May we use your office, Mr Pence?"

"Of course, Mrs Bracewell." He paused, clearing his throat with a loud *"ahem"*. "And the reward?"

At the mention of "reward" all three Newtons shamelessly thrust out their hands. Harry smacked the boys lightly on the head, a signal that he would get first pick.

She passed Mr Pence a stack of gold coins from her reticule, which he promptly handed over to Harry.

"All square, Newton?" asked Mr Pence.

"Yes, sir." Harry grinned and bowed out. "See you later, boys."

"Tommy, Alf, lessons have started." With that hint, the twins sulked their way upstairs. "I'll be just outside, madam," said Mr Pence.

"Is that really necessary?" Mrs Bracewell asked.

"The girl's a desperate creature," said Mr Pence. "I've already had to take the rod to her for lying and you saw for yourself that she won't stay with decent folk. Who knows what she's capable of?" He left the room but through the open door Sahira could see him hovering outside, listening in.

"Please, sit, child," Mrs Bracewell said.

Sahira limped to an upright chair.

"You're injured? Oh, and your feet!" The lady kneeled and looked them over, hesitant to touch her grubby skin. "You must bathe these immediately. You really must get used to wearing shoes, my dear. This is London, not the jungle. My foolish brother did you no favours not teaching you such things."

That stung more than her toes. "Baba wasn't foolish. They took the boots off me."

Mrs Bracewell stood up. "I suppose they did have a villainous look. Well, I'm pleased you know that much at least." She was talking about Sahira in her hearing as if she were some wild child raised by wolves. "I'm so sorry about your father."

"My mother died too," Sahira said pointedly.

"And her, of course. I didn't meet her, you understand?" Meaning, Sahira supposed, that she was never quite real to Mrs Bracewell. "My child, I came because John received a note from you via the little Peel boy asking for help. It said to go to the Tower of London, but that sounded most peculiar."

"It's where I work," she said defensively.

"Yes, well." The lady's tone suggested she didn't want to touch that problematic subject – a girl, working at a man's job. "He told me where you were living and was most insistent I came to see that you were all right. Imagine my shock when I found you'd been missing for a few days and no one had looked for you."

At that moment Sahira wished she could have stayed missing.

"Why did you run away?" Mrs Bracewell asked.

Where to start? Mr Pence's shadow lay across the entrance. He was listening. "I'm unhappy here."

Mrs Bracewell sat down in a chair across from Sahira. "Oh, my dear, I can imagine it's a difficult adjustment for you, but you have to accept that nothing is going to bring your parents back." She sounded like the missionary lady from the boat. "You have to make peace with your new life."

"You've not come to offer me a place in your home, have you?" she asked. She knew the answer; the lawyer had shattered any dreams she'd had of that happening.

"Me? Oh, Sahira, I... my husband... there are difficulties you wouldn't understand," her aunt answered, appearing flustered.

"I do understand," Sahira said. "You don't want to acknowledge me as a member of your family because my mother was from India and I'm different from you."

The lady looked embarrassed. "That does present a problem. People are very quick to judge and my girls are about to... well, never mind that."

"It's been explained to me. They won't make good marriages if I'm there." Sahira made herself shrug, though she was far from indifferent on the subject. It wasn't the first time she'd been treated like a leper. "My family in India on my mother's side thought I was a disgrace too."

"You're not a disgrace!" Mrs Bracewell got up and walked to the window.

"Really? Everyone treats me as if I am."

Something about the tone of her voice made Mrs Bracewell turn and look at her. "You do sound a lot like Richard when you say that. My brother always drove a coach and horses through society's conventions."

Sahira felt the anger bubbling inside her, fuelled by her disappointment that her aunt wasn't going to stand by her. It was exhausting having hope after hope stripped from her. She stood up. "Thank you for visiting, Aunt. I don't expect you to worry about me anymore. Please don't pay people to fetch me back if I run away again. I'd prefer to make my own way in the world. I won't be staying here long."

"But Sahira, we haven't talked yet about what to do –"

"I know what you're going to do," Sahira interrupted. "You're going to leave me here and tell me to be good."

"That does seem the best course of action," she said, but with a little doubt in her tone. Even she must have noticed it wasn't a nice place for a child.

"But I hate it here!" Tears came despite herself. "They are cruel and despise me, but maybe you think that's just how it is for orphans like me – that I won't get anything better anywhere else?"

"I can't help how society sees children with your background," said her aunt stiffly. "Please, don't cry."

"My father would think *you* were the disgrace – not me!" Sahira shouted.

Mr Pence stepped in, cane tapping at his side. "Madam, you can see now what I'm dealing with."

The lady cleared her throat. "Please, leave us, Mr Pence." She waited for the man to go and this time shut the door behind him. She turned to Sahira. "You're right. Richard probably would think that way – but then as a man he always had more choices than I did. If it weren't for… well, I won't burden you with my reasons. I can see you have too much pride to listen to them. Sahira, I want you to be happy."

"H… how can I b… be happy?" she spluttered. That was impossible, like asking for a sunbird or a unicorn. Sahira curled up around her boots. She felt like her aunt had taken a knife to her. This cool compassion was worse than the Newtons' and Pences' scorn.

"Time heals all wounds." Sahira felt the slightest of touches on her neck. "I will check on you regularly despite what you say and ask Mr Pence to be patient with you. I won't allow anyone to mistreat you, I promise."

There was no point in this conversation. Sahira knew that her aunt was fooling herself because she didn't really want to take responsibility. Once she left, any restraint Mr Pence was showing would leave with her.

"I really don't think you or anyone else will be able to stop them," Sahira said quietly. Still hugging her boots, she bobbed a shallow curtsey and left the room. Just like Rama and Sita, she had no choice but to return to her cage.

CHAPTER 16

June 1830. The King was dead, long live the King. In the menagerie, the lion, George Junior, was swiftly renamed William and life carried on as usual. Except, thought Sahira, idly wiping the glass in the monkey room, there was a feeling that they were all living on borrowed time. The Duke of Wellington was circling the menagerie like a wolf does an old ewe that it knows is too feeble to fight it off. The stoop to Mr Cops's shoulders was getting more pronounced even as his wife's belly grew rounder. Sahira could see him approaching across the courtyard. He must be worrying he would lose his position just as Mrs Cops gave birth to their first child.

"How do, Sahira?" he called, finding her just finishing up her cleaning.

"Well enough," she said. This had become her standard answer. She was well enough to carry on living this half life she was trapped inside. One day she would be old enough to make her own decisions about where she could live – but not yet. "How's Mrs Cops?"

"Good, thank you. Resting." He patted a stool beside him. "I want a word, so you don't hear it from anyone else first."

What now? thought Sahira bleakly. Was he going to tell her she couldn't work here any longer? The boost brought by the novelty of tigers was wearing off and visitor numbers subsiding. In summer, people were travelling further afield for their pleasures and the richer ones were going to the new zoological gardens in Regent's Park. Mr Cops was having to cut corners, buying cheaper grain for the birds and less meat for the big cats. But if he sent her away so she couldn't escape here each day, then she would have no reason to carry on.

"You won't have failed to notice that things aren't that rosy at the moment," Mr Cops said heavily.

She nodded.

"I'm thinking of making some drastic changes so the rest of the menagerie can survive."

"You want me to go?" Sahira blurted out.

"What? You? No! No, nothing like that." He shook his head. "I'm sorry, lass. I didn't realize that was what you were thinking. You work twice as hard as my other keepers. I'll keep you around as long as I can, I promise." He smiled reassuringly.

The relief felt like being washed off her feet by a warm wave of the Indian Ocean. "Thank you."

"I fear you won't like the rest of what I've got to say though so brace yourself." He gave her a challenging look.

"Ned?"

He shook his head. "Stop making wild guesses, Sahira, and let me explain."

She folded her hands in her lap and waited.

"I need to raise some money – and quickly. I've bills that could see me in gaol if I don't pay them. I have to sell some of the animals – they're the only property that I can shift quick enough. I've got a buyer for a family of marmosets, but that isn't going to solve the cash flow problem." He paused, a look of hesitation on his face. "So I've accepted Jamrach's offer for the tigers."

Sahira shot up from her seat with that hornet sting of surprise. "What!"

Mr Cops's face was the picture of guilt but he carried on regardless. "I know what they mean to you –"

"You don't!"

"But the offer is more than fair – generous – some rich man with a park. He wants them –"

"He's going to hunt them – you know that's what happens to big cats when they're bought by rich men!" She couldn't believe what she was hearing.

"That's possible. I can't control what he does with them, but I really think he'll understand that they're too valuable to sacrifice to sport," he explained, his voice wavering.

"You don't believe that – I can tell you don't."

Mr Cops hung his head. "I have no choice, Sahira."

"I thought you understood – I thought you loved these animals?"

"I do, but I have to think of the whole menagerie, not just two creatures. The new zoological gardens have also offered to take them off my hands, but for much less money. I'd prefer that but I don't think I can afford it."

"But they'd live, yes? Surely, that has to be better?" Sahira pleaded.

"The sum they're offering won't be enough to save this place."

Sahira's mind raced with anything that she could suggest to make him change his mind. "Talk to the zoological people – ask for more money!"

He shook his head.

"Let *me* bargain with them. I'm good at that – really I am. I used to do it in India all the time…"

"Sahira –"

"I'll go there right now – persuade them." She was up and running before he could stop her.

"Sahira, don't be a fool. They won't listen to you!" he called after her.

No, but they might listen to the son of the Home Secretary, she thought.

Ned caught up with her as she hurried to the gate, Nebbie trotting behind.

"Sahira, where are you going?"

"Tigers – zoological gardens or death – Bobby," she managed through pants. She had a stitch already. Since the Newtons had marched her back to the orphanage, her hip had hurt worse than ever if she rushed.

Ned was never slow. "You're going to Master Bobby's? You won't make it across town."

Sahira gritted her teeth. "Yes, I will."

Ned caught her arm. "Ride Nebbie. I'll take you. Master Bobby will definitely come down to see you if you have the zebra."

She had to admit it was a good plan – if they could get there without being mobbed by local children wanting to share the fun. There was no time for second thoughts. Sahira got on the back of the zebra, who was now used to putting up with riders and only tried to nip Ned once for his pains.

"Right, you can tell me what's going on as we go," said Ned. He looked up at her. "To think before I met you I only had Cook to worry about!"

As her initial desperation settled now she was doing something to help, Sahira had time to feel a little like the Pied Piper of Hamelin as they headed across town with a following of the curious. Carriages drew up to look, an omnibus rumbled to a stop to let them cross the road first, and workmen put down their tools to cheer and whistle. Ned turned prospective riders away with a firm shake of the head – all business today. He led them without taking a wrong turn right to the mews behind Bobby Peel's house. Leaving Sahira in charge of Nebbie, he went to the back door to deliver a message, having already done this on her behalf a few weeks ago. Then they waited, Sahira sitting on a mounting block while Ned led Nebbie to a horse trough.

They heard the voices on the back stairs before they saw the speakers.

"A zebra, you say? How fascinating! And here was I thinking I was the one invited to give the lesson on the animal kingdom!" That tone belonged to a young man in his early twenties. He came into view – straight brown hair already in retreat up his forehead, heavy eyebrows, and deep set eyes that gave the impression he peered out at the world like an animal deep in a den.

"I can't say it's a normal occurrence, Charles, but Bobby does have a way of making unusual friends," said Mr Evesham, the tutor.

Sahira now saw her cousin John and Bobby with the older men. John waved hesitantly at her and she gave him a slight smile. It wasn't his fault his mother didn't want a cuckoo in the nest.

Bobby bounded over. "Miss Clive – Ned – Nebbie!" He chose to bow to the zebra, which was so like him that Sahira's smile became a genuine one. "Have you come to tea?"

"Miss Clive." Mr Evesham nodded to her. "Please, allow me to introduce my good friend, Charles Darwin. He's a Cambridge man like me, and quite an enthusiast for all things animal and vegetable."

"Minerals are exceedingly interesting too," added Mr Darwin, bowing to her. "Don't forget that, Evie. Geology – age of the earth – all this is vital to understanding how things have come to be."

Evie? Sober Mr Evesham had that as a nickname?

John touched Sahira's arm. "How are you, Cousin?"

Sad? Lonely? Desperate? "Well enough."

He swallowed and nodded. "I –"

She had no time for his apologies. "Bobby, I need you to take me to the new zoological gardens."

Her young friend looked taken aback at the sudden demand. "What? Now?"

"Yes, now." She hadn't come across London on a zebra just to make a diary date for some distant future.

"But…" Bobby looked to his tutor.

"Perhaps you should explain?" said Mr Evesham.

"My tigers –"

"The girl has *tigers?*" asked Mr Darwin before Mr Evesham hushed him.

"– Mr Cops has to sell them but the zoological society isn't offering enough. If they don't go there, then some rich man is going to buy them and shoot them."

"Shoot them? Are you sure?" Mr Evesham asked incredulously.

She nodded. Why else would he want them?

"I see," the tutor continued. "And what do you think you can do at the zoo?"

Sahira noted the odd new word – *zoo*. "I will bargain with them. Please, I've got to try."

There was a yelp from Mr Darwin. He'd just discovered that, despite their resemblance to horses, zebras were not friendly creatures.

Mr Evesham consulted his watch.

"Please, sir," pleaded Bobby. "We were studying nature this afternoon with your friend. We can just tell Mama that you decided to take the lecture to the zoological gardens. In fact, wouldn't that be better for my education?"

"You make your case very well, Bobby," agreed the tutor. "We'll leave this creature here – who knows what they would do if we took a zebra to the gate."

"Probably try to acquire it," said Mr Darwin, shaking his hand to rid it of the pain of nipped fingers.

Bobby clapped his hands excitedly. "Thank you! Thank you! I'll get James to fetch a carriage."

"*I'll* ask James. You will be a gentleman and offer your guest refreshments," corrected the tutor. "They've come a long way already. Ned, while we go to the zoo, you will walk your charge back to the Tower. I take it he is here with permission of the keeper?"

"Not exactly," confessed Ned.

Mr Evesham sighed. "Then you'd better go back at once. I'll send a footman with you." He held up a finger. "Straight back, mind; no stops to earn a few pennies."

"Spoilsport," muttered Ned.

With Ned and Nebbie sent to the Tower in the company of a young footman, the rest of the party headed in the family coach to Regent's Park. The new zoological gardens were being constructed on the northern side, entry only for those who had permission from one of the Fellows of the Zoological Society. As expected, Sahira found that the word of Bobby Peel – a son of one of these – was enough to get them all inside the gate. The zoo did look promising: unlike the cramped quarters at the Tower, the cages were set among gardens. Families strolled along the wide paths, the animals placed in their ornate enclosures almost as an afterthought among the hoop-rolling, ball-playing children. If you ignored the small size of the cages, you could almost think it a paradise.

"We're here, Sahira. Now what?" asked Bobby brightly. John, however, looked about the place as if it no longer held any surprises for him. As a rich boy, he'd doubtless been here many times.

Sahira was aware that she didn't really have a plan. Rushing here had been more a scream of fury that her one good thing – her tigers – were about to be ripped from her. After surviving the loss of her parents, she didn't think she could bear that too. But Bobby was right: what did she have to find out first? "I need to find out if my tigers would be happy here."

"Yes, and then?"

"Get the owners to match Jamrach's offer."

Mr Evesham and Mr Darwin looked at each other, scepticism plain.

"You understand this is a scientific venture, don't you, Sahira? The aim is to educate, not make money," Mr Evesham said gently.

"He means they won't be able to stump up the money," Bobby said helpfully. "How much do you need? I could ask Papa to buy them."

His tutor clicked his tongue. "Bobby, please, don't raise your friend's hopes like that. Your father will not buy you tigers, no matter how much you badger him. He had doubts about getting you a puppy."

"I've got some money saved," Bobby added.

"Tigers cost hundreds of pounds, Bobby, not ten shillings," John said in a low voice.

Mr Evesham had caught sight of someone emerging from a pedestrian tunnel that ran under the carriageway through the gardens. "A moment. That's Charles Spooner. He's the medical attendant here. We can at least ask him about the first of your questions, Miss Clive." He beckoned the young man over. They shook hands, clearly already friends. Sahira was getting the idea that the circle of people who were interested in animal studies was a small one and they all knew each other, particularly the ones of Mr Evesham's age. The tutor made a quick introduction of the party. Spooner hesitated when he learned the little Indian serving boy was in fact a young lady, but he covered his surprise well. Mr Evesham explained the situation with a brevity that impressed Sahira.

Spooner sighed and ran his hands through his thick dark hair, dislodging his hat. "I wish I could promise they would flourish here, Miss Clive. That's the plan at least for all the animals – and why I've been appointed. The English climate, however – that's against us. The animals do well enough in the summer, but we lose so many each winter."

"How many animals are there?" asked Sahira.

"We've around 600 animals – 200 species – and yet I'm expected to know how to keep each and every one alive on just three days a week with them." He gave a disgusted laugh. "It's a battle I'm not yet winning."

"What happens in winter?" asked John.

"We can only afford to house a few in heated buildings. We put some of the smaller ones with us in offices and storerooms. The bigger ones… well, they just have to cope. Come, I'll show you." He led them toward the first row of cages shaded by trees.

"Do you have any big cats?" asked Sahira.

"We have a little tigress, an old lion, and a young one but I'm struggling to keep them healthy."

"I fear you'll continue to struggle," said Mr Darwin, frowning at a young lion cub lolling in a moveable cage, paws dangling out of the bars, no better off than a circus lion, "because it's not their natural habitat. They aren't adapted to live in a cage, being fed with no need to hunt."

"True. When I dissect our losses I find a build-up of unhealthy fat around the major organs," Spooner admitted.

"Dissect!" She couldn't bear that being the fate of her tigers.

"I'm afraid it's necessary, Miss Clive, or I'll never understand how to save the rest."

Sahira's hopes were fading. It seemed that fine gardens did not really change the plight of the animals.

They rounded a corner and came to a bear pit. A girl in a pink dress, hair arranged in tight brown ringlets, gave a vicious poke at an arctic bear with the end of her parasol, encouraged by her giggling companions. The bear, who had been resting against the railings, stumbled to its feet and roared.

Fury thundered through Sahira. "Stop it!" She grabbed the parasol from the girl and snapped it over her knee, bending thin wires and puncturing silk. She shook it at the girl. "How would you like to be poked, you… you vulture!"

"That's my best parasol!" squealed the girl. "Miss Aitkens, look what the dirty little foreigner did!"

The girl's governess swung around to take in the scene. "Arrest the boy!" she demanded, pointing at Sahira.

"Arrest the girl!" snapped back Sahira, pointing at the bear tormentor. "She hurt that bear."

The bear roared his agreement.

"Hear, hear!" cried Bobby, clapping his hands. "Send for a Peeler!"

"You'll be beaten for breaking that!" said the girl, with a sob.

"Then I'd better punch you first to make it worth it!" said Sahira.

Sahira found her fist caught by John from behind before she could land it in the middle of the girl-vulture's face. "Sahira!" he warned. "That won't help."

"But it will make me feel a lot better," she said, still seething.

"All the same. Girls don't behave like that here."

They didn't in India either, but what else could she do in the situation? Allow the girl to keep taunting a defenceless wild beast?

Mr Spooner hurried into the middle of the argument before it got any uglier. He took the broken parasol from Sahira and offered it back to the governess. "Madam, if you can't control your charges, I suggest you leave."

"There's no sign saying we can't touch the animals," whined the girl.

"Go ahead – put your stupid head in there," hissed Sahira. "Let the bear take a poke at that!"

"Miss Clive, please," said Mr Spooner.

"*Miss* Clive? That's a girl? In that outfit?" The governess bristled. "Well, I don't know what this place is coming to. I thought only decent people were allowed in here. The Fellows will hear about this!" She gathered up her little group of girls and marched them onward, looking for someone who would listen to her complaints.

Sahira turned on the medical man. "How can you let them do that to the bears?"

"How can I stop them?" Spooner asked. "I can't stand guard all day."

He was right. It was a much bigger place than the Tower menagerie; keepers could not be on hand everywhere all the time. The cages weren't designed to protect the animals but to expose them to the gaze and – it seemed – touch of the visitors. If they spent every day being tormented by the cruel and stupid then no wonder so many were dying; five minutes of such treatment had driven her to extremes. It was a terrible prison. Rama and Sita would hate it here – and they wouldn't even have her to defend them.

"They should put the people in cages and let the animals out," she said.

"A novel approach to animal handling. I'll suggest it at the next meeting," said Spooner testily. He looked down at the broken bits of parasol in his hand. "I think we'd better cut short our tour. Is there anything else I can show you on the way out?" But his tone was no longer welcoming; he was just being polite.

"No thank you. I've seen quite enough," said Sahira.

Their party was subdued as the Peel carriage took Sahira back to the Tower.

"I thought it would be different – better," said Sahira. The Regent's Park paradise was an illusion. Would it be right to argue with Mr Cops for the tigers to be sent there for a lingering death rather than a quick one at the hands of the hunters? Oh, why couldn't Mr Cops just keep them? She'd make sure they stayed healthy at the Tower.

But would they? a small voice in her head asked. What about winter? Willpower wasn't enough to keep them alive.

"The zoo will be better one day," said Mr Darwin. "The men in charge don't mean to be cruel. They're trying, but frankly, none of them know what they're doing and mistakes are inevitable. Keeping animals to study away from their homelands is a new idea."

"The animals should stay in their homes then," said Sahira.

"It's too late for that. Your tigers, you brought them here, didn't you?" Mr Darwin asked pointedly.

"I wish I hadn't!" Then they would still be in their jungle. Even if hunted, they'd have had more of a chance than here. And her parents – they'd be alive.

Mr Darwin gave her an astute look. "You mustn't blame yourself. I thought there were helpful lessons to be drawn even from what we saw today."

"Really, sir?" asked John. He looked up from his sketch of the poor Arctic bear. He'd caught the rage of the animal to perfection.

"I don't want to bore you with my ideas."

"You won't bore us," said Bobby, bouncing on his rear-facing seat.

"It was why I asked you to come today, Charles," said Mr Evesham with a smile as he laid a hand on Bobby's shoulder to stop him fidgeting.

That was all the invitation Darwin needed. "Well then. You know that the French naturalists have been telling us that the number of species we see today aren't fixed – that there have been great animals in the past that no longer live among us?"

"Really?" asked Bobby. "Like what? Dragons?"

Mr Darwin smiled. "I can't say anything about dragons, Master Peel, but Monsieur Cuvier of Paris has some excellent examples of fossilized bones of creatures who have disappeared. For example, he has some that look like they belong to a huge elephant. He named that creature a mastodon. He thinks there have been cycles of creation. Creatures live on Earth for a time and are then wiped out by a big event, like a flood."

"Like in the Bible, and Noah's ark?" asked Bobby.

"Yes, but much further back in time – and he thinks this has happened again and again."

"So the mastodon is completely gone?" asked John, now doodling an elephant-like creature on his pad.

"Yes. He believes in extinction. But that's not the only theory."

"It never is," said Mr Evesham. "You natural philosophers enjoy disagreeing with each other."

Darwin continued: "There's another idea that animals change to fit their surroundings. 'Biological evolution', they call it. Another Frenchman, Lamarck, said that animals acquire characteristics by using them, like a giraffe stretching its neck to eat the leaves higher up. He thinks using a certain part of the body makes the new abilities pass on to the next generation, and if an animal doesn't use something it withers away, like the wings on an ostrich."

"So animals change, rather than go extinct?" asked Sahira, caught up in the discussion despite herself.

"Perhaps. I'm not sure what to believe. Neither cycles of creation nor biological evolution seem complete explanations." He paused, deep in thought.

"No amount of stretching is going to make an animal flourish in a cage like that," Sahira argued.

"Agreed. Maybe the truth lies somewhere between the two ideas: extinction and change. I need to see them in their homes before I understand how this might work."

"Go travelling, Charles, that's the best way," said Mr Evesham. "Take your cue from Miss Clive here: she's seen all the Indian species in the wild. I imagine she can teach you a thing or too."

"Perhaps you can answer one of my questions then. Why are tigers striped, Miss Clive?" asked Darwin.

That was easy. "It breaks up their silhouette in the jungle. It gives them an advantage when stalking their prey," said Sahira, looking out the window at the grubby children playing in the mud. They too were camouflaged.

"Remarkable. *'Did he who made the Lamb make thee?'* – that's what the poet Blake asked about the tiger."

"Giving poetry lessons too now, Charles?" teased Mr Evesham. Sahira liked their easy friendship – envied them, in fact.

"Have tigers always had stripes?" asked Bobby. "Or did they become like that by needing it – you know, like a giraffe stretching its neck?"

Darwin smiled. "That, young Bobby, is an excellent question."

"And how would you get stripes or a long neck?" asked Sahira. "I might want to have a bigger nose like an elephant, but thinking about it, rubbing my nose, pulling it, that won't make it happen."

"Another very good observation. Lamarck looked for a special nervous fluid in the body to achieve it, but never found it," explained Mr Darwin. "We're all going to have to look and think a lot harder if we're going to solve that puzzle."

"A trunk like an elephant?" Bobby pulled hard on his nose. "That would be brilliant. I want one."

Mr Evesham smiled wryly. "You should concentrate first on developing the brain of a reasonably intelligent gentleman first."

"And the brain is something we can change," said John, holding his pencil over his completed picture of a huge elephant. "Isn't that interesting?"

The coach drew to a halt. Sahira didn't wait for anyone to hand her down like a lady as she knew John or Mr Evesham would try to do. Instead she hopped out and thanked Jenks, the coachman. She looked back at her new friends in the window. She felt a little embarrassed now, remembering how she had buffaloed her way into this outing.

"Thank you for taking me."

"It was a pleasure," said Mr Evesham.

"And an education," added Mr Darwin. "I wish you and your tigers all the best." As she turned away, she heard him add, "Evie, old chap, I don't suppose you know anyone setting off on a voyage of exploration soon, do you?"

CHAPTER 17

Ann and Emily were waiting for Sahira in the dormitory when she returned from her day at the zoo. Lately they'd been trying to be extra nice to her when she got home from work, hoping to win back her friendship. Joanna Newton had disappeared back to her life outside the orphanage so Sahira's bed was hers once more, but that hadn't repaired the broken trust between the three girls. Sahira found it hard to forget their betrayal.

"How was your day?" Ann asked tentatively. She fingered one of her black spiral curls nervously before tucking it back behind her ear under the ugly mob cap they all had to wear.

All except for Sahira. She'd refused to go back to wearing that – and, oddly, no one had argued with her.

"Great," she said sourly, "if you count learning that my tigers are to be sold and hunted for sport as good news."

"Oh, Sahira, no!" said Emily. "That's terrible!"

"Mr Cops is going to sell them to the highest bidder. I went to the zoological gardens – but that's little better and can't match the offer he already has from Jamrach."

"Would you like me to brush your hair?" asked Ann, offering what comfort she could. Clearly she thought the situation hopeless too.

Sahira nodded. She was aching. Her ride across town, the anxiety that had eaten away at her, the frustration that she was powerless, all this had combined to make her feel wretched. Having someone tackle her hair would be welcome.

Ann took the brush and began soothing strokes.

Emily flopped back on her bed and held her hands up in front of her, twirling them like a nautch girl dancing. Homesickness clawed Sahira as she remembered parties with music and ladies twirling in silken saris, doves released into the blue sky, fountains tinkling in silver basins, sherbet and cinnamon sweetmeats. There had been laughter and love in her life once upon a time.

"You know, Sahira, *you* could buy the tigers," said Emily.

The comment tripped up her memories, bringing her back to the present. "Me?"

"Mr Cops paid you for them so why not buy them back?"

Emily was right! How had Sahira not seen it for herself? "And then what do I do?"

"Give them to the menagerie or the zoological gardens, I suppose, on the condition they don't get sold again."

"That's a good idea. You could make it a temporary loan until you have enough money to ship them home," suggested Ann, beginning on a plait.

"But that will take years," said Sahira.

"Then it takes years," said Ann calmly. She was always so patient.

Emily sat up. She was more like Sahira, wanting to solve a problem today rather than wait for tomorrow. "I know: you could get your rich relatives to cough up for that part. Tell them you'll do something really embarrassing if you don't have the funds you need."

"Like what?" asked Sahira.

"There's so much you could do. Turn up at your cousins' during a ball? Make it public knowledge you're their relative? Chain yourself to the railing outside their house with a placard?"

"But wouldn't that be blackmail? And isn't that wicked?" Sahira asked. She might not have worried if it were just her aunt injured, but there were John and his sisters to consider.

"I rather thought shooting your tigers was worse. Sometimes you have to do a bad thing to prevent a worse thing happening." Emily bit her lip, looking sheepish at the admission.

Sahira guessed she was thinking about how they had reacted when Joanna was here, falling in behind the bully to save their siblings from the Newtons. Emily was right though. You did have to fight dirty at times.

John would be disappointed in her. But she wasn't actually going to carry out her threat – just make it so she could save her tigers. He'd come around eventually.

In fact, if she offered to go home with Rama and Sita, her family would probably leap at the chance to get rid of her. She could travel with the tigers, make sure they were happy on the voyage, arrange for them to be let off in an uninhabited part of the coast, and then...

Then they would disappear into the wild and she'd be alone.

Sahira closed her eyes, fists clenched. *This isn't about you,* she told herself. *This is about Rama and Sita.* She opened her eyes to find Ann and Emily both watching her in concern.

"Sorry, I didn't know you'd hate the idea that much," said Emily. "Forget I mentioned it."

She'd obviously misunderstood Sahira's anguished expression. "Thank you, Emily. It's a good idea. I'll go to Mr Cops tomorrow and get my money."

Emily smiled in relief. "Good. You can't let them kill your tigers."

"No, I can't."

"What do you mean you've already sold them?" asked Sahira as she stood with Mr Cops in Lion Yard. Rama and Sita were pacing their cell, eyes bright with concern for her. They could sense her distress.

Mr Cops wouldn't meet her gaze. "I knew you'd be upset, so I decided better to make this quick. Lop off the limb so you don't suffer. Jamrach's coming for them." He checked his pocket watch. "Any moment now."

Fury robbed Sahira of words. She had to get past this or she'd lose her very last chance to save the situation. Breathing hard, she swallowed.

"I want to buy them from you."

"You?" Mr Cops scratched his chin. "How?"

"With the money you paid for them – the money you were putting in the bank for me."

A red flush appeared on his cheeks. "About that, Sahira..."

"About what, Mr Cops?" Why had he suddenly become so shifty?

"I haven't exactly finalized putting the money in the bank for you. When Jamrach pays, I'll be able to do that – and have some left over. You'll benefit too. Ah, here he is now." He seemed grateful for the distraction.

A cart drove through Lion Gate, Jamrach holding the reins. Even worse, though, was the arrival of Harry Newton and his boys driving a second cart.

"The Newtons!" hissed Sahira. She couldn't believe this!

Mr Cops frowned. "I didn't know they were involved. Mr Jamrach, I can't say I care for your associates."

Jamrach glowered at Mr Cops. "Who I use to move these creatures is none of your business, Cops."

Harry winked at Sahira. "Special cargo in my territory. Of course I 'ave to see it moved personally."

Sahira felt sick. The boys would know that she loved those tigers – everyone at the orphanage did. This was their revenge for her keeping her boots. She sat on the ground and tugged off her sky boots.

"Here, Tommy – have them. Just leave the tigers alone."

Tommy turned his back. "No need. I'm having a pair of boots made of tiger skin next week."

Sahira jumped up and flew at Mr Cops, beating his chest with her fists. "You can't – you can't do this!"

He grabbed her wrists firmly, holding her back. "I've got no choice, Sahira."

"Right little wild cat, ain't she?" said Harry. "She's growing on me."

All reason left Sahira as she struggled and roared until her voice gave out. Mr Cops had to hand her over to two of the keepers. They dragged her away, kicking and screaming, and locked her in a storeroom.

"Sorry, Miss Clive," said Ben as he locked the door. "It's for your own good. You'll do yourself an injury carrying on so. We'll be back to let you out when the tigers are gone."

Sahira threw herself at the wooden door – but this was the Tower of London and doors were made to keep people inside. Still she scratched and kicked until exhaustion claimed her. Her nails were broken, blood trickled from a bump on her head, bruises bloomed on her shoulder where she had tried ramming the wooden panel. Nothing made any difference. The tigers were being taken and she could not stop it. She could hear their roars of distress, but then it was much worse when they fell silent.

Hurt beyond hope of healing, Sahira curled up in a corner and wished to die.

Several hours later the door opened. Sahira didn't even look up.

"I've brought you some water," said Ned.

She didn't respond.

"I'll put it beside you. I won't lock the door when I go so you can come out when you're ready." He waited for her to acknowledge him.

Somewhere deep inside Sahira knew Ned was a friend but just now she couldn't bring that thought to the surface. She kept her eyes screwed shut. This world was so horrid she didn't want to be part of it any longer.

"I'm sorry about Rama and Sita. I couldn't stop them," he said solemnly.

Of course he couldn't. She didn't blame Ned.

"Mr Cops says he's got the money for you."

Sahira growled.

"I know. That's more or less what I thought you'd say. I'll leave you alone for now."

Ned came back at the end of the day to find she hadn't moved.

"You should go home, Sahira, or you'll get in trouble," he cautioned.

The orphanage wasn't home. Nothing they could do now could touch her.

He sighed. "Right. Well, I've brought you some supper. I'll leave it with the water."

Mr Cops came next.

"Sahira, you'd better get back before it gets dark."

She curled up into a tighter ball.

"Ben, Mike." He stepped away.

As soon as she felt the touch of one of the keepers on her arm, she exploded into action, kicking and clawing. She was a tigress now, not a girl. Plate and cup went flying. Someone yelped as their shin got the brunt of a kick.

"Mr Cops, we can't move her without hurting her," said Ben.

"Yeah, leave the little lass. She's too upset to hear reason," said Mike.

"I'll make her move." That was Joseph Croney. "A little taste of a whip and she'll scurry back to that orphanage of hers."

"No! Croney, I didn't ask you to stick your nose into this business. Get you gone!" Mr Cops sighed. "All right, we'll leave her for now. One night on the floor here won't harm her. I'll send a message to explain why she hasn't gone back. Ned, keep an eye on her – and clear up that mess."

"Yes, sir."

The door closed on her and she was left alone.

"Why aren't you talking to me?" asked Ned. He sounded hurt.

Sahira opened her eyes a crack. It was morning – not that that mattered. She wasn't going to come out of here ever again.

"And you're not eating." He picked up the cup. "Or drinking." He sniffed. "You... you want to die – like Sita when she first arrived here?"

She hadn't thought of it like that, but he was right. She was pining for her tigers. Where were they now? Had they reached the estate belonging to the hunter? *Not yet*, she thought. It was no easy matter to transport two large cats across England, and longer to arrange a hunt for such special prey. Maybe, if she stayed like this, not eating or drinking, they'd die on the same day? She was fairly certain she'd know when they were gone.

"I don't want you to die, Sahira. You're my best friend."

A little prick of guilt penetrated her numbness. Ned would be all right. He had his job and the other keepers. He didn't need her.

"You can't give up." He kicked her foot. "Stop this! I'm not 'aving this!"

She almost rallied for his sake, but then she heard Mr Cops outside.

187

"How's she doing, Ned?"

"Not well, sir. I think she feels as though the tigers were the only thing worth living for."

"Humph!" Mr Cops sounded angry now. "This is taking things too far. She'll get over it – she'll have to. I don't like losing creatures any more than she does but sometimes you have to make a tough call. Leave her to stew."

"She's not eating – or drinking."

"Well, she will when she's ready. People don't just starve themselves to death. Nature takes over. She'll eat when she's hungry."

Their voices faded as they moved off.

"I really don't think she will," said Ned. "She's lost too much."

Mid-morning Sahira was startled out of her numbness when a bucket of cold water was thrown over her. She gasped and spluttered, sitting up in a pool.

"Get up, you little tyke!" Joseph Croney stood in the door. "Enough of the hysterics. The tigers are gone and good riddance!"

"Croney!" bellowed Mr Cops. "I told you to stay away from Sahira. What have you done?" He looked into the storeroom. "Good lord, man, have you no compassion? Ben, fetch a towel – Ned, dry clothes." These offerings were left inside and the door closed. "Get changed, Sahira, before you die of cold."

Sahira sat for a long time undecided as to whether she'd bother to change. She wrapped the towel around herself and shivered. Her muscles started cramping. The pain penetrated and instincts drove her to crawl to a dry spot. Slowly she changed into the shirt and loose trousers Ned had found for her. They wouldn't leave her here to die quietly, she realized. She would have to go away.

It didn't matter where.

Wringing out her hair, she draped the towel around her neck and opened the door. Ned was sitting on a bench just outside.

"Sahira!" He jumped to his feet. "You look terrible."

"Thanks, Ned." She handed him back the towel, but she meant for caring, for being her friend, for everything. "I'm going now."

"Where? Back to the orphanage?" he asked anxiously.

She shrugged.

"I bet you aren't. I bet you're going to follow the tigers and try and steal them back."

She hadn't thought of that, but what then? What would she do with two tigers in the English countryside? She could hardly let them out of their cages.

"You could bribe the carters with the money you'll get from Mr Cops." Ned had clearly been giving this a lot of thought. He shook her arm. "This isn't like you. You 'ave to try something!"

Sahira swayed, dizzy from lack of food and water. "I've tried – and I've tried, Ned. But nothing worked."

"No, you can't give up. I won't allow it. Where's the girl who took on Cook for me? Who refused to give her boots to the bullies? Those tigers are yours to protect – you've always said so."

Finally, something he said got through to her. "Ned, you're right."

He let go of her arm. "You're not giving up?"

"No – yes – I mean, they're still mine. Mr Cops never paid me for them – he broke the contract, selling them while they still belonged to me. He could only do that after he paid me – not *so* he could pay me." The fire in her belly to right the wrongs done to her tigers flamed into hot, urgent life. "They're still mine. I've not got the money even now – and I'm not taking it. I'm going to get my tigers back."

Ned danced from foot to foot, delighted to see his friend recovering her old spirit. "That's good. But how?"

"We're going on a tiger hunt."

PART 5

BURNING BRIGHT

CHAPTER 18

Sahira found Mr Cops having dinner with his wife in the kitchen at Lion House. The smell of lamb stew hit her, making her empty stomach growl and scratch.

"Ah, Sahira, good." He patted a chair beside him. "Have something to eat."

Sahira was hungry but that wasn't why she was here. It would be best to get right to it before she lost her nerve.

"Mr Cops, you've sold my tigers. Illegally. They still belong to me. I do not approve the sale." She laid down her sentences like putting a winning hand of cards on the table.

He placed his knife and fork on his plate.

"Alfred, what have you done?" asked Mrs Cops. Nearing her time, she rubbed the top of her large bump.

"I had to sell the tigers, love," he explained. "Sahira is upset."

"Of course she is! Any fool can see they're more than just tigers to her."

"But you didn't have the right to sell them. You never paid for them," said Sahira. She hated to do this to him, but it was this or the tigers. She had a solemn duty to protect them.

"I've got your money now. I'll take it to a bank later," said Mr Cops.

"But I don't accept it," she said firmly.

He frowned. "What nonsense is this?"

"Not nonsense." *Please, please support me*, she thought. "Say you made a mistake – an honest mistake. The tigers are still probably on the road. The new owner hasn't yet taken delivery so the deal isn't completed."

Mr Cops shook his head. "Take the money, girl. It's the best you can hope for out of this situation."

"It's not! I'm going to go and fetch them back."

He folded his arms, matching her stubbornness. "You'll be laughed at – Jamrach won't care what you say."

"He will when I arrive with the Home Secretary's son. I'm sure a local magistrate will side with us when I explain."

Mr Cops was slowly realizing that she was serious. "Is this all the thanks you give me? You'll get me in hot water – imprisoned for debt no doubt – and you'll make Jamrach and the Newtons my enemies – all to save those tigers."

"Oh, Alfred!" moaned his wife.

Sahira swallowed. As Emily said, it was sometimes necessary to do a bad thing to stop something worse from happening. "I'm sorry for your trouble, but I didn't do this to you. You sold the tigers, not me."

Mr Cops shoved back from the table, making the cutlery rattle. "Don't you care that you'll ruin this place?"

Sahira looked down at the caps of her blue boots, drawing strength from them. "I do care."

"No, you don't – not if you behave like this."

"I just can't let my tigers die," declared Sahira.

An eruption was building. His face flushed red. "Get out of here! I don't want to see you anywhere near my menagerie again!"

"Alfred, don't!" pleaded Mrs Cops.

He rounded on his wife. "Are you saying you take her side? You don't mind that I'll be in debtors' prison when the baby's born?"

Mrs Cops held up her hands. "Don't be absurd, Alfred. Of course I don't want that. I'm saying you'll regret you spoke to her like this as soon as your temper cools."

"That Mr Pence was right: she's trouble." He wheeled around. "Get out!"

Shaken by his fury, Sahira backed away. Even the most placid bear could turn vicious when poked too hard.

Ned was waiting for her outside, riding on the garden gate to pass the time. "Well?"

"It went as you would expect." Her voice wavered.

"That bad?"

Sahira was already heading for the exit. "We'd better get to Bobby. We can't take Nebbie this time."

Ned shoved his hand in his pocket and drew out two shillings. "We'll get a cab." Seeing her expression, he smiled. "I've got to spend my zebra-ride money on something."

The rap on the back door of Bobby's home sounded like a gunshot in the quiet mews.

"Yes? Beggars aren't welcome." It wasn't the friendly footman that Ned had hoped would answer, but a supercilious specimen of the footman species, one neither of them had met.

"We're not beggars. We're here for –" began Sahira, putting a foot in the door.

"Message for Mr Evesham," interrupted Ned.

"About?" sneered the footman. If words had been butter, he would have smeared his all over their faces.

"About something educational and very, very important for 'is lessons. Message to be delivered in person."

Ned showed a fair hand in embroidering his lie but Sahira knew it wouldn't wash with this suspicious man.

"We've word on the *Panthera tigris* from a zoological colleague," she said, giving the tigers their Latin name.

The man repeated the Latin like holding a dirty rag by its corner. "*Panthera tigris?*"

"And please add that Miss Clive says it's about *adiuva me,*" Sahira added. This meant "help me" in Latin – Mr Evesham would know.

A little less doubtfully, the man looked behind them, expecting to see the respectable sounding Miss Clive, not this duet of street urchins, one dressed in Indian garb. "Miss Clive?"

"That's right. She's asking for him. *Adiuva me.* Have you got that?"

The implication that he couldn't remember a message poked him into action. "I believe I can retain that information as far as the schoolroom – *Panthera tigris, adiuva me.* Will Miss Clive be expecting a reply?"

"I should 'ope so," muttered Ned.

"Yes, we'll wait," said Sahira, planting herself on the mounting block with no intention of moving until her message produced results.

The message made its slow way upstairs in the capacious brain of the footman – and received a short answer in the form of the running legs of Bobby, and the statelier progress of his tutor.

"Miss Clive, what's happened?" asked Bobby, bursting out into the yard. He looked them both over like a farmer checking his herd. "You both look all right – bit rough around the edges but not in need of saving."

"Mr Cops..." But Sahira couldn't speak past the lump in her throat.

"'E sold her tigers – for shootin'," said Ned with admirable succinctness as Mr Evesham approached. "But thing is, they ain't 'is to sell, but 'ers, so we're fetching them back."

Bobby rubbed his hands. "Good-o. Let's get the carriage."

Mr Evesham put his hand on Bobby's shoulder before he went off like a rocket to fetch the coachman. "Miss Clive? What's going on?"

Sahira could tell that he was about to throw a bucket of cold water on the fire of their rescue plan. "It's true, Mr Evesham. Mr Cops never paid me for my tigers but went and sold them to some rich man with an estate. I'm going to get them back from Mr Jamrach."

He raised a brow. "And then?"

"It's not as mad as it sounds. I thought I'd lend them to the menagerie or the zoo while I get the money to ship them back to India – back home."

"With what money?"

She thought it better not to mention her plans to blackmail her family. "I have connections who might help."

Mr Evesham sighed. "Miss Clive, I think I understand how much the tigers mean to you –"

How could he? she thought.

"– And your plan sounds a commendable one, even achievable given time, but you can't wrest the tigers from the grip of men like Jamrach just by telling him they're yours. You need an order from a judge – and proof, something showing that they are indeed your possessions. Look, I'll talk to a friend of mine who practises law and ask his advice how best to proceed."

"But how long will that take?"

"A few days – I can be quite persuasive when I put my mind to it. That will give you time to see if you can arrange the matter of money with your *connections*." The way Mr Evesham said it made it clear he didn't believe in the promised money, which was fair as she was living in an orphanage – the very definition of a child without connections.

"But my tigers might only have days – or hours – and I don't even know where they've been taken!"

"It's the best I can do – and I'll leave right now if that will set your mind at rest. Bobby, see to your guests and then finish your geometry. I'll be back by the end of the afternoon with news."

Mr Evesham headed to the gate and they heard him whistle for a cab on the street outside.

The three friends looked at each other.

"Hours, you say?" asked Bobby.

Sahira nodded.

"You don't know where they've been taken?"

She shook her head. It wasn't enough. She prayed desperately to God under her breath. *You didn't answer my prayers before, but please, please, answer this one! Help me help my tigers!*

It wasn't God who answered, or not directly. Bobby gave a decisive nod. "Right. We'll leave Mr Evesham doing his bit but that's bound to be too slow. We need your cousin John. Wait here." He followed the tutor out onto the street.

"Why fetch John?" asked Sahira, reluctant to get him involved.

Bobby glanced around him, checking no one was listening. "Jenks has been giving us lessons around the square. If we're going to take the coach without permission, we'll need someone to help me drive."

Very uncertain as to whether this was a good idea, Sahira sat with her knees to her chest on the mounting block. She was alone as Ned had also gone off to the orphanage to fetch her a change of clothes and leave word with Ann and Emily that Sahira might be out of town for a day or two. The pause gave her long enough to consider the rashness of what they were about to attempt. Could she be arrested for carriage theft if the son of the owner was the one behind it? It seemed very likely that Ned and she, as the ones without impressive families to back them, would probably catch the worst of the blame when it was splashed about like a cartwheel through a puddle. Should she tell Ned to stay behind? In fact, shouldn't she tell him to do so anyway, as absconding with her would lose him his job at the menagerie?

Ned returned within the hour, thanks to lavishing more of his zebra money on cabs. However, he didn't return alone. Ann and Emily had squeezed in with him in the hackney carriage.

"What are you all doing here?" asked Sahira, jumping up. Her legs had gone to sleep sitting hunched up on a cold stone and she stumbled as she rushed toward them.

Ann caught her elbow to steady her. "We know what the tigers mean to you, Sahira. You're our friend."

"I know that but what about Mr Pence?" Was she dragging all her friends into disaster?

"Not to worry. I told 'im the Constable of the Tower needed 'em for a special cleaning job at the menagerie and not to expect them back till tomorrow night," said Ned proudly.

"Mr Pence didn't believe him until Ned showed him the down payment," said Emily with a cynical roll of her eyes.

"Oh Ned, your zebra money!" said Sahira. He had to have spent it all on their comings and goings today.

"Always more where that came from," said Ned. "I'll just take Nebbie on a little stroll along the river one sunny day."

If Mr Cops lets him have his job back, thought Sahira glumly.

Bobby and Cousin John entered the mews at a fast pace, both with flushed faces from running.

"Sorry, sorry, had to track John down. He was at a drawing class," said Bobby, waving. "Good heavens, who is everyone?"

Sahira quickly made the introductions. John nodded gravely to the girls as if they were duchesses while Bobby shook hands as if they were his school fellows. Sahira couldn't have been prouder of her well-to-do friends.

"Are we ready now?" she asked. "I am."

"Good-o," Bobby said chirpily. "Let's go rescue some tigers."

From her previous encounters, Sahira had expected her cousin to be among those urging caution, like Mr Evesham, and was surprised to see John was as quick to arrange for the stealing of the family carriage as Bobby.

"I believe the ladies and Ned should wait around the corner," he advised Bobby. "Just in case."

Just in case they got stopped. John was trying to save them from getting into worse trouble.

"Will they let you take it out?" Sahira asked in a low voice.

John checked his pocket watch. "It's the servants' dinner. Unless we are very unlucky and Bobby's parents call for the carriage unexpectedly, we should have time to harness the horses and get free of the mews before anyone notices."

"Father's in Westminster," said Bobby blithely. "Mother's with her friends in the front parlour."

With that, Sahira decided her role was not to put any more doubts in their minds. They would have to face the consequences, but not now. Now her tigers were their primary concern.

Five minutes later, as the three girls and Ned waited on the corner of the street, they saw a familiar carriage clop out of the mews. John was on the driver's box, dressed in Jenks's coat so that he looked like a grown man if you didn't examine him too closely. He was handling the pair of horses with care, despite Bobby bouncing beside him.

"Get in, get in!" Bobby urged. "I think Henry saw us."

"Henry?" asked Sahira as Ned opened the door to the compartment and helped Ann inside.

"The footman on duty."

Sahira muttered a little prayer that Henry would not hurry with that message either, giving them enough time to get lost in the London traffic.

The four orphans made themselves comfortable inside the carriage while the young gentlemen drove them. Buoyed by the success, so far, of their escape with the carriage, the reversal of ordinary roles struck Sahira as so absurd that she laughed softly.

"What's so funny?" asked Emily. She had arranged the carriage rug delicately over her ankles like the very finest and most pernickety of ladies.

"Us," said Sahira, pointing to the occupants of the carriage. "Them." She pointed to the roof.

Ann gave one of her warm smiles. "They're fine friends you've got there, Sahira. They'll both be in hot water when we get caught." She shook her head as second thoughts edged in. "As will we."

Ned shrugged. "That won't matter. By then we'll have tigers. No one will worry about a little matter of borrowing a carriage when we have two tigers on our side."

It wasn't hard to follow in Jamrach's tracks. Stop at any inn on the way and ask if someone had seen two tigers in cages and they were inundated with people wanting to give a full account of what they'd witnessed that very day.

"*Striped like a sunset*," said one farmer on the outskirts of the city.

"*Roaring like devils*," according to a washerwoman, as they crossed the Thames.

"*Big old tabby cats*," said another, perhaps short-sighted, old man at a village crossroads.

All agreed that they were headed toward Maidenhead.

"Why were the Newtons driving the carts?" mused Ann after a long stretch on a good road across Heath Row. "I didn't think they'd stoop to such things."

"Pr'haps the money was good," suggested Ned.

"Perhaps they wanted to see more of the county?" asked Emily.

The others groaned at this sunny interpretation and shook their head.

"I wager it's because of the boots – and my trunk. They didn't get the boots in the end, and I told them I hid the trunk with the tigers. Being the ones to take away my tigers gives them revenge and a chance at getting my things from me."

"Yeah, that sounds like them. They like nothing better than bearing a very long grudge against someone. I think it's their way of entertaining themselves," said Ned glumly.

Sahira played with the cord on the window blind, drawing it down and up against the long shafts of late afternoon sunshine. "I suppose

I'll have to take the trunk back to the orphanage now. I never did find out who broke into it."

"Wasn't it Joanna?" asked Ned.

"No, that was before she came," said Sahira.

"Matron?"

"That's who I thought did it, but I don't know for sure."

"It was me!" The confession was blurted out so rapidly Sahira wondered if she'd imagined it.

"Emily?" She let go of the cord and the blind descended with a snap.

"It was me. I did it. And I'm pleased I couldn't open it!"

Sahira's confidence in her friend took a new blow. "Why?"

A curl of blonde hair slid from under her hat. Emily tugged off the cap altogether in a despairing gesture like she was revealing her true unvarnished self to them after so long hiding the truth. "They threatened my brother, told me I'd be on their enemies' list if I didn't, but the truth was… the truth was, I wanted to see all your lovely dresses. I envied you having them. That trunk is like the best costume store in the world. It was mad, I know, but I thought for a wild moment that I could wear one and go to Covent Garden and offer myself as an actress. They'd have to pay attention if I looked like a princess." She bit her lip. "I'm sorry."

Sahira blinked uncomprehendingly. "But Emily, you only had to ask me and I would've given you one to wear."

Emily nodded miserably. "I think I knew that. It's just that I was so tempted – and they were so pretty. I let my fear of the Newtons push me into doing something I really wanted to do."

Sahira had to allow that Emily was honest to a fault. She could have hidden behind the threat and not explained her other motives. And here she was, risking everything to help Sahira now, even with her brother in the orphanage nursery and her place there in danger if this came out.

"Then I forgive you," said Sahira.

"You do?" Emily's eyes shone with tears. "Thank you! I've been feeling like a worm for months now."

"Worms are very useful creatures," said Sahira seriously. "They help break down the fallen leaves, making the soil more fertile."

Emily gave a huffing laugh and swiped at some escaped droplets. "Only you, Sahira. It's a saying."

"I know."

After all, part of Sahira felt like a worm for having treated Mr Cops the way she had that very morning. You can want to be someone's friend and yet still go on to hurt them gravely, Sahira had learned. Mr Cops had wanted to be her friend, and she had meant to be his, and yet they had still fallen out over the tigers.

"Hold up!" The gruff shout came from behind them. Sahira stuck her head out of the window, then flopped back on the seat.

"It's Jenks. He's catching us up on horseback."

"Can we outrun him?" asked Ned.

Sahira shook her head. They'd changed horses at the post-house at Longford, sending a boy back with the Peels' pair, but even two fresh hired ones couldn't outpace a single rider.

"What are we going to do?" asked Ann.

"Anyone got a marmoset?" asked Sahira. At their confused expressions, she just shook her head. "Brazen it out, of course."

The boys on the driving seat must have reached a similar conclusion to Sahira because the carriage pulled to the side of the road to allow Jenks to catch up.

"What do you think, Jenks?" called Bobby. "Isn't John a capital hand on the ribbons? That's all thanks to your teaching."

"Master Bobby, you'd better have a good reason for taking my carriage without my say-so!" Jenks swung down from the back of his horse and strode toward them. He caught sight of the occupants inside. "What's this? Some lark to impress your friends? You're all in big trouble, young masters!"

"You said I should practise," said John.

"I didn't mean by taking the carriage on a thirty-mile journey on your own!" thundered Jenks.

"He's not on his own," chirped Bobby.

Sahira could tell the "only-took-it-for-driving-practice" argument was about to be struck down by a flash of Jenks's lightning temper. She pushed open the door and hopped to the ground.

"Mr Jenks?"

The coachman was holding the horses' heads, ordering John and Bobby to climb down so he could take over and return them all to town for their long overdue thrashing.

"What?" he said curtly.

"They're doing this for me." She stood in front of him, offering herself as a target for his anger. He, no doubt, was driven by concern for his horses, left back at the last post-house. She too in his position would feel indignant that her animal friends had suffered.

"We sent Carrie and Ridley home with a reliable boy," she said reassuringly.

"I know," he said gruffly. "Saw them myself when I stopped to ask after you."

"We didn't drive them too hard. John's been very careful. He really is a very good coachman."

Jenks blinked at her. "You think this is about my horses? My horses?" he repeated in astonishment.

Sahira recalculated. "We've not put a scratch on the carriage either."

He looked up to the heavens, appealing for assistance. "I don't care about the carriage. I don't even care about the horses. I care that the Home Secretary's son has disappeared with a bunch of ne'er-do-wells on some wild jaunt across England!"

Sahira let it pass that he had just called them "ne'er-do-wells" when they were trying to do their very best. "It's not a wild jaunt. We're saving my tigers from certain death!" she countered.

"Tigers!" Now Jenks exploded. "*Tigers*? Is the girl mad? Shall we take her direct to Bedlam hospital?"

"I certainly am not mad. I own two tigers. Jamrach has stolen them from me – not that he knows he's stealing," she admitted.

John had reached her side and touched her arm. "May I have a turn at explaining, Cousin?"

His version of the story was not the same as the one Sahira would have told. He started with her, rather than the tigers, how she had been abandoned by everyone who should have taken care of her: her parents by death, the East India Company through carelessness, the orphanage through cruelty, Mr Cops through penury, and her family because…

"Because my father is a man of rigid, unforgiving views. My mother is unable to act independently, my grandfather is sick, and my remaining relatives are unwilling to acknowledge Sahira."

Sahira could feel her blush creep from her cheeks right down her neck. She must look like a cherry.

"I couldn't stand for it any longer, so when I heard that the last thing that she owns, the last thing that means anything to her, had been taken from her, I knew we had to act," continued John. "That's why we're all here. It would be a crime much worse than taking the carriage to let those magnificent creatures be shot for sport. I appeal to you, sir, to your sense of justice, to help us."

Sahira wanted to applaud his final sentence. Bobby actually did, adding "Hear, hear!"

Jenks swept them all with an uncompromising stare. "Humph!"

That didn't sound hopeful.

He held out his hand. "My coat."

Sending Sahira an apologetic look, John slipped out of the coat and passed it over. Jenks shrugged it on.

"Right. Which way did you say they were going?"

Emily gave a squeal of excitement and hugged Ann. The boys grinned. Sahira, however, too moved to say anything, just pointed.

"That way, is it?" Jenks headed for the driver's seat. "You'd better not hang around on the side of the road: we've got some tigers to catch."

CHAPTER 19

After having driven the horses for several hours over unfamiliar roads, John took a rest inside, leaving Bobby and Ned to entertain Jenks on top of the carriage.

"Thank you for speaking up for me," said Sahira while Ann and Emily made quiet conversation between themselves. They did it, she knew, to give her a moment apart with her cousin.

"You don't have to thank me," admitted John. "I've been feeling wretched about my family's treatment of you. We've been having some terrible arguments, my mother and I on one side, my father on the other. He won't budge – for my sisters' sake, he claims."

Sahira glanced out at the woodland through which they were passing. "I understand."

John shrugged. "I don't. I know he never met your father – and you aren't his blood relation – but you're family." He spoke as if this should be enough for anyone.

"So you came for me – not the tigers?"

He nodded. "I came for you. You realize this plan to save your tigers isn't likely to work, don't you?"

"I'll make it work."

"I know you'll try – and we'll help you. It's good we've got Jenks with us now, but Jamrach is likely to drive us off, not to mention what the Newtons will do."

"I don't care about those jackals."

"Well, you should. Even *I* have heard of Harry Newton – and I live in Mayfair. We'll be taking on some powerful enemies."

"But we're in the right."

He sighed. "Being right is rarely enough."

Sahira knew he was only telling the truth but it still made her angry. "Do you want to go home then?"

John gave her a rueful smile. "Not if you need me."

That made her feel better. "John, you're quite my favourite cousin."

He shook his head. "Sadly, I don't think my competition is very strong, but thank you, all the same."

Twenty minutes later, John sat up.

"Wait a moment: I think I recognize this farm!" he exclaimed.

Taking directions from a tinker, they'd turned off the main road and headed north away from Maidenhead.

"Been here before, sir?" asked Ann, who couldn't be persuaded to call the young gentleman "John" like Emily and Sahira.

"We're near my family's estate. Most of the land round here on the left belongs to Fenton Park, and on the right is our neighbour's land."

Sahira knew that local knowledge would be very helpful. When on an expedition with her parents, they'd always relied on natives from that region to direct where they should go. Surely this would be the same?

"Who lives round here who would want some tigers?" asked Sahira.

John furrowed his brow. "Colonel Wilmot rents Tinsbury Court from your grandfather, one of the minor houses, only eighteen rooms. It's just down here, a mile or so to the turn-off."

"*Only* eighteen?" said Emily with a laugh. "That's more than twice as many as the orphanage."

"He's an old East India hand, retired to the countryside. It could be him."

"Does he hunt?" asked Sahira.

"Everyone around here hunts. It is the main pastime in the winter. He –" John broke off.

"He what?" Sahira didn't like where this conversation was heading.

"I was going to say that he already has a tiger-skin rug in his study. I used to play on it when I was little, pretending I was riding on its back. Why would he want any more? But, of course, a hunter always wants more trophies." John rapped on the roof. "I'd better go up top and keep an eye out for someone to ask. They'll be more likely to give me an answer, knowing I'm connected to the big family at Fenton Park."

Yet when they reached the fork in the road that led to Tinsbury Court, a local shepherd swore that the carts had carried on straight.

"They're going to Fenton Park," the shepherd said in his rolling country accent. "I heard how the old lord thinks they killed his son, but that don't make no sense. His son died of a fever, not as a meal for some big cats."

Sahira gulped. Her grandfather had bought the tigers so he could punish them? That was even worse than giving them some slight chance of escape in a hunt.

"Are you sure, sir?" she asked, standing beside her cousin, who had been doing the questioning.

"Oh aye."

"But I thought my… the old lord was ill?"

"Ah, you're right." The shepherd pointed a finger at her. "Maybe it were that sister of his. Lady Dorothy. She don't like those exotic creatures, not like poor old Captain Dickie Clive, God rest his soul."

John and Sahira exchanged a look.

"You could stay in the carriage – I could talk to Great-Aunt Dorothy without her even knowing you're there," John offered.

It was tempting to leave it to John but Sahira asked herself what her father would have wanted. He had intended to present her to his father in her swallow dress and she was coming dressed in a work-stained tunic and Indian trousers. He had hoped her relatives would love her and care for her; so far they – with the honourable exception of John – had done nothing but reject and ignore her. He had given her responsibility for the tigers as a sacred duty to care for God's creatures.

"No, John, I'll argue my own case. You never know, wanting to get rid of me as quickly as possible might mean they just hand over the tigers. We might not even need to argue with Mr Jamrach about who owns them."

"Jenks, we're heading for the big house," called John.

"Right you are, Master Bracewell."

It was a bittersweet homecoming for Sahira. She had heard so much about Fenton Park that she felt she knew the copses, the ponds, the meadows, from her father's tales. Even the pheasants that flew up as they passed, the deer scattering across the hills, the squirrel that leaped from branch to branch to keep up with them, seemed familiar, like storybook characters stepping out to make her acquaintance at long last. As for the house, this was exactly as she had pictured it: an expanse of honeyed stone, layered like a ziggurat temple from Persia. It was a fit home for a pantheon of gods, not one little noble family.

"How many rooms?" asked Emily, even her usual spark somewhat quashed by the formidable prospect.

"I'm not sure anyone has ever managed to count. Three hundred?" guessed John.

And they didn't even have one spare for her, thought Sahira, refusing to let the view daunt her. She would take her tigers and go.

Jenks drew the coach up at the bottom of an impressive flight of steps. A footman hurried toward them, ready to receive the important guests. He looked somewhat taken aback when the visitors proved to be two young gentlemen, two girls in the simplest of uniforms, a rather ragged boy, and an Indian young person.

"Where are the tigers?" asked John.

"Master Bracewell!" The footman finally recognized one of the party. "The tigers? They're by the stables."

At least they had come to the right place.

An elderly lady now appeared at the top of the flight of stairs.

"John, what on earth are you doing here? And who are these with you? Is your mother quite well?"

John bowed. "Great-Aunt Dorothy. Mother is well, thank you. We're here for the tigers."

The lady came nearer, using a stick to help her on the stairs. The footman rushed up to provide support. Sahira could now see that she looked as formidable as her reputation: iron-grey hair twisted and curled into a style of yesteryear when there was still an emperor in France. Her dress was of similar vintage: high-waisted and in a navy blue silk, trimmed with black. Was that a sign that the house was observing a period of mourning for her father?

The lady was inspecting her visitors more closely. "Who is that?" she asked, pointing with her stick at Sahira. "And who are they?" The stick now pointed to a second carriage rattling down the drive.

"This is Sahira Clive, your great-niece," said John stoutly. "As for the other visitors, I've no idea."

But Sahira did. She could see the unmistakable uniforms of Robert Peel's new policemen, crowded on the roof of the carriage, which meant the inside must be full already of the same. The Home Secretary had sent his best men after his errant son, possibly fearing the worst.

"Peelers," said Ned in horror.

"Bobbies," said Bobby, looking pleased rather than aghast at the prospect. "Isn't that splendid? We can get them to arrest the Newtons!"

Sahira did not think it would turn out that way.

The coach slowed then stopped at the bottom of the steps and an officer with ginger sideburns jumped down.

"Master Peel, we've come to rescue you!" The police officer clicked his fingers at his entourage. "Arrest them!"

"What? All of 'em?" asked one young constable, looking at Great-Aunt Dorothy warily.

"Not the lady, numbskull – or the young gentleman – or the footman," the officer clarified after further thought. "The gang of kidnappers." He picked out the three girls and Ned in a waving gesture to say that their clothing spoke for itself.

"Hang on a moment," said Bobby. "But I haven't been kidnapped. We're on a tiger hunt."

"According to a member of staff at your father's house you were kidnapped. He saw you leave in the company of disreputable types and raised the alarm. Arrest them. We'll sort this out later in London."

The young constable went so far as to put his hand on Sahira's shoulder.

Lady Dorothy rapped her cane on the bottom step. "Unhand that child, officer!" Sahira thought for a wild moment that maybe her great-aunt was coming to her rescue. "You have no power over anyone on our land. Lord Chalmers is a magistrate. If anyone is doing any arresting it will be under his orders, and not yours!"

"But I'm acting on the instructions of the Home Secretary," protested the policeman.

"I don't care if your orders were handed down on tablets of stone by Moses himself: this is our estate and you will abide by our rules!"

The policeman glowered. "Then fetch his lordship and we'll see if we can get this settled."

"I don't like your tone, young man," sniffed Lady Dorothy. The policeman was far from young but to a woman of her advanced years she could get away with this set down. "And Lord Chalmers is indisposed."

During the ensuing argument about landowners' rights and the laws of England, a third delegation arrived – this time on a hired hack, a big brown horse capable of pushing on through miles of mud and potholes. Mr Cops swung from the horse's back and came forward, cap in hand. He took a quick survey of the quarrellers, much as he would the monkeys in the menagerie, noted the children standing helpless while the adults argued, and the absence of tigers. Sahira couldn't anticipate what frame of mind he was in as he had been so angry with her that morning. He was the last person she expected to turn up here – unless, that was, he came to claim that she was lying about owning the tigers? He cleared his throat.

Neither the policeman nor Lady Dorothy noticed.

He took more drastic action.

"Excuse me, your ladyship? But I've come about the delivery of tigers. You see, there's been a mistake."

The two quarrellers paused and turned to him.

"Tigers, what tigers? This is about a kidnapping!" said the policeman.

"Those horrible beasts!" said Lady Dorothy. "What kind of mistake? Please say you've come to take them away."

Her friends were quick to fill in the slight pause in hostilities with suggestions and explanations.

"There's no kidnapping but there are tigers," said Bobby helpfully.

"They're not 'is," said Ned, "but 'ers." He pointed to Sahira.

"She really is your great-niece, Aunt Dorothy," added John.

"You should arrest the lady for buying stolen goods," said Ned for good measure.

A slow clapping came from the top of the flight of steps. So unexpected, so disrespectful was the sound that they all looked up. An elderly man sat in an invalid chair wheeled by a muscular footman. He waved a wrinkled hand at them.

"Please, do carry on. This is the most fun I've had in ages!"

"Grandfather!" John bounded up the steps. Sahira was riveted to the spot in shock: her father's father, the very man whom she had hoped would take her in, was well enough to be out and about, looking quite fit despite the wheelchair. Why then hadn't he sent for her – or even come to the orphanage himself?

"John, my boy: this is a scrape worthy of your Uncle Dickie. I'm so proud of you!" the old man exclaimed.

Lady Dorothy forgot her argument and also hastened to his side. "Samuel, shouldn't you be inside?"

"That quack you keep sending to me would have me muffled up against every little breeze and miss all the fun, but that's not the way a Clive behaves, even if he's at death's door. So, tell me, John, what've I missed?" Lord Chalmers rubbed his bony hands together.

The policeman cottoned on to the fact that the very lord he had asked to see was among them so he approached with his hat doffed in deference.

"My lord, I've come to arrest the kidnappers of the son of Robert Peel."

"Very good. Where are they?" asked the lord, his eyes glowing.

The policeman turned and looked down at the children from the orphanage. From his perspective they must have looked very small indeed, all of them shorter than their supposed kidnap victim. "Those four."

"I wasn't kidnapped," repeated Bobby. "I came of my own accord."

"Hmm. Now if you'd said the kidnappers were any of the shifty-looking fellows who delivered my tigers just an hour ago then I would've believed you. They went off with their gold and a couple of smaller silver objects from my study, thinking my age meant I wasn't wise to their game. I've men chasing them, but if you want to make yourself useful I suggest you give my people a hand."

"He's talking about the Newtons," added Bobby.

"*The* Newtons?" repeated the policeman.

"Yes, Harry and his sons, Tommy and Alf."

"You have a chance to arrest the Newtons out of London with the stolen items on their person," said John. "They're driving two carts with Mr Jamrach from Ratcliffe Highway."

"Really?" asked the policeman and for a moment he looked lost in thought. Then, making up his mind, he reached for his whistle and issued a sharp blast, unnecessarily, as all his men were within earshot. "About turn, lads. We're off for bigger prey!" The policemen piled back into their carriage and the driver manoeuvred it on the drive to face the way they had come. "Master Peel, I trust you will send word to your father of our chase – and that you are unharmed?"

"Indeed. What's your name, officer?" said Bobby soberly.

"Mulgrave, Josiah Mulgrave."

Bobby gave him a military salute and the policeman climbed up beside his driver.

"Follow those carts!" Mulgrave ordered. The carriage surged away with its cargo of swaying policemen.

"That got rid of them," said Lord Chalmers with satisfaction. "Now, where were we? You children came for the tigers, thinking they're yours; and this man... who are you exactly?" He beckoned Mr Cops.

"Cops, sir, His Majesty's Keeper of the Lions," said the man.

"How splendid. That sounds like the best job in the world," said Lord Chalmers, clearly thoroughly enjoying himself. "And, let me guess, you think the tigers are yours and that you were within your rights to sell them to me?"

Mr Cops looked down at Sahira, who by now was standing quite alone at the bottom of the steps as the others drifted up to surround the old man.

"No, sir, I came to admit to a mistake. I should never've sold them, not only because I'd not paid for them, but because I let down that young lady there. They belong to her in spirit and in law."

"That's a young lady?" marvelled Lord Chalmers. "Good gracious. I thought her an Indian servant boy. Come closer, my dear. Who exactly are you? An Indian princess? A character from the tales of *Arabian Nights*?"

Sahira took the slow climb up the stairs, hampered by her bad leg.

"No, sir. I'm your granddaughter." She took the turban from her hair. "Sahira Eleanor Clive. And I won't let you shoot my tigers."

The old man stared at her in wonder, as if she were a magician who'd conjured herself out of a hat.

"Sahira? Dickie's girl?" asked Lord Chalmers in the tone of one asking if an angel had just appeared in the courtyard. "You're here – in England?"

"I am. But I'm only here to fetch Sita and Rama. You don't have to worry: I won't stay long."

"What do you mean, you won't stay long? Dorothy, what's going on? Why is Dickie's girl here? You said she'd gone back to India to be with her mother's people."

Great-Aunt Dorothy glared at Sahira as if she were a viper that had slithered out from under a bush. "I said she… she was preparing to go back," she stammered.

"You said no such thing! I may be frail, but I'm not foolish. When I asked what had happened to the girl, you said she'd gone back on the same boat that brought her with a kind lady escort from the Company. Where have you been, child?" Lord Chalmers held out his hand. "Why didn't you come before?"

Is this a trick? wondered Sahira. Was he just pretending not to know about her?

"Go on, Sahira," whispered Ann. Emily nudged her forward. With feet like lead weights, Sahira came to his side and he gripped her hand like it was his last handhold on a cliff edge before he fell.

"My Dickie!" he said reverently, tracing the shape of her eyebrows that she knew were so like her father's. "You've got his eyes." He smiled, his own eyes damp with tears. "Thankfully, you don't have his – or should I say our – chin." He tapped hers, which was rounded like her mother's, not the square one of the Clives.

"You really didn't know?" whispered Sahira.

"Know what, dearest?"

So he hadn't known. "You're not going to shoot my tigers?"

"Now why would I do that? I thought they were the last link to my dear boy. I bought them so I could look on them and be reminded of him – but now I have you – and you, my dear, I have to say, are so much better than tigers, however fine they are in their own way."

EPILOGUE

Sahira pushed her grandfather along the path outside the tigers' enclosure, Jeoffry curled up on the old man's lap as he hitched a ride. The Garden of Eden, that's what they'd called the tigers' new enclosure when the workmen put the sign up over the gate. When God answered her prayer, he had done so generously. She could not have imagined this: a home for both her and the tigers that went beyond all hopes.

"Will we see them today, do you think?" Grandfather asked, using a telescope to peer into the further reaches of their woodland.

"We may see Rama, but Sita will probably stay with the cubs," said Sahira.

"Quite right. The proud mother has her hands full." Grandfather paused to allow a coughing fit to pass. "Do you think the enclosure is big enough for them now they've got a family?" Together Sahira and her grandfather had drawn up the plans to section off a portion of the parkland to make a home for the tigers. It had a high fence and many warning signs. So far the tigers had stayed within and trespassers without.

"For now I think it'll be enough. When the cubs grow up we'll have to find new homes for them – or a bigger park."

Grandfather chuckled. "Perhaps we should just fence off the house and leave them to it?"

"I don't think your farmers or gamekeepers would approve."

Even this was not a perfect paradise for the tigers, Sahira knew that, but it was the best she could provide outside of India – better than the menagerie, better than the zoo. She felt that this was the best way to keep them if they had to be caged and confined – and she believed in her heart that they agreed, for they had gone on to produce a litter of cubs almost immediately after they'd moved into their new home.

Sahira and her grandfather trundled under an oak tree, old acorns crunching underfoot. Sahira kicked at the hem of her favourite dress, trimmed with swallows. The birds would be flying away soon but she was staying put. The summer had passed and Sahira's life had blossomed. As her grandfather's companion and cherished granddaughter, she had a family, a home, and not a cloud in her sky. The Newtons had been arrested in Windsor and sentenced to be transported; Mr Pence had been dismissed for pocketing the money meant for care of the orphans; even Great-Aunt Dorothy had taken herself away to Bath to grumble and thunder at a distance.

"My secretary said you heard from Mr Cops this morning." Grandfather had taken an interest in the man's welfare since he had been the first to help his granddaughter.

"A lovely long letter. His little girl is four months now – and they're still at the Tower. Most of the big animals have gone but he's allowed to keep a small collection and is making do, he says. He sends his thanks to you. What did you do, Grandfather?"

"I told Wellington that if he tried to get rid of the Keeper of the Lions he'd have a battle to rival Waterloo on his hands in the Lords."

Sahira steered around a tree root to ensure her grandfather wasn't jostled. He was lively in spirit, but his poor health was no invention on the family's part. "I was ready to set the tigers on the duke," he continued.

"So was I!" They laughed together as only Clives could, knowing they were not joking.

"It's kind of you to take me out, Sahira. Am I keeping you from your lessons?" the old lord asked.

"You know this is my favourite part of the day. Besides, Cousin John, Bobby, and Mr Evesham are expected later so our governess is preparing a special nature table. Ann and Emily are helping her." Grandfather had insisted her friends, plus their little brothers and sisters, join Sahira at Fenton Park with promise of work on the estate when they were older. It wasn't good for a child to be educated alone, he said, though Sahira suspected it was mainly because he missed having lots of young people rattling about the mansion. Her grandfather thrived on company and mischief.

Speaking of mischief... Sahira thought. "What have you done with Ned, Grandfather? I saw you send him off this morning."

He reached up and patted her hand where it rested on the handle of the chair. "I arranged a special delivery from the menagerie."

"You did?"

"A certain zebra that Ned said he missed – and who apparently was making himself a nuisance without his keeper."

"You didn't?"

Lord Chalmers nodded.

Sahira groaned. If her grandfather had a fault, it was falling in with Ned's schemes far too easily. Ned reminded Grandfather of her own father in that way, so Lord Chalmers rarely said no. "Grandfather, no bonnet will be safe, no mug of beer untouched, no rose left with a flower!"

"Splendid!" declared Lord Chalmers. "We've plenty of beer, a surfeit of roses, and bonnets are quite the stupidest of inventions."

And then, just as they were turning for home, Rama padded out of the trees and came to the path he had worn on the boundary of his enclosure. He sniffed and yawned, like a monarch acknowledging the obeisance of his minions. Something stretched and yawned in response inside Sahira, a feeling of rightness that the tiger had all this room to patrol, woods to hunt, hidden places to keep out of human gaze if he so wished.

"Good Morning, Rama," she said softly in Persian.

Then, magically, Sita appeared from the trees, two cubs close to her heels. She flicked her whiskers once in Sahira's direction, then processed past. The cubs didn't manage her regal poise, but gambolled after her with kittenish bounds and tumbles. This was the first time Sahira had seen them.

"Oh my goodness," she murmured.

"Oh indeed," echoed Grandfather.

They watched as the family of tigers wound their way back into the trees, swallowed up by the shadows with a last flicker of orange, white, and black from the tips of their tails.

Sahira's Glossary for Bobby

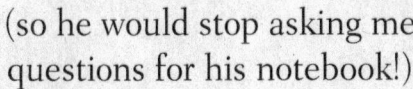

(so he would stop asking me questions for his notebook!)

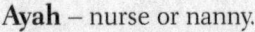

Ayah – nurse or nanny.

Brahmin – top caste in Hindu society.

The Company – or the East India Company, British trading company that has grown to be so much more – in fact it practically runs parts of India!

Diwan – a collection of poetry, such as the one my father made me.

Durbar – a ruler's court.

Fakir – a Muslim holy man who has taken a vow of poverty.

Khansaman – our camp cook.

Memsahib – upper-class European wife, title of respect.

Nabobs – the name given for Company men who go to India and bring home a fortune.

Nautch girl – a dancing girl.

Nizam – the ruler of Hyderabad.

Resident – chief representative of the East India Company.

ACKNOWLEDGMENTS

I would like to thank those who have written so entertainingly about the history of wild animals in England, London Zoo, and the menagerie in the Tower of London, particularly Isobel Charman, author of *The Zoo: The Wild and Wonderful Tale of the Founding of London Zoo*, and Daniel Hahn, author of *The Tower Menagerie: The Amazing and True Story of the Royal Collection of Wild Beasts*. Also very enlightening was John Simon's *The Tiger that Swallowed the Boy: Exotic Animals in Victorian England*. Thank you. And a big thank you to Siddo Deva for helping me on the details of the Indian setting. He also pointed out that there is no such thing as a Bengal Lion, but the Tower Menagerie poster is a copy of the wording on a real one so I decided to let that oddity remain. I think this description was chosen for its dramatic flourish rather than accuracy!